BODY & SOUL

John Harvey

PEGASUS BOOKS
NEW YORK LONDON

BODY & SOUL

Pegasus Books, Ltd.
148 West 37th Street, 13th Floor
New York, NY 10018

First Pegasus Books hardcover edition November 2018

ISBN: 978-1-68177-873-0

10 9 8 7 6 5 4 3 2 1

Printed in the United States of America
Distributed by W. W. Norton & Company, Inc.

The separating years approached them both, like a station down the line, all gain for her and all loss for him.

Graham Greene, *Our Man in Havana*

1

1

The house was at the edge of the village, the last in a row of stubby stone-built cottages backing onto fields which led down to the sea. Elder pulled the front door firmly closed, edged his coat collar up against the wind and, with a last look at his watch, set out on the path that would take him across open country to the headland. Up ahead, the sky was slowly darkening, scudded with cloud. The ground became increasingly stony and uneven underfoot, the fields giving way to granite cliffs. Rabbits ran, startled, helter skelter as he passed. A little way out, a small fishing boat wavered on the tide. Gulls wheeled overhead.

At the headland, he stopped and turned, looking back. Above the village, the road on which she would come curved steeply between the high moor and the fields beneath, a scrimmage of rock and stone, rough bushes of heather and gorse. The lights of cars, soft, as in a mist.

How long since he'd seen her? Katherine. His daughter. A degree ceremony that had turned sour when, misjudging the moment, he'd been unable to find the right words. Since then there'd been phone calls, his mostly, and mostly filled with protracted silences, terse answers, laboured sighs. His occasional emails went largely unacknowledged, as did his even more occasional texts. What did he expect? Twenty-three, rising twenty-four, she had a life of her own.

Then, out of the blue: 'I thought I might come down for a bit. If it's okay. Just – you know – a few days. A bit of a break, that's all.'

'Yes, yes, of course, but . . .'

'And no questions, Dad, okay? Interrogation. Or I'm on the first train back home.'

He'd realised, after she'd rung off, he no longer knew for certain where her home was.

When he'd said he'd drive in and meet her at the station, she'd said there was no need, she'd catch the bus. Lengthening his stride, he was in time to see its headlights as it rounded the hill; time to see her step down and walk towards him – ankle boots, padded jacket, jeans, rucksack on her back – uncertainty flickering in her eyes even as she summoned up a smile.

'Kate . . . It's good to see you.'

When she reached out her hands towards his, he struggled not to stare at the bandages on her wrists.

At the cottage he pulled open the door and stepped aside and, ducking her head, she walked in past him, shrugging off her rucksack and jacket almost in one.

'Just dump stuff anywhere for now. You can take it upstairs later.'

Katherine stooped to unlace her boots and handed them over for him to set alongside his own, beneath the barometer in the hall.

'Tea? Coffee? There's juice if you'd rather. Orange or . . .'

'Tea's fine. But first I need to pee.'

He pointed her through the kitchen to the bathroom, filled the kettle at the tap and set it to boil. Did she look any different? Her face, certainly; thinner, cheekbones more prominent, almost gaunt. And she'd lost weight. At least, so he thought. It wasn't easy to tell. Tall like her mother, she'd always been slender, long-limbed and slim. Distance, that's what you should be concentrating on, the coach at her athletic club used to say. The five thousand, maybe even the ten. You've got the build for it, not this four-hundred lark.

She hadn't listened to him either.

'I thought we'd get something out tonight,' Elder said. ''Stead of eating here. If that's all right.'

The living room was small: a single easy chair, coffee table, TV, two-seater settee. Katherine held her mug in both hands, dark lines around her eyes. Outside it was all but black, the evening closing steadily in.

'That's fine. Just let me crash for an hour first. It's been a long day.'

'As long as you're sure.'

'Dad, I said it's fine, okay?'

Fine. Not so many years ago it would have been accompanied by a rolling of the eyes.

The pub was further along the coast, sprawling, low-ceilinged, the car park all but full. Elder found them a table in a side room, hunched up against the wall.

'Music night,' he explained, nodding in the direction of the doors leading to the lounge bar. 'Gets busy. We could go in later, have a listen.'

'What kind of music?'

'Jazz, I think.'

5

'You don't even like jazz.'

Elder shrugged and opened the menu. Hake; corn-fed chicken breast; goat's cheese tart; scampi; rump of beef.

'You still veggie?'

Katherine answered him by ordering the beef. Wearing the same skinny jeans she'd travelled in, she'd changed into a red turtleneck top with long sleeves, the bandages only showing when she moved her hands towards her plate. He still hadn't asked.

'So where exactly are you living now?'

'Dalston.'

Elder nodded. East London. He had been stationed near there for a while in his early days in the Met. Stoke Newington, Borough of Hackney. He imagined it had changed a great deal.

'So, what? You're in a flat?'

'Flat share, yes. Ex-council. Nice. Not one of those tower blocks.'

'You should let me have your address.'

'Don't suppose I'll be there that long.'

Whenever the doors to the main bar opened, music drifted out. Trumpet and saxophone. Applause. A woman's voice.

'Still working in the same place?' Elder asked.

'Sports centre?'

'Yes.'

Katherine shook her head. 'Got laid off. Ages ago now.'

'I didn't know.'

She shrugged, looked down at her plate.

'You're managing okay, though? Rent and that?'

'S'okay. Mum helps out occasionally.'

'She does?'

'She didn't tell you?'

'No.'

If she'd asked him, he couldn't have told her the last time he and Joanne had spoken. Around the time of Katherine's birthday most probably, but that was months ago and since then . . . He had his life, such as it was, and she had hers.

Main courses finished, they were contemplating desserts when a woman on her way through from the lounge bar stopped at their table, a hand on Elder's shoulder. Black dress, pumps, serious hair.

'Frank. Didn't know you were in tonight.'

Elder turned, half rose, some small embarrassment on his face. 'Vicki, hi. This is my daughter, Katherine. Katherine — Vicki. Vicki sings with the band.'

Katherine squeezed out a smile.

'Kate's staying with me for a few days.'

'That's nice.' Vicki took a step away. 'You'll pop in? Second set's just starting.'

'Wouldn't miss it.'

When he sat back down, there was no mistaking the grin on Katherine's face.

'What?'

Katherine laughed.

The band were playing 'Bag's Groove', the trumpeter soloing, eyes tightly closed, while the alto player stood listening intently, bell of his saxophone cupped in both hands. Piano, bass and drums. Elder led Katherine to a couple of empty seats down near the side of the makeshift stage.

When the number finished and the applause faded, the trumpeter leaned towards the microphone. 'Ladies and gentlemen, the pride of the Penwith Peninsula, Vicki Parsons.'

Her voice was deep and full, smoky round the edges. She moved her body as she sang, feet planted firmly, one hand fast around the mike stand, the other hanging free. 'Honeysuckle

Rose' was slow and lazy, hips swaying; 'Route 66' swung hard. 'Can't We be Friends' was knowing and, with a quick glance in Elder's direction, playful. For an encore there was a rolling, bluesy 'Tain't Nobody's Business if I Do'.

'Well,' Katherine said when it was over. 'Hands full there, I dare say.'

Clouds crossed the moon where it hung low over Zennor Hill. A bird shifted in the trees at the end of the lane and something scuttled past them in the dark.

Katherine shuddered. 'At least in Dalston if someone's out to mug you, you can see them coming.'

'I think you're safe here.'

'Really?'

'Really.'

He reached out a hand but she was already turning away. No need to read the expression in her eyes. One thing she'd learned the hard way, he knew, there was no such thing as safety. Anywhere.

The interior of the cottage struck cold.

'You want anything before you go up?'

'I'm good, thanks.'

'Sleep well, then.'

'You, too.' Partway up the stairs, she paused. 'If I hadn't been here, would she have come back?'

'Vicki?'

'Unless you've got someone else.'

'Maybe. Not necessarily, no.'

'I'm sorry if I'm getting in the way of your love life.'

'You're not.'

He made tea, sat and watched the news on TV, sound turned low. It had started suddenly, as these things were wont to, an after-hours party, a lock-in at the pub; too much alcohol and, in Vicki's case, a little weed; when she brushed up against him the third time in thirty minutes he read it for what it was. They progressed awkwardly from the side wall of the pub to the front seat of her car and from there to the king-sized bed in her flat in Marazion, a view out through the window next morning across the tideline to St Michael's Mount. That had been — what? — six months or so ago, and Elder was beginning to wonder if the spark, the sense of anticipation that had passed between them, was already in danger of fading.

Can't we be friends, indeed.

He woke up on the settee with a start. A little after half past two. Switched off the TV. Turned the key in the front door.

Quietly climbing the stairs, he hesitated outside the second bedroom; after a few moments, eased open the door. The curtains had been left undrawn. Katherine lay on her side, fingers of one hand clutching a length of her hair, holding it close towards one corner of her mouth. A gesture from childhood. The other hand was wrapped around an end of the sheet where she had gathered it fast. Her breathing was even, her shoulder bare. Elder stood watching her for a while longer, then went to his room, climbed into bed and fell, immediately, fast asleep.

2

The next day broke fair. When Elder got back from his morning run, Katherine was making coffee, readying toast.

'How far d'you go?' she asked.

'Ten K, give or take.'

'Every day?'

'Bar Sundays.'

'Day of rest.'

'Something like that.'

'Still, not bad considering.'

'Considering my age, you mean.'

Katherine laughed. 'Something like that.'

'Maybe tomorrow you can come with me?'

'Maybe.'

'I thought later, if the weather holds, we might go for a walk.'

'I'd like that.'

'Okay. Just let me get a quick shower before you put on that toast.'

*

They drove out on the Morvah to Penzance road, parked, and made the slow, winding climb up past the Seven Maidens to the derelict engine house at the centre of the old Ding Dong mine. Down below, the distant curve of Mounts Bay stretched out towards Lizard Point; above them, a patchwork sky and a buzzard hovering on a current of air.

Elder took the thermos of coffee from his backpack and they sat on a remnant of stone wall, backs to the wind. When Katherine reached out to take the cup from his hand, the words were out of his mouth before he could swallow them back.

'Kate, your wrists . . .'

'Dad . . .'

'I just . . .'

'Dad, I told you, no questions, right?'

'I just want to know what happened, that's all.'

Spilling the coffee across her fingers, Katherine rose sharply and walked away. Fifteen metres on, she stopped, head bowed.

'Kate . . .' He rested his hand gently on her arm and she shrugged it off.

'No questions, that's what I said. What you agreed.'

'I know, but . . .'

'But what?' Facing him now.

'That was before . . . You can't expect me not to ask.'

'Can't I?'

Elder shook his head and sighed.

'I cut my wrists, okay? It was an accident.'

'An accident?'

'Yes.'

'How on earth . . . ?'

'It doesn't matter.'

She stared back at him, daring him to say another word. The same stubborn face he remembered from the playground when she was four or five and he'd say it was time to leave, time to put your things away, stop reading, stop writing, get ready for bed.

'I don't want to go to bed.'

'Why not?'

'Because I have dreams. Bad dreams.'

Worse now, he was sure. He went back and sat down and after a few minutes she came and sat beside him. Somewhere in the middle distance a tractor started up and came gradually into view, ploughing its way up and back along one of the fields north towards St Just, a small squall of gulls following in its wake.

'I thought things were a little better now.'

'Better?'

'You know what I mean.'

'Do I?'

'I thought, after the therapy and everything . . .'

She laughed. 'The therapy?'

'Yes. I thought it was going well. Thought you'd found a way of coming to terms . . .'

'What? As in forgetting? You think that's possible? A few sessions with some shrink and it all goes away?'

'No, just . . .'

'Just what?'

'I don't know.'

'No, you don't, do you? Don't know a fucking thing. About me or anything. Hide yourself away down here and you don't fucking care!'

Swivelling on her heels, she stomped off through the heather the way they'd come, and Elder slowly levered himself up and set out after her, careful to keep his distance.

That evening, peace restored, they went to the cinema, the Filmhouse in Newlyn, ate fish and chips leaning over the harbour wall. Katherine had changed the bandages on her arms, while the questions continued to reverberate, unabated, unasked. Accidental? Both arms? The result of self-harming or something more potentially serious, final? If she wants to tell me, Elder persuaded himself with difficulty, she will.

On the way back across the peninsula, relaxed, Katherine chatted about the movie they'd just seen; about friends, flatmates – Abike, who was a teaching assistant in a local primary school; Stelina, who worked as a ward clerk in Mile End Hospital and was studying for a degree part-time; Chrissy, who juggled working behind a bar with being an artists' model. When Elder got out a bottle of Scotch back at the cottage, Katherine shook her head and made tea instead. It was quite late by the time tiredness took over and they were away to their beds.

Elder slept fitfully, riven by familiar dreams. A fisherman's makeshift hut fashioned from timber and tarpaulin and held together with nails and rope. The lapping of water. Seaweed. Ash. The remains of a fire further back along the beach. The carcass of a seabird plucked clean. When he pressed his weight against the door, the rotting wood gave way and he stumbled into darkness.

A scream shrilled through him and he was instantly awake.

A scream from the next-door room.

Katherine was sitting bolt upright in bed, eyes wide open, staring towards the open window, her body shaking. When he touched her gently, she whimpered and pulled her knees closer to her chest. Her eyes flickered, dilated, then closed.

'It's all right, Kate,' he said, easing her back down. 'It's just a dream.'

Her dreams, his dreams: one of the things they shared.

When she was just sixteen Katherine had been kidnapped by a man named Adam Keach, forced into a van and driven to

13

an isolated location on the North Yorks coast, a ramshackle hut where she had been held prisoner, tortured and raped. It had been Elder who had found her, naked, blood blisters on her arms and legs, bruises discolouring her shoulders and her back.

Stooping, he kissed her hair now, as he had then.

Squeezed her hand and left her sleeping.

Next morning she was gone.

3

No matter how hard he tried to shake off Katherine's words, they continued to sting. Hide yourself away down here and you don't fucking care! Well, there was truth in that, he supposed, more than he might readily admit. And, like most truths, it was hemmed in by circumstance and things that had, at the time, seemed beyond his control.

If only we'd stayed in London, he might have said, none of this would have happened. This. The past ten years.

In response to Joanne's pleading – it's a great opportunity, Frank, once in a lifetime; the chance to run her own salon in the high-flying Martyn Miles beauty and fashion empire – he had grudgingly transferred north from London and his job as a detective sergeant in the Met. Not even the proper north: Nottingham, the East Midlands; the Major Crime Unit, detective inspector. Promotion, at least. The pair of them dragging their fourteen-year-old, hormone-battered daughter reluctantly with them.

How long had it taken for Katherine to kick off at school,

collecting last warnings and temporary suspensions like trophies; for Elder, frustrated by what he saw as muddled provincial inefficiency, to shoot his mouth off at his superiors one time too often; and for Joanne, with all the grace and alacrity of the bloody obvious, to fall into the arms of Martyn Miles, self-made multimillionaire and Midlands Businessman of the Year?

Faced with probable disciplinary action and his wife's flaunting infidelity, a teenage daughter he no longer seemed to recognise, never mind understand, Elder had done the sensible, adult thing. Thrown his toys out of the pram. Handed in his resignation and, with only a few small savings and a foreshortened police pension behind him, hastened himself as far away as he could without leaving the country entirely. Hied himself off down to Cornwall, the far west, close enough almost to Land's End to smell the tang of the Atlantic, feel the spray. And with a few exceptions and excursions, there he'd stayed.

Odd jobs, a bit of manual labour, helping out at harvest, breaking his back alongside crews of Eastern Europeans picking daffodils in the spring. More recently and, with time, less resistant, he'd built upon a friendship fostered over a pint or two, the odd glass of single malt, with a local DI, Trevor Cordon, and for the last couple of years had worked sporadically as a civilian attached to the Devon and Cornwall Police Major Incident Support Team, providing training and assistance for investigations into serious crimes. A double murder, two cases of arson, one of serious sexual assault.

'Shame,' as Cordon had said, topping up his glass, 'to let all that experience go to waste.'

Elder wasn't so sure. But it kept his mind occupied, helped to pay the rent.

When he dialled Joanne's mobile it went straight to voicemail, but within minutes she called him back.

'Frank, what's wrong?'

'Does something have to be?'

'Usually, yes. Either that or it's my birthday. It's not my birthday, is it?'

'I was wondering if you had Kate's address?'

'Yes, of course. But I thought she was down there with you.'

'She was.'

'Don't tell me. You had a row.'

'Not exactly.'

'Oh, Frank . . .'

'She's been cutting herself, that's what it looks like. Maybe you knew. She had these bandages on her arms.'

He heard Joanne light a cigarette, slowly exhale. 'I had a phone call from London, just over a week ago. Homerton Hospital. Someone had found her collapsed on the street and called an ambulance. They were phoning from A & E. She'd cut her wrists.'

'Why on earth didn't you tell me?'

'She asked me not to. Almost the first thing she said when I saw her. Told me she'd tell you herself in her own time.'

Elder looked out to where two crows were worrying a buzzard away from their nest. If that had been her intention in coming down to see him, then, for whatever reason, it had failed.

'What was it all about, d'you know?'

'She wasn't exactly forthcoming. Well, you can imagine. But something to do with a relationship, I think. Someone she'd got involved with who'd messed her around, let her down. I'm really not sure.'

'And what she did, was it . . . was it serious? I mean . . .'

'Was she trying to take her own life?'

'Yes.'

'Frank, I don't know. I just don't know. From what I could tell she was pretty much out of it at the time . . .'

'Out of it how?'

'She'd been drinking. Quite heavily, I think. Pills, too . . .'

'Christ!'

'I tried to talk to her, but you know what she's like . . .'

Silence filled the air between them.

'I thought I might get the train up to London tomorrow,' Elder said. 'Go and see her.'

'You're sure that's a such good idea?'

'No. But I don't want to just leave it. Do nothing.'

'If you could get her to consider going back into therapy, that would be something.'

'Yes, maybe. But after what she said the other day, I don't think that's very likely.'

He wrote down the address on the back of an old receipt.

'You know where it is?' Joanne asked.

'Dalston, somewhere. I'll find it.'

'Tread carefully, Frank. Don't make things any worse than they already are.'

When Elder stepped outside, the birds had disappeared, leaving an empty sky. What kind of a father didn't know his only daughter's address? How many couples did he know who were truly happy and for how long? How many families?

It's being a copper, Frank, Trevor Cordon had said, one of too many nights when they'd closed the pub between them. It's the job. It skews your way of thinking, the way you see the world. Kids, fourteen, fifteen, out of their heads on heroin. Nine-year-olds giddy on laughing gas. Love as a fist in the face, a form of abuse.

Elder knew about abuse.

Used to think he knew about love.

What had Katherine said? You don't, do you? Don't know a fucking thing. About me or anything.

4

For all the day had started off fair, by the time the train reached the outskirts of London the skies had darkened and it was threatening rain. Elder followed the crowd down into the Tube, took the Victoria line to Highbury and Islington and changed onto the overground. The address Joanne had given him was ten minutes' walk from Dalston Junction. The Wilton Estate.

When he stepped out onto the street it was brightening again and the sun was trying to break through the remaining clouds. A woman with a black-and-white spaniel came towards him and he stopped her to ask for directions, the dog jumping up enthusiastically and leaving damp pawprints on his trousers.

At the corner of Lansdowne Drive and Forest Road, Elder passed between two low-rise blocks of flats and crossed towards a third. The flat where Katherine was living was on the upper floor, the paint on the front door flaking and in need of a fresh coat, the bell making a small chirruping sound that suggested the battery was running low. After two rings, a young woman in T-shirt and jeans snapped open the door and looked at Elder, surprised.

'You're not from UPS?'

'Afraid not.'

'I'm expecting a delivery.'

'Sorry.'

'They said between twelve and one.'

Elder glanced at his watch. 'Still twenty minutes to go.'

'So . . .' She stepped back and gave him an appraising look. 'You're not UPS, not here to read the meter, not smart or smarmy enough to be a Jehovah's Witness, besides which you're not holding a bible – you must be the police.'

'Not any more.'

'Okay, I give in.'

'I'm Katherine's father.'

'Really?'

'I don't suppose she's here?'

'Not now, no. But look, you're really Kate's dad, yes?'

'Yes.'

'She didn't say anything.'

'She doesn't know.'

The young woman looked at him keenly. 'You've got some kind of identification? I mean, you could be just about anyone.'

'Apart from UPS.'

'Apart from that.'

Elder took out his wallet and showed her his driving licence.

'Well,' she said, 'I suppose you'd better come in.'

The living room was busy with too many chairs, a television set, bookshelves, a table; what Elder assumed to be a sofa bed, covered with cushions, newspapers and magazines; an over-crowded clothes drier in front of the radiator.

'I'm Stelina.'

'Frank.'

Her hand was firm and cool.

'I'm not sure where she is. Kate. Seeing someone about a job, perhaps. I shouldn't think she'll be long.'

He nodded in the direction of the table, where an open lap-top lay surrounded by loose sheets of paper, a notebook, several large textbooks. 'Don't let me stop you, whatever you're doing.'

Stelina grimaced. 'Trying to finish an essay. Only two weeks overdue.'

'You're studying for what? A degree?'

'Community Development and Public Policy.'

Elder raised an eyebrow. 'Good luck with that.'

She laughed. 'I was just about to make coffee when the door went.'

'Thanks. If you're offering.'

'Instant okay?'

'Instant's fine.'

'There is some of the real stuff but it's Chrissy's and she gets antsy if anyone else uses it. Counts the grains. Besides, it's a faff.'

Elder opened the door on to the cantilevered balcony and stepped outside. Someone had decided to grow herbs in an old sink with indifferent success. Geraniums fared better, red and white, a long window box attached to the edge of the corrugated-steel shuttering. Below, the same woman he had seen before was walking slowly back across the courtyard, dragging her dog reluctantly behind her.

Stelina brought two mugs out onto the balcony and stood beside him. 'Kate, she's been through a bad time.'

'I know.'

'Must be a worry.'

'Yes.'

'When she . . .' The sentence hung, unfinished.

'Cut her wrists?'

'Yes. She'd been acting sort of strangely for a while. Not speaking. Shutting herself in her room. And drinking. I mean, more than normal. And she looked, well, she looked dreadful. Chrissy tried talking to her. She's the closest to Kate, I suppose, closer than the rest of us, the one she's known longest. But she just told her to F off and mind her own fucking business. Then . . .' She glanced away. 'The next thing any of us knew was this phone call from the hospital. You know the rest.'

'I'm not sure if I do.'

'That bastard,' Stelina said quietly.

'Who? Who d'you mean?'

'Winter. Anthony Winter.'

'Who's he?'

'Some artist. Painter. Kate was modelling for him . . .'

'Modelling?'

'Yes, they had some kind of thing going. I don't know . . .'

Someone knocked on the glass and when they turned it was Katherine.

'What the hell are you doing here?'

'Came to see you,' Elder said.

They walked, not heading anywhere in particular, talking sporadically, both careful, for now, to avoid the elephant in the room. That morning Katherine had been for an interview at a shop in Stoke Newington that had advertised for someone to work part-time.

'One of those trendy little places that sells everything you don't need at extravagant prices.'

'How'd it go?'

Katherine scowled. 'They wanted someone with retail experience. Bar work, apparently, doesn't count as retail experience. Not as far as they're concerned.'

'Bar work? Is that what you've been doing?'

'When I can.'

'You can always ask, you know. If you need help with the rent.'

'It's fine. Really.'

'I know your mum's been . . .'

'Dad, just leave it, okay?'

They bought a couple of sandwiches, a can of Coke and a ginger beer on Kingsland High Street and sat in Gillett Square, watching the skateboarders manoeuvre back and forth at speed.

'I'm sorry about running out on you like that,' Katherine said eventually.

'That's okay.'

'It was a lot of pressure, you know?'

'Not what I intended.'

'My fault, I should have realised.' Katherine smiled. 'You were a copper for how long?'

'I don't know. Twenty, twenty five years.'

'And I expected you not to ask questions? Begin an investigation?'

'That's not what I was doing. I just . . .'

'That's what you're here for now, though, isn't it? Why you've come all this way? You can't leave well enough alone.'

Elder nodded in the direction of Katherine's arms. 'Something like that, it's not so easy.'

'It's happened, Dad. It's over. I'm not going to do it again in a hurry.'

Elder bit into his sandwich; watched as a youth of maybe sixteen, tall, no helmet, pirouetted in the middle of a jump, missed the centre of his board and wobbled dangerously, flailing with both arms, before finally regaining his balance and executing a near-perfect turn.

'Stelina mentioned someone you'd been seeing.'

'Stelina should learn to mind her own business.'

'Some artist? Winter? Anthony Winter?'

'Dad . . .'

'You were modelling for him, she said.'

'She said too bloody much.'

Not wanting to fall into the same trap, Elder waited. A small, birdlike woman walked past, pushing two small, straggle-haired dogs in a pram.

'There was a thing, right?' Katherine said. 'Between us. Anthony and myself. No big deal. Not for him anyway. Obviously. But it was for me. At least, that's what I thought. Now it's over, okay? I never need to see him again and that's fine.'

'Fine?'

'Dad, it's what happens. Relationships end. You know that better than me. You and Mum.' Swallowing the last mouthful of Coke, she got to her feet. 'You'll want to make sure you don't miss your train home.'

5

The first time she'd seen him was at the art school. Central St Martin's. CSM. She'd been waiting for Chrissy, sitting under the glass-and-metal canopy by the entrance from Granary Square, flicking through the pages of a magazine.

'Come and meet me,' Chrissy had said. 'I'll be finished by four. Just after. We can get coffee or something. Maybe a drink later.'

Why not? Katherine had thought. It wasn't as if she had any thing much else to do. Not then.

A little way down from where she was sitting, a small crowd had gathered around one of the table-tennis tables; two blokes having a right go at it, smashing the ball and shouting. People egging them on.

Years ago, the last time she'd played. On holiday. Italy some-where. The Garfagnana? A villa, so-called. Nothing special, no pool or anything, but there had been a table-tennis table. Full-size. Hidden away in the barn, as if the owners, for whatever reason, hadn't wanted anyone to find it. Use it. Once they'd realised it was there, they'd played all the time. Her and her dad especially. Her mum getting more and more worked up and angry. 'Is that what we paid all that money for? To come all this way just to play ping-pong?'

It had given them something to argue about, Katherine thought, her mum and dad, that's what it had done. Ping-pong! They didn't give a shit about ping-pong, who played and how often. Neither of them. That hadn't been it at all.

A cheer went up as one of the players smashed home the final point and someone else stepped forward to take him on. She wondered if Chrissy might fancy a game later, after they'd finished? But then, Katherine thought, knowing Chrissy she was almost certain to say no. Me? You kidding, right? All those people watching? Chrissy, who took off her clothes regular as clockwork in front of a bunch of students with never, as far as she knew, a second thought about it.

She checked her phone: no new messages, no texts. There were plenty of art students coming out now, arty bags on their shoulders, pausing to fiddle with their phones, texting, lighting roll-ups, but still no sign of Chrissy. Katherine shoved her magazine back down into her bag and wandered over towards the doors. Which was when she bumped into him. Walking with his head turned, calling out to someone behind him, laughing.

'Watch it!' Katherine shouted, but by then he'd gone clattering into her, knocking the bag from her shoulder and spinning her round.

'Oh, God!' he said in that voice of his. 'I'm so sorry.'

'You should look where you're going!'

'I know, I know. Here, let me . . .'

'No, it's okay.'

He started to bend down towards the bag and the magazine that had gone shooting out across the floor, but Katherine scrambled after them and retrieved them both.

When she'd set them to rights he was still standing there and she got a proper look at him for the first time. Not tall, but not short either. Late forties, maybe? She'd never been very good with ages. Men's ages. Bald. Completely. Not that that was any kind of sign nowadays. Wearing what looked like an expensive overcoat, cashmere; flecks of paint on his shoes.

'You'll accept my apologies?'

She nodded, mumbled something, and he turned swiftly away, striding off towards Granary Square. Then there was Chrissy, coming through the crowd.

'What were you doing, talking to Anthony Winter?'

'Who?'

'Anthony Winter.'

'Who's he?'

6

Paddington to Penzance, five hours, twenty-seven minutes. A lot of time to think. Too much. Thoughts churning round and round. Whatever her intentions, Kate had come within — what? — an inch, an hour of taking her own life. And why? Because she was depressed? Because she'd been out of her head on booze and worse? Because of — what had she called it? — a thing? Because a thing with a man she'd become involved with, a relationship, had gone wrong.

Relationships end. You know that better than me. You and Mum.

He walked down to the buffet car and bought two minibar-sized bottles of whisky, drank one there, two swallows, the burning at the back of his throat, took the other to his seat. At first the Wi-Fi wasn't working and then it was.

The Wikipedia page for Anthony Winter was nicely succinct. British artist, born March 1966, Salisbury, Wilts. Best known initially as a painter of urban landscapes and, latterly, portraits, his work often mixes figuration with symbolism, ultra-realism with elements of the surreal. He studied at the Slade School of Fine Art (1984–87), briefly at Goldsmiths College (1987–88) and at the Royal College of Art (1988–90). After taking part in several group shows, including one in the British Pavilion at the Venice Biennale (1998), his first solo exhibition was at Abernathy Fine Art in 1999. Solo exhibitions since then include the National Gallery of Scotland (2004), the Museum Brandhorst in Munich (2009), the Irish Museum of Modern Art (2011) and the Serpentine Gallery (2015).

His marriage to the painter Susannah Fielding (b. 1969, Beccles, Suffolk) ended in divorce. They have one son, Matthew (b. 1992) and a daughter, Melissa (b. 1994).

His photograph showed a strong face, a quite prominent, chiselled nose; the mouth set, the barest suggestion of a smile; blue eyes, dark blue, unfettered and clear. The head close-shaven and smooth. Nothing to suggest, as he stared back into the camera's lens, anything less than absolute confidence, self-belief.

No big deal.

Elder could picture him, picture the scene.

No big deal, Kate, okay? And smiling. Even as he turned away. Job done. No big deal.

Not for him anyway. But it was for me.

Kate's words became lost in the broken rhythm of the train. Bristol Temple Meads. Exeter St Davids. By the lock gates of a canal, a heron stared down into the water with perfect concentration. Glimpsed then gone.

Dad, it's what happens.

Is it? Did it have to be? And was there nothing he could do?

He finished the second whisky, closed his eyes.

7

At the cottage there was a note tucked under the door. *Just in case you don't check your messages, we've a gig tonight. The Acorn. See you there? Vicki xxx.* The last thing Elder fancied right then: music, noise, a crowd, the need to be sociable, respond. But by evening he'd changed his mind. A walk to the headland. Wind coursing around his head. Water driving against the rocks below. What was it someone had said? Loneliness is just solitude taken a step too far. Or was that the other way round?

The Acorn was two-thirds full, not a bad crowd, most of the tables taken, a few people standing at the back and along the sides, blokes mostly, pints in hand. The band had been augmented for the occasion by a couple more musicians, a trombonist down from London and a second saxophone; the sound fuller and, to Elder's ears, more satisfying. Midway through an arrangement of Ellington's 'A Train', he felt a finger pressing gently against the nape of his neck.

'You made it then.'

When he turned to face her, she kissed him close by the side of his mouth.

'When are you on?'

Vicki's smile broadened. 'They're saving me till the second half.'

'Secret weapon?'

'Something like that.'

She began with 'Honeysuckle Rose', no surprises there, just the double bass behind her at the beginning, that and her thumb and finger clicking on the beat, and then the drummer coming softly in on brushes when they reached the middle eight. Vicki singing, as she usually did, with her eyes closed much of the time, body swinging easy – a velvet dress in deepest blue, full at the hips, close at the waist and loose above – a woman, Elder thought, not for the first time, for whom cleavage could have been invented.

A blues next, then an up-tempo chase through 'What a Little Moonlight Can Do', and then . . .

'This is a song I learned from a recording by Billie Holiday that she made way back in nineteen forty and which I first heard when I was eighteen or nineteen and I've been plucking up the courage to sing it ever since. So fingers crossed and here goes. Body and Soul.'

A few bars of sparse piano and then the lyric . . . My days have grown so lonely . . . nailing Elder from the first line, a threnody of helplessness, love and despair. Vicki's voice by the final verse, the final chorus, beaten, defeated, little more than a whisper. Silence. And then the applause. Elder walked out into the night.

Walked down towards the harbour, lights on the water.

How long he'd been standing there before Vicki came and stood alongside him, he couldn't say, save that his face and hands were cold and his mind was numb.

'You didn't like it?'

'What do you think?'

'You never walked out on me before.' Her hand slid into his. 'Actually, that's a lie.'

He put his arm around her waist.

After a few moments she said, 'It doesn't have to be true love, you know. Not at our age.'

He didn't need to look to know she was smiling.

'Shall we go in my car,' she said, 'or yours?'

When Elder woke it was still dark. Vicki lay curled towards him, her hand twitching involuntarily, the faint whistle of her breathing almost at one with the tide as it beat back along the shore. Careful not to wake her, he padded to the window and looked out: the longer he stood there the more clearly he could make out the contours of St Michael's Mount, bulking up against the grey of the sky.

'Come back to bed, Frank.'

She slipped one of her legs across his and rested her head on his chest. 'What was it about the song?'

It was a while before he could formulate an answer.

'The helplessness of it, I suppose. The if-I-can't-have-you-my-life-isn't-worth-living-ness of it. And the way you sing it, so bloody believable.'

'It's a song, Frank, just a song. And if I can't make you believe in it for the time I'm singing it, then I'm doing it all wrong. But that's not me. That's not who I am.'

'I know.'

She stroked his arm. 'You're thinking of Kate, aren't you?'

He nodded, told her about the relationship with Winter, what little he knew.

'I'm sorry, Frank,' she said.

He sat up, swinging his legs round from the bed. 'I'll make tea.'

'And bring it back?'
'And bring it back.'

Elder had had a girlfriend once, before he was married, who'd insisted, every morning, rain or shine, weekday or weekend, on making tea and toast and bringing them back to bed on a tray. It didn't matter if they'd been out late the night before and not got back, exhausted, till two or three; didn't matter if the alarm went off at some godforsaken early hour because she'd drawn first shift, there it was, where it had to be, tea and toast. Some mornings it was not unknown for the tray to capsize, crumbs to be found days later, deep down in the crevices of the sheets.

Just when he'd brought himself around to thinking it was really serious, true love perhaps, maybe they should get engaged – well, he was only twenty-three at most – she'd made it clear she had other ideas entirely, other fish to fry.

He'd scarcely thought of her in years.

At twenty-three that hadn't seemed possible; hadn't felt that way at all.

Sitting, the pair of them propped up against pillows, Vicki listened while he told her about Katherine and Anthony Winter, what little he knew, what little more he could surmise.

'First serious relationship I had,' Vicki said, 'was with my teacher, music teacher. I was at college, seventeen. He was forty, forty-one. Married, of course. And for – what? – nine months, a little more, it took over my whole life. Being with him, thinking about him, thinking about being with him again. Then one day it was over. As quickly as it had begun. I was bereft, angry; cried myself to sleep, cried myself awake. Hung around outside his office, outside his house. Wrote letters to his wife that never got sent. God knows what would have happened in these days of instant emails, instant texts.'

She shook her head, exhaled slowly, sipped her tea.

'And what did happen?' Elder asked.

Vicki smiled. 'I always think . . . There's this story I read, short story, Hemingway, maybe? I think it's Hemingway. Anyway, there's this boy, Nick, he's young, no more than fourteen or fifteen. And he learns that the girl he's in love with has been seen with this other boy. When he goes to bed that night, he's feeling so bad about it, so upset, he thinks his heart must be broken. But then, when he wakes up in the morning the first things he hears are the waves outside and the wind – they must live by a lake or the sea or something – and all he can think about is going fishing. It's a long time before he remembers his heart is broken.'

'And that's what it was like? For you?'

'Not overnight, not exactly. But that's not the point.'

'Then what is?'

'The point is, he thinks his heart is broken because that's what he's been taught to think.'

'Taught how?'

'By what you were talking about before. Partly that, anyway. Songs. Stuff he's heard on the radio. Films. TV. Things he's seen. I mean, don't get me wrong, he's upset, feeling wretched, anyone would be. But, like it says, his heart isn't really broken.'

'And you're saying that's what it's like for Kate? She's just overreacting?'

'I don't mean what she's feeling isn't real, of course it is. She was hurt, angry, upset, she had every right to be. I just mean, given a little time, it may not be quite as serious as she thought it was. She'll get over it, that's what I'm saying. And maybe' – squeezing Elder's hand – 'maybe by dwelling on it, drawing attention to it, asking too many questions, you're preventing that from happening.'

'So I should shut up, say nothing, mind my own business?'

'Not exactly.'

'What then?'

'Back off a little.'

'And if I can't stop thinking about it? Worrying?'

'Then that's your problem. Don't make it hers.'

Elder felt as if he'd been stung, slapped; his body tensed, his breathing changed. 'I'd better be getting ready,' he said.

She came up behind him as he was tucking his shirt down into his trousers and rested her hand on his shoulder. 'The trouble is, you're a man. And not just a man – for most of your adult life you've been a policeman. You feel the need to do something, get things sorted, solve the problem. And I think this is something she's got to do on her own. You can help, of course. Be supportive. But other than that . . .'

She stepped away and he turned towards her. 'That relationship you were talking about, with the teacher, didn't you think he was using you?'

'Frank, I knew what I was doing, knew he was married; I think we were both using each other.'

He thought about it later, what Vicki had said, and yes, it made sense, a skewed sort of sense perhaps, but sense nonetheless, and he knew that what he was doing could be construed as interfering, making things worse instead of better. He understood, with the clarity of hindsight and common sense, that he should leave well enough alone. Let time do its thing, allow wounds to heal. But Winter was a significantly older, presumably experienced and sophisticated man, and Katherine, in his eyes, was still little more than a child.

His child.

And that made all the difference in the world. Whatever Vicki and Ernest fucking Hemingway might say.

8

They were at this club. Shoreditch. All four of them. Abike's birthday. They'd had a meal first, some new burger place; patties in brioche for God's sake, hot sauce, sweet-potato fries. Then the pub. And then this. Cosmopolitans. Screwdrivers. Vodka Martinis. Abike, who didn't drink, sticking to Shirley Temples, virgin pina coladas. The DJ heading off on some kind of mild retro kick. Missy Elliott, Jamiroquai, Jack 'N' Chill. 'Fuck off!' Chrissy yelled at the umpteenth bloke to start hitting on them. 'Fuck off and take your sorry dick with you!'

At two in the morning the streets were cold and Stelina's Uber app kept refusing to recognise her location. Linking arms, they half-danced, half-hobbled as far as the high street, Chrissy and Katherine with their heels in their hands, and hailed a black cab.

Back at the flat, Katherine came close to crashing out, but Stelina brought her round with peppermint tea and the promise of chocolate digestives. Chrissy presented Abike with two

Weetabix in warm milk topped with a pink cake candle and announced she was off to bed.

'I'm sorry,' she said over loud protests, 'but I have to be looking my best for a roomful of final-year students in the morning and I need all the beauty sleep I can get.'

Half an hour or so later, when Katherine went into the room they shared, single beds a few metres apart, Chrissy's eyes blinked open.

'I don't know how you can,' Katherine said.

'Can what?'

'In front of all those people. Naked.'

'It's not naked, it's nude. There's a difference. And besides, it's like sex. Most sex. After the first few times you barely give it a second thought.'

With that, she turned over and, within minutes, she was fast asleep.

'What did you mean?' Katherine said. 'What you said last night?'

They were in the kitchen, oddly early, Abike and Stelina still dead to the world. Chrissy measuring out the coffee.

'I probably said a lot of things.'

'No, I mean last thing. About posing.'

'Posing?'

'Not naked but nude.'

'I said that?'

'Uh-huh.'

Chrissy laughed. 'I probably read it somewhere. Some magazine.'

'But is it true?'

'Yes, I think so. More or less, anyway.'

'So explain.'

Chrissy screwed the lid down on the stovetop pot and set it on the gas.

'Naked, it's like ordinary, everyday. In the bathroom, the shower. Or, you know, when you're with someone. But nude, it's . . . well, it's professional, for one thing. The way it's set up, everything. Posing for a group especially. When it's for someone on their own, just the one person, I suppose that's a bit different, or it can be, but with a class you're the model and they're the artists, well, trying to be, and what they're doing – they might be sketching or painting, whatever – what they're concentrating on, it's not really you, not you at all – you could be a bunch of flowers or some old vase or something – what they're concentrating on is getting it right, getting it down properly. They don't even see you, most of the time. Just bits of you. A knee or an arm . . .'

'A breast?'

'Yes, but not . . .' She paused to turn up the flame. 'The way they look at you, it's not . . . If they were looking at you as if you were naked, you'd know, believe me.'

'And that never happens?'

'Hardly ever.'

'And when it does?'

'Give 'em the same look you would if they were coming on to you in some club, they get the message. Once, there was this one guy, I had a word with the woman taking the class – just so happened it was a woman – next week she'd moved him, back of the room, out of my eyeline, end of problem.'

She lifted the pot from the stove while Katherine got the milk from the fridge.

'I've told you before, if you're interested, there's always people looking for models. Good ones. That drawing class, Wednesdays . . . Be a shoe-in, figure like yours, all those inter-esting little curves . . .'

'Fuck off!' Katherine said and laughed.

'That's a no, then?'

'Yes, it's a no.'

'Rent's due end of the month again. Can't bank on your mum bailing you out for ever.'

'I'll get it sorted.'

'Suit yourself.'

They took their mugs of coffee into the living room. Katherine checked her emails, Facebook, Tumblr. Chrissy seemed to be alternately staring at her toes or out of the window.

'How much d'you get an hour again?' Katherine asked.

9

It was an old building, grand at the front, pillars and a decorated arch above the door; far grander than the street it was in: a mini-supermarket at either end, a workman's café, betting shop, dry cleaner's, an old-fashioned ironmonger's that doubled as a locksmith and shoe repairer. Inside the entrance to the building the paint was starting to flake away from the walls; a number of the tiles in the hallway were chipped and in need of being replaced. The lift wobbled and shook a little as it took Katherine up to the topmost floor.

'It'll be a doddle,' Chrissy had said. 'If you're going to start somewhere, you can't do better than this. A drawing class for old biddies and granddads. And the bloke who teaches it, he's a sweetie.'

The sweetie met her at the door: moleskin trousers, Aran sweater, a mane of white hair.

'You must be Katherine. It's lovely to meet you. And every bit as beautiful as Chrissy said.'

Camp, Katherine thought, as Christmas.

She followed him along the corridor and into a wide room with windows on two sides; a dozen or more tables set out in a broad curve around a raised platform where she assumed she would pose. A few of the class had arrived already; a pair of grey-haired ladies chatting amiably, a tall man with a slightly hunched back taking off his coat and draping it carefully over his chair.

'The changing room's over here,' the teacher said, pointing off along another short corridor. 'Just pop back out when you're ready. We usually try to start on time.'

Katherine let herself in and closed the door. There was a sink with a skimpy towel pegged alongside, a toilet in a separate cubicle. Table, chair, worn boards, a mirror on the wall. Her face looked pale, the colour bleached away. From outside, she could hear voices raised in greeting as more of the class arrived.

She could leave now, say it was all a mistake, there was still time.

Some kind of robe and something on your feet, Chrissy had said, that's all you need. Katherine had brought along a silky dressing gown with a design of peacock feathers that had been her mother's; a pair of scuffed pink trainers. After using the toilet – 'You don't want to be jumping up every five minutes to pee' – she undressed quickly, hanging some of her clothes on the hooks behind the door, folding the rest over the chair.

One last glance in the mirror – she looked terrible, she thought, a waxwork of herself – she stepped out and closed the door.

'Katherine,' the teacher said, his voice deliberately louder to attract the class's attention. 'This is Katherine, everyone, she's going to model for us today.'

Amongst murmured greetings, a few calls of 'Hello, Katherine', clutching her robe closed, she followed the teacher

41

through the tables and on to the platform, on which there was now a chair.

'What I like to do is give the students the chance to get their eye in, as it were, so we usually start off making two or three quick drawings and then move on to something more concentrated, detailed, forty minutes or so – a longer pose for you – after which we'll all take a little break. Then, when we're refreshed, we'll finish by asking you to do a longer pose, standing. If that all sounds hunky-dory?'

He smiled, waiting for Katherine to nod agreement.

'Lovely. Well, seated first then. Back quite straight and sort of half-turned away, the body at an interesting angle.'

Stepping back, he smiled again, encouragingly.

'Whenever you're ready.'

Katherine would say, telling her friends later, it was the longest moment of her life, but, in fact, it was a matter of seconds: an awareness, blurred, of faces looking up at her expectantly, and then, kicking off her shoes, she let the robe slide over her shoulders, down her back and to the floor.

After the first time it was easy. Well, no, but easier, certainly. Aside from those few occasions when one of the students directed a remark to her directly, Katherine contrived to keep herself apart; as if she'd been able to erect some kind of shield, invisible, between the class and herself. Compartmentalisation, she'd learned to be good at that. Had to be. Thinking her own thoughts, projecting herself back and forwards in time, anything and everything from the name of the girl who'd been mean to her in the first year of primary school to the mental shopping list to take with her to Tesco's on the way home. Thoughts interrupted by the slight pain that was spreading from her hip down along her thigh, caused by being in the same position for too long; the desire to scratch that itch on the left side of her cheek; the need, despite adhering to Chrissy's advice, to pee. When she glanced, almost accident-ally, at the drawing tables as she passed, it was as if those nicely contoured lines in ink or charcoal, those limbs, belonged to someone else, not her.

After just a month, the same teacher asked her if she would model for a class he taught over in Chelsea, beginners, a longer session but he could afford to pay a little more per hour.

Katherine agreed.

Soon, if things continued this way, she might be able to give up bar work altogether. Have a few more early nights. Spend more time in the gym. Start to think again seriously about what she wanted to do with her life, longer term. Take after Stelina and study: another degree, maybe. Something more useful this time.

Chrissy woke her at seven, sitting on the edge of the bed, pained, blotchy-faced, a hot-water bottle pressed against her tummy.

'What? What is it?'

'You've got to go in for me. The art school. I've got my period.'

'That's okay, surely. You can always . . .'

'I feel like shit. This bastard hurts like hell and I can't face four and a half hours of lying on my side with swollen tits, worrying if the string from my tampon's showing.'

'Then cancel.'

'I can't. It's too late. And besides . . .' The thought got lost in a gasp of pain. 'Kate, please. Just this once. I won't ask you again, I promise.'

Katherine was careful to arrive in plenty of time; Chrissy had messaged the tutor who took the class, explained, apologised, introduced. She was around her mother's age, Katherine thought, the tutor, dark hair cut almost savagely short, a white shirt under paint-smirched dungarees, sitting cross-legged on the wall outside the studio, assiduously working on a roll-up as Katherine approached.

'I'm Vida,' she said, holding out a hand. 'Stupid name. Call me V.'

The tips of her fingers were calloused and hard, the palms fleshy and soft.

'Classic pose this morning. You on a nice length of purple velvet, arse cheeks outwards, hip raised. *Rokeby Venus*, that kind of thing. And let's see' — reaching round, she bunched Katherine's hair in her hand and raised it higher — 'if we can't clip this up somehow, see what they can do with this neck of yours.'

Was it any more strange, twenty pairs of eyes fixed on your back view as opposed to your front? At least, Katherine thought, she still exercised enough that her rear didn't sag; there was firm flesh and muscle in her thighs and running had left her with well-defined triceps.

'How was that?' Vida asked at the lunch break.

'Okay, thanks. Fine.'

'We've got a visitor this afternoon. Anthony Winter. Heard of him?'

Katherine nodded. 'Yes, I think so.' She didn't say, he almost knocked me flying once, not looking where he was going.

'Won't affect you particularly. Just means there might be a bit more chat than usual. Students getting nervous. Oh, and we'll do the thing with the mirror.'

'The mirror?'

Vida slid a postcard from the pocket of her dungarees.

'The lady herself.'

In the painting, the woman lay in the same position Katherine had adopted, but with the addition of some kind of winged cherub holding a mirror which reflected her face. 'That's what we've got for you this afternoon, a nice framed mirror. But only resting against the wall, I'm afraid, no cherub.'

Did she feel any more nervous that afternoon, knowing that Winter was there? Not at all, why should she? What was Winter to her? She couldn't help but be aware of his presence, nonetheless. Sense him as he moved amongst the students, pausing to look at their work, pontificating, cajoling, occasionally laughing, his laugh a rough-edged kind of sound, akin to growling. The voice resonant and deep; the voice of a man well used to being listened to, expecting attention.

Staring, as she had to, at her own face in the mirror, she was less able to drift off into a world of her own, as she sometimes did when posing; consequently, time passed more slowly and she felt herself becoming increasingly conscious of the tiredness that came from being restricted to the same position, the dull ache in the arm on which she was leaning.

At last, she heard Vida thanking Winter on her students' behalf for giving over so much of his time to look at their work and for all the encouragement he had given, the expertise he'd passed on.

'Nothing, nothing. A pleasure, a pleasure.'

And she thought he had gone. Until, glancing back into the mirror, she saw him standing, perfectly still, his eyes staring into hers.

10

'He wants you.'

'What?'

'He wants you – Winter. To model for him.'

'What? No way.'

'Why ever not?'

They were sitting on a low wall overlooking the canal, Katherine with a salted caramel ice cream from Ruby Violet, Vida smoking a particularly evil-looking black roll-up. Lunch break the following day, Chrissy still indisposed.

'I don't know,' Katherine said. 'It's different. Just one person, it wouldn't feel . . . it just wouldn't feel right.'

'You know it's a big deal, though, right? Anthony Winter. He doesn't just ask anybody. I know girls'd give their eye teeth for the chance. I mean, he's not Damien Hirst or anything. But up there. Getting to be. Couple of paintings sold recently at close to six figures.'

Katherine swore beneath her breath as a piece of ice cream rolled off the edge of the cone and down on to her jeans.

'I'm happy doing what I'd doing. Just the odd class here and there, filling in.' She smiled. 'I don't exactly see it as a career.'

'What is?'

'My choice of career? I'm still not sure. I thought I did, but now . . .'

'You went to uni, right?'

'Uh-huh. Sheffield. Sports management.' A small laugh. 'Seemed a good idea at the time.'

'And have you thought what you might really want to do?'

'I'm afraid not, no.'

Vida looked at her watch. 'We should be getting back.'

Katherine dabbed again at her jeans and dropped the napkin into a convenient bin; licked the stickiness from her fingers as they walked back inside.

'So what do you want me to tell Winter when he calls?'

'Tell him no. I'm sorry, but no. No way.'

A week or so later, after spending the best part of an hour burrowing through the maze of clothes that is TK Maxx, hunting down that elusive bargain, Katherine found herself crossing the street towards Foyles bookshop, the art department right there on the ground floor, monographs on the shelves in alphabetical order. She had to bend low to slide the book she was looking for out and into her hands. *Anthony Winter: Paintings 2004 – 2016*, published to coincide with his show at the Serpentine Gallery.

The first group of paintings were of street scenes, rows of anonymous-looking houses, at night for the most part, sombre, dark: always a single light somewhere burning, a street lamp or bedroom window; and then, as you looked longer, more carefully, something else came into view – something that had been there all along, but had somehow remained unseen – the silhouette on an animal sneaking along beside the wall, a cat, perhaps, or fox; someone in deep shadow behind a curtain, a downstairs window; a couple pressed together in a furtive embrace by the corner wall.

Then, fewer these, paintings of fields, barren, bare, speckled here and there, some of them, with snow. A skeleton of trees piercing the fierce blue of the horizon. A car at the end of a lane that seemed to have petered out in the middle of nowhere; dusk, a lowering sky, the car facing away, the red of its tail lights burning brightly, the contours of two people, just visible through the rear window.

From there onwards the focus shifted: interior replaced exterior; people no longer in shadow but in furious close-up; people laid bare, the paint thicker than before, more extreme. A man's face, mouth wide, screaming silently from the canvas, his eyes dark and drained of colour; a child in ragged clothing pressed back against a brick wall, crying, wrought by tears; an elderly woman with her shoulders bent, one withered hand reaching towards the viewer – the artist – as if pleading to be released.

In contrast, the first of the nudes was gentle, soft, a blurring of the light; the model young, Katherine thought, no more than fourteen or fifteen, breasts barely formed, eyes closed as if sleeping. Then several paintings in which parts of the body were shown in close-up: pendulous breasts, riven by purple veins; a partly engorged penis above a tangle of pubic hair. No face. No mercy shown.

The book opened out into a double-page: on either side of the fold a young woman, naked, strikingly beautiful, dark hair that fell towards her shoulders, lipsticked mouth, standing in front of a floor-length mirror; the identical pose in both, save that on the left her hands hung down empty, relaxed, and in the other her right hand held what Katherine knew from her brief early passion with horses to be a riding crop, its narrow shaft ending in a leather tongue known as the keeper.

In the first painting, the model's back, reflected in the mirror, was smooth and bare; in the second, the upper half, across and below the shoulders, was scored with red, narrow lines, biting into the skin and edged with blood.

Katherine shut the book firmly closed.

An image in her mind, hooking her back: Adam Keach, the stink of slowly rotting fish, the cry of gulls, his hands on her skin.

Standing, she was dizzy, needing air.

Out on the pavement, she steadied herself against the glass of the shopfront, waited until passing traffic, passers-by, had come into focus, then made her way slowly, steadily towards the Tube.

That night and nights after, the usual dreams. The ones that had been haunting her since she was sixteen. She went to the GP, who prescribed pills to help her sleep. Bought more pills of her own. She contacted the therapist she'd seen previously and made an appointment, cancelling it at the last moment. A week or so later, she picked up another session with the same teacher, this in the upstairs room above an old Victorian pub in Walthamstow. Almost enough to pay her share of the rent but still not quite. She put off calling her mum until it was well overdue. With a sigh and a warning that this would have to be the last time, Joanne transferred the money into her account. A little extra on top so you can go out and treat yourself.

Katherine bought herself a black velvet dress from Zara and wore it to the party she and Chrissy had been invited to in Soho, Vida and Justine celebrating the fifth anniversary of their civil partnership.

The party was in a private club, a DJ on one floor, live music on another, just bass and guitar; everywhere crowded, couples sitting on the stairs. Katherine found herself squashed up into a corner with a couple of gay men animatedly trying to remember the names of all the characters from *The Magic Roundabout*. Florence? Dylan?

Edging narrowly between them, she extricated herself back into the twenty-first century.

Chrissy seemed to have disappeared.

Picking up a glass of wine, she made her way cautiously down the stairs and out into the street.

It was late, later than she'd thought. A straggle of people, cars, the glare of lights.

'You know what they say about parties?'

She recognised the voice before turning her head. Unstructured suit, blue shirt, brown shoes.

'No, what do they say?'

'Arrive late, leave early.'

'How about just don't go?'

'There is always that, of course. The denial school of orthodoxy.' Winter reached into his pocket for cigarettes; offered one to Katherine and when she refused, lit one for himself and leaned back against the wall.

Katherine drank a little more wine.

'You're refusing to model for me, V says.'

'That's right.'

'Any particular reason?'

Katherine shrugged.

'You don't like my work, perhaps?'

'I don't know your work.'

'You don't like me then?'

'I don't know you either.'

'Shame.'

The lights from the restaurant across the street reflected green and red across his face, deflecting the blue of his eyes.

'How much d'you get per session, at the college?'

'Ten pounds an hour.'

'I'll pay you twelve. Fifteen. Lunch thrown in.'

Katherine shook her head. A couple came out of the club, drunk, laughing, and pushed their way between them, almost knocking Katherine's glass from her hand.

'Why?' she said. 'Why's it so important?'

'Is it?'

'You seem to think so.'

Winter flicked his cigarette away into the road. 'Here,' he said, taking a card from his pocket. 'The address of my studio. Come round, any time, get a sense of things. If you still feel uncomfortable with the idea, then as the French say, *tant pis.*'

He left her with the card in her hand.

11

Trevor Cordon lived in a converted sail loft in Newlyn, together with a springer spaniel, a small library of mainly nineteenth-century novels – he was on his way through the *Barsetshire Chronicles* for the third time – and several teetering piles of cassettes and CDs, picked up at charity shops across the county, Penzance to Redruth and beyond. Cordon and the springer were both getting on a little, starting to creak at the knees.

A detective inspector in the Devon and Cornwall police, further promotion stalled by a mixture of his own intransigence and a lack of ambition, Cordon was content enough to ply the local brand of neighbourhood policing, spiced up as it was, from time to time, by excursions in the company of the Major Incident Team – in which context he'd met Frank Elder, Elder having been drafted in to help with training, and assist, in a civilian capacity, in the pursuance of the occasional serious investigation. Most recently, a double murder, mother and daughter, initially thought to be victims of a fire; the house in which they'd lived, on a secluded spot deep into the peninsula, had gone up in flames, a dozen fire appliances to deal with the blaze; only later, when the charred bodies were autopsied, was the true cause of death revealed, asphyxia caused by a combination of smothering and severe chest compressions, rather than, as had been assumed, by smoke inhalation.

Elder had helped to plot a path through a circuitous trail of potential witnesses, unravel a complex family tree. Who had the most to gain, the least to lose? What slights, what jealousies had grown, festering through the years? More and more, Cordon had said, like a Daphne du Maurier novel.

The daughter had been in her late fifties, twice divorced, twice remarried, five children, three living within a hundred-mile radius; her mother, in her eighties, had been a minor celebrity in her day, a poet and painter in her own right and the muse and lover of one of the latter-day Lamorna colony of artists.

Art, Elder said as if it were an infection, it gets bloody everywhere.

In the end, the perpetrators proved to be a pair of drugged-up sixteen-year-olds, lured to the house by rumours of hoarded cash, the prospect of easy money, and acting out their angry disappointment before setting fire to the place in an attempt to cover up their crime. They were caught when one of them attempted to sell a silver watch at a pawnbroker's in Camborne and the owner, checking his list of stolen goods, phoned the local police.

Little or nothing either Elder or Cordon had done amounted to much more than the expense of police time and money. That was how it was sometimes. An apparent waste of diminishing resources. Still, it was the job; you did what you could.

'Miss it, don't you?' Cordon said. They were in the Star Inn, not far shy of closing. 'Wish you'd never chucked it in, I'll be bound.'

'Do I, buggery! What little I'm doing now, that's quite

enough, thank you very much. And I'd not be doing that if it weren't for the money.'

Cordon chuckled. 'I'll believe you, millions wouldn't.'

Outside, a narrow strip of pavement facing towards the harbour, the air struck cold. Stars plentiful overhead.

'Nightcap?'

'Best not.'

'Taxi, is it?'

Elder laughed. 'It's a long bloody walk else. And I'll not be driving. Last thing I want, one of your lads breathalysing me, making me walk a straight line.'

'Come back and help me crack this new bottle of Bushmills, then. Call a cab from there.'

The interior of the old sail loft was warm and smelt faintly of dog. Cordon poured two good shots of Irish whiskey into appropriate glasses; sliced bread and cut generous chunks from a hunk of cheese.

There was a photograph, faded a little now, fixed to the fridge door, Cordon and a youth of fourteen or fifteen side by side on a small boat out to sea, wind catching the boy's hair, sunlight glinting off the surface of the water. No disguising the look of pleasure on Cordon's face, the smile.

'Your lad?' Elder said. 'See him at all?'

'Not since he was over a few years back. I say a few, must be five now, maybe six. Talk once in a while. Christmas and New Year. Birthdays.' Cordon shrugged. 'You know how it is.'

'You've not been out to see him?'

'Australia? Too bloody far by half. Scillies, that's far enough for me.' His face creased in a smile. 'He used to say, when he'd got settled, it's great here, you'd love it, you should come, and I'd be yes, yes, of course, but not just now. Both of us knowing it'd never happen.' He reached for his glass. 'His mother went the one time, I believe.'

'Miss him, though?'

'Once in a while. You? Your lass? Katherine, is it?'

Elder shrugged. 'London, not Australia.'

'See quite a bit of her then?'

'Not really.'

'Comes a time. Live their own lives.'

'She was down not so long back.'

'Like to have met her.'

'Only here a couple of days.'

'Maybe next time then.'

He refilled Elder's glass and then his own. Time to talk about something that didn't matter. What was going on in the Premiership. The current state of Cornish rugby. Twenty minutes or so later, Elder's phone beeped with a text from the driver; he was waiting at the end of the street.

As soon as Elder was back from his morning run and showered, coffee on the stove, he switched on the computer. Three email messages, one from Vicki.

If you haven't already seen it, there's something about that Anthony Winter in the news.

A link to the BBC News website. *British artist Anthony Winter threatened with legal action over alleged breach of contract.*

The gist of what followed being that Winter had apparently walked out on a long-standing agreement with one gallery in favour of exhibiting with another. Rebecca Johnson, described as an art consultant, was quoted as saying, *'Anthony is only interested in having his work displayed in the most sympathetic settings and the most appropriate circumstances. As regards the galleries concerned, I'm sure that any disagreements can be resolved to everyone's mutual advantage.'* There followed extracts from conflicting interviews with Rupert Morland-Davis, owner of Mayfair-based Abernathy Fine Art, and Tom Hecklington of the Hecklington and Wearing gallery in Shoreditch. From Anthony Winter himself there was no word.

Elder typed *Hecklington and Wearing* into the search bar.

The gallery was pleased to announce a major exhibition of New and Recent Work by the renowned British Artist, Anthony Winter, opening in three weeks' time.

Legal action, Elder assumed, notwithstanding.

12

Winter's studio was in a former piano factory in Kentish Town. An elongated two-storey building between a builder's yard and a new development of mixed-use office and living space, there was nothing to mark it out as what it now was. No sign, no name plate above the door. Only a circular bell push that didn't seem to work.

Katherine stepped back. The windows on the upper floor were bare. The way round to the back was blocked on one side by a brick wall topped with nasty-looking barbed wire, on the other by a tall mesh fence. Nothing to do but bang on the door and shout.

After several minutes that yielded nothing aside from making herself hoarse, Katherine kicked at the ground in annoyance and turned away. Almost as if he'd been waiting, Winter unlocked and opened the door.

'What's all the hullabaloo? Noise enough to wake the dead.'

'The bell's not working.'

'Of course it's not working.'

'Then how d'you expect people to let you know they're here?'

'I don't.'

'Fine. In that case don't ask them to come round.'

She was approaching the side entrance to the new building, the narrow strip leading out onto the street, before he called her back.

'Katherine, wait.'

If she'd carried on walking, perhaps it would have been different. But instead she stopped, hesitated, slowly turned and walked back.

'I was busy, working. Any distraction . . .' Winter made a vague gesture with his hand. 'You're here now. Better come in.'

He went back inside, expecting her to follow.

The room ran the length of the building, save for one end which had been partitioned off. A curved staircase led up to a second floor which was open and stretched less than a third of the way across. At the rear, broad arched windows reached down towards the ground. The bare boards were shiny with use and thickly speckled with paint. Canvases, turned inwards, rested in twos and threes against the walls. Tins of paint in various sizes were piled on top of one another on a metal plan chest and others sat abandoned here and there across the floor.

By the central window a large easel was angled towards an empty bed, in front of which a glass vase of failing poppies, purple, white and red, stems arching outwards, stood on a tall three-legged stool draped with a velvet cloth.

'Just give me a minute. A minute. Look around. Make yourself useful. There's coffee. Down at the end there. Black for me.'

The partitioned area divided into two: toilet and shower to one side; small, overcrowded kitchen to the other. A toaster sat uneasily on a pile of books; the lead from the electric kettle trailed down towards the floor. The remains of what looked like lasagne was encrusted round the inside of an oval dish on the stove. Katherine found a jar of ground coffee in the cupboard above the sink; a coffee pot – the kind that Chrissy swore by – in the sink itself, waiting to be washed. Milk was in the small fridge on the counter, a Roberts radio resting on top.

Newspaper clippings and postcard reproductions of paintings overlapped on the wall.

Katherine thought she recognised a Picasso – a woman's body splintered into ugly segments and then put back clumsily together again. The other artists she couldn't identify. A blotchy portrait of a man reflected in a bathroom mirror, head shaven, dark holes where the eyes were meant to be. A naked man on a brown settee, legs spread wide, genitals showing, holding a small black rat in his right hand. The clippings seemed to be a mixture of reviews of other artists' work, recipes, and odd news items – three people fall to their deaths from same clifftop in a single day; epidemic of flying ants drives family from their home.

When it was ready, Katherine poured the coffee into mugs and added milk to her own.

Hesitated, uncertain.

'Shit!' came the sudden shout from behind. 'Shit and fuck again!' And the sound of something being hurled to the ground.

When she stepped out from behind the partition, Winter was standing away from the easel, wiping the end of a paintbrush on a torn piece of rag. 'Just when you think you've got it cracked, another fucking petal falls.'

They sat up on the mezzanine floor. A day bed and two canvas chairs either side of a small folding table. Winter pressed buttons on a remote control and music started up from speakers above their heads, something classical, some kind of string quartet Katherine thought, the sort of thing Abike went sneaking off to see, Sunday mornings at Wigmore Hall.

'So, tell me about yourself,' Winter said.

'There's nothing to tell.'

'I find that hard to believe.'

Katherine shrugged and turned her head away, avoiding his gaze.

'Where are you from? Originally, I mean.'

'London, I suppose. We moved up to Nottingham when I was just starting secondary.'

'We?'

'My mum and dad. My mum's still there. My dad's in Cornwall. Well, mostly.'

'And you, you're . . .'

'Stuck in a holding pattern, Stelina says . . .'

'Who's Stelina?'

'One of my flatmates.'

'Works for an airline, does she? Air-traffic control?'

'The NHS.'

'Currently going down without a parachute.'

Katherine wasn't sure if she was meant to laugh. It felt awkward, strange, sitting there talking to someone she hardly knew. Someone close to her father's age; partway, she supposed, to being some kind of celebrity. Made her feel as if she were sixteen again. Not a good feeling at all.

'So, modelling, for you it's a sideline, not a career?'

'I suppose.'

'V says you're very good. And she's an excellent judge.'

'I don't even know enough to know what being good is.'

'Maybe that's better. More instinctive.'

'I doubt that.' She drank some of her coffee, hooked one ankle over the other. Whatever movement she made, no matter how small, his eyes followed. 'What's it mean anyway, being a good model? Aside from how you look?'

Winter leaned forward, fingers loosely interlaced, elbows resting on the edges of the chair. 'What distinguishes a good model, a really good model – above all else they want to give the artist what he or she needs. And the closer they come to one other, the more they work together – the good model knows what that is without a word having to be passed between them.'

'And does that happen often?'

'Hardly at all.'

His mobile rang and he glanced at the screen. 'I'll have to take this.'

Downstairs, he paced the length of the room. 'Rebecca, I understand . . . I've got it . . . Of course I've fucking got it. You think I'm some kind of naive . . . ? Yes. Yes, I know.'

Katherine stood, went to the window. On the far side of the builder's yard the railway line ran west towards Hampstead and the Finchley Road. Beyond that she could see the beginnings of the Heath, Parliament Hill Fields, grass and trees; people, little more than matchstick figures, out running, pushing buggies, walking their dogs.

Winter's voice, louder, closer to exasperation. 'Well, tell Rupert he can . . . Yes . . . I don't know, anyway you can. Just make sure it gets done.'

By accident or design, he kicked over a pot of paint on his way back to the stairs.

'Sorry about that. Business, I'm afraid. I'm supposed to have this show coming up, a year, eighteen months from now. Maybe sooner, I don't know. And now it's got mired in all these fucking negotiations . . .'

He lowered himself back down into his chair. 'It used to be, once upon a time, when I started, all I had to do was paint.

That was it, get up, go to the easel, dip a brush, paint. Hockney . . . You've heard of Hockney?'

'Yes, I think so.'

'When he was a young man, still a student, he made this sign, like a poster, and stuck it on the chest of drawers beside his bed so it would be the first thing he saw when he woke. *Get Up and Work Immediately.* Lucky bastard, to be able to do that. Could then, can now.'

'And you can't?'

Winter laughed. 'Yes. Yes, I can. Except, you know, life . . . life fucking intervenes. Life and money. Reputation. Lack of it. Hockney now, what is he? Eighty? He's got it made. Has for years. Decades. Do what he likes. Always has. Dye his hair, smoke like a fucking chimney in the face of all the available advice; flaunt the fact that he was gay before it was practically bloody essential. Except now it's bisexual that's the thing. Bisexual and then some. Fluidly fucking gendered, whatever the fuck that is. LGB fucking T. And no matter what, he's still a national fucking treasure. Hockney. He could pose naked save for a piss pot on his head on top of the plinth in Trafalgar Square and everyone would cheer.'

'You sound as if you're jealous.'

'Jealous? That's not the word. A certain amount of envy perhaps. Not for the work, though I like the work, some of it, quite a lot in fact, the early stuff especially, not this iPad nonsense. No, it's that somehow he's earned the right to do what he likes, say what he likes, without having to manoeuvre, second-guess, smarm up to the right people, the right collectors.'

Katherine didn't know what to say, how to respond to the flurry of angry words. She picked up the empty mugs and moved towards the stairs. 'Why don't I just take these down and . . .'

'And come back.'

'What?'

'Come back tomorrow. Early. We'll get an early start. Eight, can you make it by then? Eight-thirty?'

'But I haven't said . . .'

'This show, the one I was on the phone about earlier, it's going to be big. A big deal. And there's at least another three canvases I've got to have finished by then, if not four. And I can't do that on my own.'

She made the mistake of looking into his eyes.

'What do you say then? Eight sharp?'

'Okay.'

Back outside, she was slightly unsteady on her feet without knowing quite why.

13

She thought of a hundred and one reasons for not going. Convinced herself that she had no obligation, no need; woke at half past four rehearsing what she might say by way of an excuse. Somehow she'd been talked into agreeing to something she didn't really want to do and if, in the cold light of day, she changed her mind, well, that was fine. Posing naked before one man, one pair of eyes. She flinched at the thought.

'Kate, you don't have to do this,' she said aloud.

She was still saying it as she folded her robe into her shoulder bag, along with a pair of ballet shoes she'd borrowed from Chrissy, and a change of underwear. Make-up, mobile, headphones. The overground from Dalston Kingsland to Kentish Town West and then a fifteen-minute walk.

Coming out of the station, she joined the small queue at The Fields Beneath and bought a latte and a croissant, breakfast on the hoof.

The door to the studio was ajar. Winter was bending down close by the easel, mixing paint. The vase and its flowers had disappeared and the bed now had an oversized white sheet stretched loosely across it, falling in narrow folds towards the floor.

Without looking at her, Winter pointed his brush at a hessian screen standing off to one side. 'You can change behind there.'

She came out in her robe and shoes and stood in front of the bed, arms folded across her waist, the sides of the robe pulled closed.

'What is this? Some kind of striptease? We don't have the time.'

Katherine closed her eyes for the briefest of moments, bit down into her lip and slipped the robe from her shoulders. Slid the ballet shoes from her feet.

'Okay, now I want you to sit. Just sit. Centre of the bed. That's it. And hunch forward, just a little. A little more. Good. Head slightly down. Arms resting . . . yes, that's it . . . resting on your thighs. And now move your legs further apart. More. More. Good, good. But keep your head down. I don't want to see . . . don't want to see that much of your face. Just . . . Yes. Pick out a spot on the floor to focus on. And hold that, hold that there. Can you do that? Hold that?'

After the first thirty minutes or so Katherine's shoulders were starting to ache due to the position of her arms; after twenty more there was an itch at the back of her left knee she desperately wanted to scratch; close to the hour and she was beginning to feel the frame of the bed biting into the backs of her thighs.

How much longer?

'Right. Take a break. Stretch, whatever.'

Leaving her to it, he marched outside and she saw him pacing up and down with a cigarette, mobile to one ear. Part of her wanted to step round and look at the canvas, see what he'd done, how she looked, but she knew that, without his express permission, that was prohibited, forbidden.

She peed, drank a glass of water from the tap, did a few rudimentary stretches and, as soon as she heard Winter return, resumed the pose.

At lunchtime there was a delivery from the Vietnamese café close by: noodle soup and prawn summer rolls. Winter ate quickly and, grabbing his phone and his cigarettes, headed for the door. Katherine checked her own phone for messages. Facebook, Instagram. Chrissy: *How's it going?* Stelina: *Good luck!* One of the few girls she'd kept in touch with from athletics had broken her PB for the 400 metres, an indoor meeting in Sheffield. Her mum, nothing special, just wanting to know she was okay. Tomorrow, if she remembered, Katherine thought, she'd bring a book.

'Okay,' Winter said, closing the door with a bang. 'Let's get back to work.'

On the train going home, busy with people of all ages, bicycles, prams, Katherine found the words of a song slipping through her mind, one of those morose guys Abike would play late at night, when she wasn't sentencing them to Beethoven or whoever: something about aching in the places where I used to lay, was that it? Used to play?

At Dalston Kingsland she came close to losing her footing as she stepped down from the train, the feeling in her left leg all but gone. Back at the flat, she ran a bath, sneaked some of Stelina's bath salts, borrowed Abike's little portable radio, slid down into the warm water and closed her eyes.

The next few days followed the same pattern.

One of the things that had worried her about being so long in Winter's company, just the two of them, was the need to hold her own in conversation, but she soon realised that now the work had started in earnest there would be precious little conversation at all. Instructions aside, Winter restricted himself to the occasional grudging query, when the pose had been held longer than usual, as to how she was feeling, that and violent imprecations called down upon himself when a mark on the canvas failed to tally with the one he had in mind.

'Fuck, fuck, fuck and fuck again. Call yourself a fucking painter? You can no more render skin tones on fucking canvas than you can flap your fucking wings and fly.' With a swing of a foot he sent an open paint can skidding wildly, splashing Cadmium Orange across the studio floor. 'Take a break. Take five, ten, I don't fucking care.'

She found it difficult, hearing him berate himself, not to feel, in some way she couldn't properly articulate, responsible. A good model, she remembered him saying, was the one who knew how to give the artist what was needed without having to be told. She would try harder, if only she knew how.

When she arrived on the fifth day, the bed had been turned at right angles, pointing towards the easel, and the sheet removed, leaving just the blue-and-grey striped mattress. Winter told her to lie back with her legs hooked over the end of the bed, a pillow behind her head.

'My eyes,' Katherine said. 'Open or closed?'

'I can't see your eyes.'

At least, in that particular pose, exposed as she was, she couldn't see his eyes either, could only feel but not see his gaze.

He worked in silence, just the sounds, faint, of brush against canvas, the scrape of a palette knife, the rise and fall of his breathing merging occasionally with hers.

'Wait,' he said abruptly and she realised she'd been drifting towards sleep. 'Something not quite right. Those shoes, trainers, whatever you were wearing earlier. Where are they?'

Sitting up, she pointed. A pair of faded green Converse she'd come close several times to throwing away.

'Here . . .' He threw them, one by one, for her to catch. 'Put them on, then let's see. Now lay back. No, that's still not . . . the laces, lose the laces, that's it. Now pull back the sides. Open. Good. Fine. Try that.'

Katherine lowered herself back down and closed her eyes. Outside, the wind was getting up and she could hear it rolling around the top of the building, causing the windows to shift in their frames.

At the end of the session, she plucked up courage for the first time to ask if she could see what he'd done.

''Course fucking not! Some other time, maybe. When I'm further along. Just don't ask. I'll tell you when.'

'So,' Chrissy said some days later, Stelina off at lectures, Abike at a movie, the pair of them on the sofa watching TV, 'is it as bad as you thought it was going to be?'

'I didn't think it was going to be bad, exactly. More awkward, I suppose. You know, one pair of eyes.'

'And is it?'

'No, not really. I mean it was. It was. But, no, not so much. Not any more. You sort of forget about it, don't you?'

'Zone out, you mean?'

'Something like that, yes.'

Chrissy smiled. 'After all the fuss you made, you sound as if you're almost enjoying it.'

'Yes,' Katherine said hesitantly. 'In a way I suppose I am.'

And it was true. Winter no longer swore at himself as frequently when he was working and, during their breaks, if he wasn't talking on his phone, he'd chat to her about seemingly trivial incidents, tell her anecdotes involving other artists she thought she might have heard of but she wasn't sure. He'd started to look at her differently, too: watch her in a different way as she moved around the studio, following her reflection, window to window, in the glass. Look at her and, just occasionally, smile. She came to cherish that smile. And the more it happened, the more willing she was to do as he asked, the more eager she became to please, hold herself in this uncomfortable pose or that until she was almost enjoying the discomfort, the lower levels of pain.

'Good news,' Winter said one morning. 'That show I mentioned, new gallery, looks as if it might be happening after all. Could be as much as nine months, a year off, but it means upping the ante, even so. Working a whole lot harder. Tomorrow we'd better try something new.'

The new pose had Katherine standing side on, the upper half of the body angled back towards the artist, the viewer, at the waist, both arms raised high above the head.

'Your arms. You think you can hold them in that position?'

'I'll try.'

It wasn't long before the muscles at the backs of her calves, her thighs, were tight and there was a pain like a stitch, but not a stitch, in the small of her back where she was forced to turn. Her arms were starting to shake and drift apart.

'Here, look. Maybe this will help.'

Winter looped one of the pieces of rag he'd been using to clean his brushes around her wrists and tied them loosely together in a knot.

'There.'

When he stepped away, his arm accidentally brushed against her breast.

After another thirty minutes she started to sway and then, without further warning, her knees gave way and she collapsed to the floor.

In the moments between consciousness and waking that followed, she was back in another place, a place she'd taught herself to keep shut away; the shape leaning over hers another shape, the voice another voice. 'Sit up, can't you? Come on, sit up straight.' As she opened her eyes, Adam Keach's words came tumbling from Anthony Winter's mouth.

Katherine vomited.

Choked. Bile stuck in the back of her throat.

Winter plucked another piece of rag from the ground and gave it to her to wipe her mouth; when she moved the rag away it had left a gash of paint across her cheek.

'You all right?'

She blinked, nodded, blinked again.

Something about the way he was looking at her was different now, something about his look, his gaze; looking at her as if she were naked not nude.

'All right?' he asked again and smiled.

She thought that he must touch her now, but no.

That was later . . .

14

Vicki told him in no uncertain terms, don't go. Why on earth would you want to do that? A private view? What have you got to gain? It's as if you've got this sore place and instead of letting it heal, what you want to do is take something sharp, stick it in and scrape it round. And what about Kathcrine? Have you thought about her? How she might feel? Are you even going to tell her what you're doing?

Elder listened, thanked her for the advice, a quick kiss on the cheek and he booked return tickets on the Penzance to London train.

As far as Katherine was concerned, there was no reason she had to know. He had thought, at one point, of texting her, telling her he was going to be up in London, but then, if he did that it would be difficult to avoid telling her the reason why. Her response to which he could readily imagine. So there he was, window seat in the quiet coach, today's paper, an indifferent cup of coffee and a KitKat for company.

*

By the time he arrived in London it was early evening, the blur of slow-moving headlights as he stepped out from the station, the threat or promise of rain. After all that time sitting, he needed to stretch his legs. Praed Street led him on to the Marylebone Road and from there he knew it to be a straight line past Baker Street and Madame Tussauds to Euston. No more than a couple of miles.

Passing the intersection with Gloucester Place, something jarred in his memory. A shop, wasn't there a shop with some Italian-sounding name? Gandolfini, was that it? Gandolfi? Tutus, ballet dresses, leotards and ballet shoes. Katherine's best friend at primary school at the time went to ballet lessons every week, every Thursday after school, and she had to do the same. The letter that came home after her first visit listed quite clearly what was necessary for her to wear to class, a list of stockists appended. Marylebone the closest to the salon off Lisson Grove where Joanne was working.

It had been a Saturday, Elder remembered, raining; not a faint drizzle like today, but unremitting, serious rain. Crossing the street, Katherine had stumbled and, reaching out for her arm, he'd only succeeded in knocking her further off balance so that she stumbled against the kerb, her coat trailing in the wet, one gloved hand going down into a puddle. Joanne 's voice rising above the escalating thrum of traffic as she helped her to her feet. Couldn't he be more careful? What did he think he was doing? And Katherine crying, Elder turning away from them both with a shake of the head.

'There it is,' Joanne said brightly a moment or so later, doing her best to pull things together. 'The shop. See, Frank, look. Right there.'

'I don't give a fuck about the fucking shop,' he barked back, louder than intended.

'Great! That's lovely, Frank. Really sweet.'

And all the time the crying getting louder. Katherine staring up at him with helpless eyes; wet, bedraggled and bereft.

In the end he'd waited outside while they went in and spent what seemed to him a ludicrous amount on a pink skirt and turquoise leotard, shoes for ballet, shoes for tap, and a pink dance bag to carry them all away in.

Within little more than six months *Ballet Shoes* had been replaced by *Black Beauty*; they were driving Katherine up the A1 to stables north of London and anything pink had been consigned to the bin.

'Excuse me,' someone said brusquely, brushing past, and Elder realised he had come to a standstill, mid-pavement, mid-reverie, embarrassed even now by how childishly he'd behaved. Knowing, in the same circumstances, there was a good chance he'd respond in the same way again. And the shop itself, he could now see, was no longer in business, the front boarded over, *For Sale* sign overhead; most people nowadays, he assumed, preferring to buy their tutus online.

Rain starting to fall more heavily, he pulled up his collar, hunched his shoulders and continued on his way.

At Euston, he took the Northern line three overcrowded stops to Old Street. The Hecklington and Wearing gallery was close by Arnold Circus, between Shoreditch High Street and Bethnal Green Road; *Anthony Winter: New & Recent Work* stencilled across the window in two-foot-high type.

Between the letters, Elder could see the first scattering of people starting to gather; paintings, at this distance without definition, on the walls. A young man in a black overcoat stood in the doorway, discreetly checking invitations as people arrived, the overhead light reflecting in the polished toes of his shoes.

The notice had been clear: *Private View. Admittance by invitation only.*

At a smart-looking burger place on Bethnal Green Road, Elder found a seat by the window and took his time over a chilli burger with fries and two bottles of pale ale. Manoeuvring his way to the bar in a busy pub a little further down the street, he ordered a large Scotch, no ice, water on the side. And then another. Still taking his time.

'Invitation, sir?' The voice was polite, just this side of insolent; young face unmarked save for a snail trail of scar tissue over one eye.

Elder grinned. 'Must have left it at home.'

'Then I'm sorry, sir . . .'

He held out his hand, a twenty-pound note curled between finger and thumb. 'I've come all the way up from Cornwall for this. Wouldn't like to miss it.'

'Of course, sir. I understand.' While one hand disappeared the note from sight, the other pushed open the door. 'Enjoy your evening.'

Elder hadn't known quite what to expect, but it hadn't been exactly this. Long and low-ceilinged, the central section of the L-shaped gallery was busy with knots of smartly dressed people, the women mostly in slim black, the men, many of them, richly bearded, the occasional tattoo, small gold earrings, silver studs. The buzz of conversation reverberated loudly, waiters and waitresses in matching uniforms filtering their way with difficulty through the crowd, carrying trays loaded with canapés and glasses of what Elder assumed to be champagne.

A pair of security men, similarly attired to the one on the door, but older, bigger, altogether a more serious proposition, stood at either end of the gallery, stationed there, presumably, in case anyone should take it into their head to try walking off with one of the artworks – not that many people seemed to be paying very much attention to the paintings at all.

Elder accepted a puff-pastry-wrapped prawn and, skirting the edges of the crowd, made his way towards the rear wall. Two portraits, head and shoulders, richly contoured, of a middle-aged man Elder thought he should recognise. An author perhaps? Actor? He wasn't sure. Further along a land-scape, barren, no trees, a lowering sky. A factory, derelict, rusted machinery, fractured glass. Advancing between two more groups of people, Elder swallowed hard.

There, unmistakable, two paintings of his daughter, side by side.

In the first, she was sitting on the edge of a bed, leaning for-ward, naked, head down so that her face was partly hidden, but even so he could tell it was her; in the second she lay stretched out on her back, face just visible and legs splayed wide, a thin line of blood running from her vagina down along her thigh.

For a moment, Elder thought he might throw up.

Turning sharply, he narrowly avoided colliding with one of the waiters, apologised and pushed his way through into the centre of the crowd. More people than ever now and the sound of overlapping conversations more high-pitched, more intense.

Go, just go. Leave well enough alone.

The doorman looked at him in surprise. 'Not leaving already?'

'Just after a bit of fresh air.'

When he reached the end of the street he hesitated, turned slowly around, went back inside. Crowd hushed, one of the gallery owners making a speech, how proud he was to be showing such vibrant new work by one of the most gifted painters on the contemporary scene. At his urging, Anthony Winter stepped reluctantly forward to prolonged applause. Elder's first sight of him, around the same height as himself but heavier, broad-shouldered, fleshy. Shaven head glistening in the gallery lights.

Winter thanked Tom Hecklington for his kind words, thanked everyone at Hecklington and Wearing for their hard work, thanked his friend and advisor Rebecca Johnson without whom none of this would have been possible. As for the paintings themselves, he preferred to let the work do the talking for him.

More applause.

Elder made his way towards the other end of the gallery and turned into the foot of the L.

A single canvas, bigger than the rest, hung spotlit on the far wall. At the centre, Katherine stood naked, her body twisted sharply at the waist; hands raised high above her head, her wrists tightly manacled, chains holding her arms aloft.

Elder was finding it difficult to breathe.

Kate's face staring down at him, the pain alive in her eyes.

He knew that look; recognised that pain.

Turning quickly away, he pushed himself through the centre of the crowd.

'Anthony Winter?'

The artist was surrounded by a dozen or more people, women in their little black dresses, men with their sharp suits and beards.

'Yes?'

'The painting round the corner. In the spotlight. The girl in chains.'

'Yes?'

'That's my daughter, you sick fuck!'

Winter glanced anxiously over his shoulder. Elder punched him in the solar plexus and then, when he doubled forward, punched him in the face, hard enough almost to break his nose.

Blood spurted freely. Men shouted and women screamed.

The security men muscled their way through the crowd. The camera flashes from a dozen or more mobile phones.

Winter was crouching forward on his knees, one hand to his face, blood leaking between his fingers to the floor.

Elder moved in to hit him again but hands hauled him roughly back and propelled him, feet scarcely touching the ground, towards the door and out on to the street. Off balance, a well-judged elbow struck him in the temple and he fell headlong. Two precise kicks in the ribs and he rolled into the gutter, the final swing of a boot opening a gash down one side of his face.

'More'n your twenty pounds' worth there,' the young doorman said and laughed.

Elder levered himself awkwardly to his feet and stumbled across to the other side of the road.

Less than forty-five minutes later he was at Paddington station, waiting to board the sleeper train to Penzance. His ribs were sore and, despite the painkillers he'd taken, his face throbbed beneath the plaster on his cheek.

He would have had difficulty, at that moment, remembering the last time he had felt quite as good.

2

15

Hadley woke in the dark. The sound of Rachel's breathing; a sliver of street light through the curtains; the cat curled in the space between their legs. Six, a little after. It had been late when they'd got back, the roads at that hour close to empty till they were inside the M25. It had been Rachel's turn to drive, Hadley dozing fitfully alongside, blinking at the occasional oncoming headlight; the radio playing music, as the announcer said, long into the night.

It had been a weekend away with friends, mates of Rachel's from university, sand and shingle, the best part of two spring days on the Suffolk coast.

'Stay till tomorrow, why don't you? Leave after breakfast, first thing.'

'Work, I'm afraid,' Hadley had said. 'Early start.'

'And besides,' Rachel added, 'there's the cat. Leave her too long, she'll wander off.'

'That cat of yours,' the friend said with a laugh, 'child substitute, you do realise that?'

Yes, well, Hadley thought, we tried that, the child thing, didn't work out. Sensing movement, the cat jumped down to the floor and began to purr.

How was it, Hadley thought, marooned behind the wheel of the car halfway along Hornsey Lane, some mornings it seemed to take as long to travel the few miles from Crouch End to Kentish Town as it did to drive all the way back from Southwold? A major disadvantage of the part of London where they lived – and there were others – being the paucity of public transport. Though that, at least, had the effect of keeping property prices just the right side of affordable. Affordable now that Rachel had swallowed her principles sufficiently to start taking on private clients outside her work with the NHS.

Seizing the opportunity, Hadley cut round a four-by-four delivering a child to school, accelerated through the lights and turned left past the church and down the hill.

Dwindling resources and yet another reorganisation had already closed several police stations in the area and, according to all available rumours, Holmes Road's days were numbered. But for now it was still home to one of the Met's Major Investigation Teams, one of four in the north-west, and Hadley's to command.

The last incident they'd dealt with had been a multiple stabbing, the result of an argument that had started at the school gates and escalated rapidly, ending up outside Argos on the Holloway Road. One youth seriously wounded, another pronounced dead on arrival at hospital. More witnesses than you could shake a stick at, most of them unwilling to talk. Those that did, some of them, only too keen to lay blame in the wrong places. Settle old scores. Eventually, five arrests were made, charges ranging from possession of an offensive weapon in a public place up to and including murder. The case was still to come to trial.

Since then it had been oddly quiet, two of the team being temporarily seconded to burglary, one transferred permanently south of the river, a fourth quitting to retrain as a paramedic.

Hadley riffled through the latest batch of Home Office directives, initialling where necessary. Chris Phillips, recently promoted to detective sergeant, had been first in as usual: direct line, lucky bastard, from Walthamstow and then a brisk walk from Gospel Oak.

The call came at 8.37, one of the officers in the Homicide Assessment Team, Brian O'Connor, Hadley recognised the voice. MIT presence required. A matter of minutes away, local. Phillips drove. The scene was already cordoned off, the building itself and the area immediately surrounding. Hadley ducked under the tape as the HAT officer approached.

'Ma'am.'

Hadley nodded acknowledgement. 'Brian, what've we got?'

The body lay in the middle of what was obviously an artist's studio, curled on its side; severe damage to one side of the face and the back of the head. The floorboards close around were stained with what could be paint, could be blood. The woman who'd found him and contacted the police had identified him as Anthony Winter: even allowing for his injuries, verifiable by a quick search on Google.

'Medical examiner's on his way,' O'Connor said. 'Stuck in traffic.'

'SOCO?'

'Likewise.'

Hadley shook her head. 'Anything interesting meanwhile?'

'Like a murder weapon, you mean?'

'Something like that would be nice, yes. Acceptable.'

O'Connor grinned. 'Pair of old-fashioned rigid handcuffs – real collectors' item – manacles, I suppose you might call 'em, kind they used to shackle those poor bastards they shipped off to Botany Bay. Over in the far corner, chain attached. Like they'd been hurled there. Might be what you're after.'

'Chris,' Hadley said, 'take a look.'

'Boss.'

'Whoever it was,' O'Connor said, turning back towards the body, 'went at him with a vengeance and no mistake.'

The blood had long clotted, the wounds deep and thickly scabbed, darkening at the edges. Twenty-four hours? Hadley wondered. More? She nodded in the direction of the woman sitting off to one side, the other HAT officer finishing taking a provisional statement. 'Friend? Relative?'

'Some kind of business associate. Johnson. Rebecca Johnson.'

'I'll talk to her when your colleague's through.'

Chris Phillips was back at her shoulder. 'SOCOs're here, boss.'

'The words fine, tooth and comb come to mind.'

'Understood.'

The Italian café set back from the main road was open for breakfast. They sat at one of the tables outside, their conversation less likely to be overheard. They'd been there a while, coffees starting to grow cold.

Rebecca Johnson, Hadley thought, was in her early forties, around the same age as herself. But whereas after several years of trying to hold it at bay, she'd decided to hell with it and allowed the encroaching grey to show through, Johnson had a full head of dark hair, nicely shaped and cut and, doubtless, dyed. Everything about her, save for the redness of her eyes where she'd been crying, the mascara rubbed away and not yet replaced, suggested smart, fashionable, businesslike.

'So, just to be clear,' Hadley said, 'your relationship with Winter? You're his agent, is that the term?'

'Consultant might be more accurate.'

'You advised him where to show his work, helped arrange the sale of his paintings, that kind of thing?'

'Yes.'

'And you'd been doing this for how long?'

'For Anthony? Three, almost four years.'

'You knew him well, then?'

'Professionally, yes.'

'And otherwise?'

'Anthony?' Something showed in her eyes, difficult to read. 'Perhaps I knew him as well as most people, I don't know.'

'He was private, then? A private person, is that what you'd say?'

'Yes, I . . .' She stopped abruptly, face angled away.

Hadley waited, happy for now to let things take their own time.

'I'm sorry, it's just . . . talking about him like this, when's he only just . . . It's hard.'

'Of course. We can stop, take a break. Maybe you could come into the station this afternoon?'

'No, no. It's . . . it's fine.'

'Another coffee perhaps?'

'No, thank you.'

'I think I will if you don't mind.' She signalled to the waiter, hovering by the door.

'The thing to understand about Anthony,' Johnson said, 'the most important thing in his life was the work. It's what he did, what he . . .' She shook her head. 'I was about to say, what he lived for.'

'So, no relationships? Significant others?'

'He was married, a long time ago. Two children? I'm really not sure. I don't think there was much contact between them, if any.'

'And more recently?'

Johnson moved her head a little to one side, non-committal. 'I think there were relationships from time to time, but as far as I know, nothing long-lasting or particularly serious. Not since I've known him, anyway.'

'And sexually, again as far as you know, he was . . .'

'He wasn't gay, if that's what you're suggesting.'

Hadley reined in a smile. 'I didn't think I was.'

'There's this assumption, isn't there?'

'Which assumption's that?'

'Artists, being gay.'

'They say the same about police officers,' Hadley said, straight-faced. 'Female ones, that is. And I'm sorry if it seemed I was reaching for the stereotype. It's just that sometimes it helps to get these thing clear from the off.'

'Well,' Johnson said, 'if only they were. Clear, I mean.' She smiled. 'I think I'll have that coffee now.'

Hadley sat back and sipped her espresso. A small covey of students went past on their way to the girls' school: head-scarves, headphones, rucksacks, skirts trailing the ground.

'I'd just like to recap,' Hadley said, flipping through her notebook. 'The reason you came round this morning, to the studio, you were concerned because you hadn't heard from Winter in a couple of days?'

'That's correct.'

'And that was unusual?'

Johnson nodded. 'The one thing Anthony was good at, even if he'd shut himself away, working on something he felt wouldn't come right, he'd always get back to me by the end of the day. Now especially, with the show opening, buyers interested, collectors. It's one of those times we'd keep closely in touch.'

'And, to be more precise, the last time you'd heard from him was when?'

'That would have been Friday. Friday afternoon. I wanted to make sure he was okay. After, you know, the incident I told you about at the gallery. The private view, the day before. I'd been with him at A & E that evening. What an experience that was! But Anthony, they patched him up, took some X-rays — there was some concern his nose might have been broken. I don't suppose we left there until, oh, half past two in the morning. Maybe later. Three.'

'And from there he went home?'

'As far as I know.'

'You didn't feel the need to go with him?'

'No. I mean, I offered, of course, but he assured me he'd be fine. I ordered a taxi for him — for both of us — we live in opposite directions. Made sure he got into it okay and that was that.'

'His house . . . flat, I think you said . . .'

'It's in Camden. Well, Chalk Farm really. Not so far from the studio. Walkable. Thirty minutes or so. A little more. He did it most days. Thinking time, that's what he called it.'

The waiter arrived with Johnson's cappuccino; looked questioningly at Hadley, who shook her head. Caffeine enough for one morning already.

'The incident, as you called it, in the gallery . . .'

'Extraordinary. I've never known anything like it.'

'The man who attacked Winter . . .'

'Drunk, I imagine.'

'He was shouting something, you said.'

'Something about his daughter. And one of the paintings. I didn't hear it all clearly. Apart from anything else, it all happened so fast.'

'This was one particular painting?'

'Yes, I think so.'

'And the daughter? She was involved how?'

'I assume she was the model. I can't think what else . . .'

'Is there any chance I can see it? The painting?'

Johnson took her iPad from her bag. Found a connection, clicked on to the image and swivelled the screen.

Hadley looked closely. The face. The pose. The girl's hands cuffed together, arms stretched awkwardly high above her head. Pain in her eyes.

'And that's the daughter?' Hadley said.

'Yes.'

'You know her name?'

'Katherine, I think. I'm pretty sure. Katherine what, I don't know.'

Hadley looked closer. The heavy manacles around the girl's wrists, perhaps not surprisingly, looked very much like the ones that had been found on the studio floor. For a moment, she had a vision of the chain to which they were attached being swung through the air, taking on force and speed before striking home. Then swung again.

16

By the time Hadley had the team assembled she had spoken briefly to Alistair McKeon, the detective superintendent with overall responsibility for the north-west unit of Homicide Command, and he had left two messages on her phone, as yet unanswered. All, Hadley thought, in good time. First, let's get the ducks in a row.

The room was stuffy, windows closed, tables and desks at odd angles. A large whiteboard, currently blank save for Anthony Winter's name, stood alongside a large-screen television, also blank but for reflecting the faces of the assembled team. Half a dozen of them, mostly familiar, only one, Mark Foster, a young DC recently transferred in from uniform, still pretty much an unknown quantity.

Howard Dean and Terry Mitchell, heads together, arguing, no doubt, the respective merits and demerits of Spurs and Arsenal, the old north London rivalry. Alice Atkins, some fifteen years Hadley's junior and seeing her as a role model, keen and conscientious almost to a fault. Richard Cresswell, the oldest of the group, much of his career, before he resigned early, spent in uniform; after an unsuccessful attempt to set up a landscape-gardening business with his brother, he'd rejoined the force relatively recently.

With Chris Phillips occasionally chipping in, Hadley laid out the facts as they were then known. The victim, Anthony Winter, a fifty-one-year-old artist, had been found dead in his Kentish Town studio early that morning; an artist with, apparently, something of a reputation, so they could expect more media attention than usual. Cause of death, awaiting confirmation, most likely blunt-force trauma to the head; the potential murder weapon, a pair of old-fashioned handcuffs – manacles – which had been found near the body attached to a length of chain and were currently undergoing tests. Time of death, at a best guess, anywhere between Saturday night and Sunday morning.

'There are no obvious signs,' Hadley said, 'of a break-in at the studio, so the assumption for now is whoever was responsible was known to Winter in some way or other – which could mean known well, as in mother or lover, could mean someone from Deliveroo.'

A brief smile, there and then gone.

Chris Phillips got to his feet.

'We're waiting on the usual RIPA authorisations before starting the process of retrieving call data and email records from the laptop and mobile phone found in the studio, along with compiling an Internet search history. As well as the studio where he worked, Winter had a flat in a mansion block between Gospel Oak and Chalk Farm. We'll see what a search turns up there, but, my guess, at least one more computer, in all probability a landline phone. More to add to the mix.'

'Okay, Chris, thanks. Richard, keep an eye on how that's progressing. Give CIU a nudge if needs be.'

'Boss.'

'And Chris, you'll liaise with the Coroner's Office. Post-mortem results.'

'Right, boss.'

'Mitch, chase up SOCO, the forensics. Anything potentially useful, prints, whatever, check it through HOLMES, keep me informed.'

'Yes, boss.'

'Howie, there's some CCTV out there, traffic cameras on the main road certainly, ANPR, I'm not sure what else. But it would be nice to think, the heaviest surveillance in Western Europe, we've got something covering exits and entrances.'

'Right, boss. I'll get to it.'

'One more thing worth noting,' Hadley said, 'might be relevant, maybe not, but last Thursday evening Winter was victim of an attack at a gallery in Shoreditch showing his work. Punched and knocked to the ground. There are bits and pieces of this on social media. Some video. The man responsible seems to have had some kind of grievance about Winter using his daughter as a model in his paintings. And, having seen one of them, I'm not too surprised. So, Alice, get yourself down there, find out what you can. Trace him, the assailant, and it could be that's all we need, look no further.'

'Chance'd be a fine thing,' Mitchell said, half under his breath.

'Wouldn't it just. Meantime, Mark . . .'

'Thought you'd forgotten me, ma'am.'

'Could I ever?'

Mark Foster blushed.

'You started a history degree, didn't you? Chance to put all that research work into practice. See what you can dig up on Winter's private life, family, relationships, anything nasty lurking in the woodshed.'

'Will do.'

'Okay, everyone, as you all know, we're understaffed and overstretched and about to be even more so, which means working all the hours it takes without as much as a whisper of overtime. But then, I know that would be the last thing on your minds . . .'

Groans, laughter . . .

Hadley stepped outside into the corridor just as a call came in on her mobile. 'Yes, sir. Sorry I missed you earlier . . .'

17

Katherine had slept in late, vaguely aware of movement around her, sounds from other parts of the flat: voices, the opening and closing of doors. Until the drawing class in Walthamstow that afternoon, there was little she had to do, few demands on her time. Somewhere around ten-thirty she rolled over, looked at her phone and lay back down. Just five minutes more and then she'd get up, take a shower, wash her hair.

The next thing she knew someone was gently shaking her shoulder, telling her she needed to wake up.

Stelina.

A quarter to twelve.

'Sorry, I must have dropped off again.' She drew her knees back so that Stelina could sit on the bed, read the concern on her face.

'What is it?'

'There's something . . .'

'What?'

'Something's happened.'

'What? What kind of thing?'

'Winter. Anthony Winter.'

'What about him?'

'He's . . . he's dead.'

'Don't be stupid! He can't be.'

With a sigh, Stelina clicked on her phone and passed it across. Katherine blinked, stared at the screen, unable to believe. But there it was. The words. Irrefutable. Body dis-covered. Exact circumstances as yet unknown. She dropped the phone, threw aside the covers and, brushing past Stelina, rushed for the bathroom and slammed the door.

The white enamel cold against her forehead. Hands pushing her hair away from her face. Eyes clenched tight, clutching the sides of the bowl, she retched stale air, retched again, raw on the back of the throat, and brought up a thin veil of yellow vomit, vile to the roof of the mouth, the tongue.

'Kate, are you okay in there?'

Vision blurred, broken by tears, Katherine leaned slowly back till she was sitting on her heels.

The world continued to spin.

'Kate . . .'

'It's okay, I'll just be a minute.'

Cautiously, she levered herself to her feet, ran water from the tap and splashed it on her face; flushed the toilet and lowered the lid. Her legs were still unsteady as she opened the door and stepped out into the main room.

'Here,' Stelina said, reaching out to take her arm, 'come and sit down. I'll get you some water. There now, just sit there.'

Katherine shivered and clutched her arms across her chest, stared at the floor.

'I've got this class this afternoon . . .'

'I'll call them.'

'The number, it's on my phone.'

She sipped the water, set the glass back down, covered her face in her hands. A brutal attack. Circumstances unknown. Quietly, almost soundlessly, she began to cry.

It had been a sunny morning, the first after several overcast days, the sun so bright through the high windows she had to shield her eyes as she moved into position.

Anthony, some small impatience in his voice, asking her to turn her body a shade more to the right. 'That's good, now straighten your back just a little. No, no, too much. That's it. That's right. Hold that − can you hold that? Yes, yes. There. Good. There. Just don't . . . don't budge. Not one inch, okay? Good girl. Not one fucking inch!'

A smile in his voice when he swore. A laugh, almost. Not angry, like sometimes. Angry at himself always more than with her. Pleased even, she thought. Pleased with what she was doing, the pose she was holding. Obeying his instructions to the letter.

Blinking into the light, head turned away, she saw him without really looking. Black trousers, loose at the waist, black shirt open at the neck, two buttons, no, three. Chest hair, dark, tightly curled. Bending towards the easel, then straightening, stepping away, stepping back. Looking. Always looking. How many days had she had lain bare for him like this? Open, on display. A muscle, somewhere in the small of her back, was beginning to ache. Ache sharply. Touching her tongue to the underside of her lip, she controlled her breathing, absorbed the pain.

Good girl. Not one fucking inch!

He was beside her before she realised. The smell of paint and tobacco strong on his fingers; his breath, as he leaned towards her, warm on her skin.

18

Elder had taken it reasonably easy over the weekend, relegated his usual morning run to a walk and a slow one at that, his ribs still sore from the kicking they'd received. The bruising was gradually darkening into several distinct shades of brown. Vicki was off with the band on a brief tour of south Wales – Cardiff, Swansea, Newport – and Trevor Cordon was visiting friends in Redruth, so social engagements were few. An hour or so in the local pub, the Tinners' Arms, a chat with a neighbour and that was about that. Not for the first time he fell asleep in front of the TV.

Come Monday, encouraged by a brightening sky, he pulled on his running gear, but after jogging for no more than half a mile, he shook his head and walked slowly back home. The rest of the morning passed aimlessly: loading up the washing machine, dislodging leaves from the guttering; a little reading, a quick drive into Penzance to replenish supplies.

He was putting things away, contemplating making soup of some kind for supper later – leek and potato? Mushroom and barley? – Radio 4 droning away in the background, the lunch-time news, when he heard Winter's name. Artist found dead in his studio, victim, according to a police spokesman, of an attack by assailant or assailants unknown.

Elder fetched his laptop from the other room.

Details were sparse and he picked his way between the lines. Some reports were cagey as to the cause of death, others not above taking a punt in the dark. A possible intruder. The result of a struggle. Badly beaten. Bludgeoned. A good old-fashioned word for a good old-fashioned crime. Bludgeoned to death. Dickens, Elder thought. What little Dickens he knew. The copy of *Oliver Twist* that had spent years beside first his father's bed and then his own. A version of *Bleak House* he'd watched on television some years before. Inspector Bucket, he would have known bludgeoned, Elder thought. Bill Sykes, too. The police, the reports said, were currently following several lines of inquiry.

On several of the sites there were reproductions of Winter's paintings, none, as far as Elder could see, involving Katherine.

He wondered if she'd heard the news; when she did, how she might respond? No reply from her mobile number, the landline at the flat rang out unanswered. He started to send an email and realised anything he might say only ran the risk of making things worse. Better to wait, contact her later. He poured himself a small whisky and set to peeling the potatoes.

Hadley could tell from Chris Phillips' face when he came into her office that he'd struck some kind of gold.

'Just spoken to Alice, boss. That set-to at the gallery, a couple of nights before Winter was killed. The man who attacked him, she's got a name. Elder. Frank Elder. Ran it on the computer. He's only ex-job, isn't he? Detective sergeant in the Met. A good few years back now. Transferred up to Nottingham around two thousand and four, five. Detective Inspector, Serious Crime. Took early retirement, six or seven years back.'

'We've got an address? Current?'

'Cornwall. Village on the north coast, few miles outside St Ives. Ends of the bloody earth, looks like.'

Hadley smiled. 'Rachel and I went down there a couple of years back. That part of Cornwall. For some reason I never fathomed she'd taken it into her head she wanted to see Land's End. Not that, in the event, we need to have bothered. The day we were there you could scarcely make out your hand in front of your face.'

'I've been in touch with the local nick,' Phillips said. 'Penzance. No stranger to them, Elder. Seems he's been helping out once in a while, training, that kind of thing.'

'Be all the more anxious to help us then. Help you.'

'Me?' Phillips' face was a picture. 'More one for Alice, surely? Carry on from where she's started?'

'I don't know, Chris. This Elder, what rank did you say he had last? Detective inspector? Don't want to risk him getting up on his high horse, having to talk to a young DC. Besides which, if you go down, shows Devon and Cornwall we're treating it seriously. More likely to get the cooperation we need.'

'No way of me getting out of this, is there?'

Hadley smiled. 'Chalk it up to experience. Another country down there.'

'That's what I've heard.'

The wind was getting up, the kitchen window rattling loose in its frame, one of the many small tasks Elder kept neglecting. Fitting a new washer on the bathroom tap was another. Maybe later, maybe not. He'd tried Katherine's flat again and her friend Abike had answered: Kate was sleeping and she thought it was best if she didn't wake her. As far as she understood, she'd been upset by the news of Anthony Winter's death, but not uncontrollably so. She didn't tell Elder that when she'd looked there'd been a half-empty bottle of vodka beside the bed.

Elder heated up the soup he'd made earlier, toasted some bread, ladled the soup into a bowl and carried it, along with the toast, into the small living room. Vicki had lent him a batch of CDs – Ernestine Anderson, Dianne Reeves – he thought he'd give those a listen while he was eating.

'Let me know what you think,' she'd said, 'make a nice change from that mournful stuff you listen to.'

That mournful stuff, he had informed her, was Mozart's *Requiem* and he didn't find it mournful at all. Quite the opposite, in fact. A woman he'd been briefly seeing at the time, a music teacher from Mounts Bay Academy, had talked him into accompanying her to a live performance in Truro cathedral and he'd gone under sufferance. Only to emerge elated. He'd bought a CD the next chance he got and now it was what he played when he couldn't sleep.

Dusk settling in, he took a walk down the lane to stretch his legs a little after finishing his supper. He was on his way back when he saw the headlights coming over the hill.

It wasn't until the car came past the church and turned towards the cottages that he recognised it for certain.

'Trevor, social call?'

'Not exactly.'

'You'll come inside?'

Cordon followed Elder down the path to the front door, ducked his head and entered, accepted the glass of whisky pressed into his hand.

'Anthony Winter,' Cordon said, 'name familiar?'

Elder nodded.

'Came to a nasty end, maybe you'd heard?'

He nodded again.

'Someone's coming down from the Met. Wants to talk to you. "Person of interest".'

The expression on Elder's face didn't change.

'You're okay with that?'

'Sure. Why not?' He could tell there were things Cordon wanted to ask and thought he understood why, for now at least, he was keeping them to himself.

'Eleven-thirty, then? At the station?'

'I'll be there.'

Cordon raised his glass. 'Thanks for this. Keep out the cold.'

'Any time.'

When the sound of the car had faded away there was nothing but the familiar rattle of the window and, more distant, the trees in the churchyard moving uneasily in the wind.

19

Cornwall, the homeland of the Cornish people and recognised as one of the Celtic nations: Chris Phillips had done a little basic research on the journey. A population of close to 550,000, of whom 95.7 per cent were white British: not much chance, he thought, of bumping into one of the brothers. Living in London as long as he had, thirty-one of his thirty-five years, it was possible to go for days, sometimes, without being reminded of the colour of his skin.

The police station was a long, low, grey building, unattractive and unprepossessing, and when Phillips went to present himself at the front desk he discovered it was permanently closed.

He was about to dial the number he'd been given, when Cordon appeared. 'Cost-cutting exercise. Either that or toilet paper. Close call.' Cordon held out a hand. 'Welcome to Penzance.'

'Thanks.'

'Frank's here already.'

'Frank?'

'He's ex-job, I thought you knew.'

'Mates, though?'

'Share a jar or two, time to time.'

'Conflict of interest then, surely?'

Cordon shrugged. 'Friendly interview, background, strictly voluntary, that's what I thought. No way I'm going to interfere. But if it makes you uncomfortable . . .'

Phillips was already shaking his head. 'Let's not keep Frank waiting.'

He followed Cordon up the stairs and along a blank corridor on the upper floor; the room was little different from interview rooms he was well used to, the same fading paintwork on the walls, the same lingering smell of sweat and disinfectant.

Elder was already seated, comfortable enough in familiar surroundings – jeans, roll-neck sweater – rising half out of his seat to offer Phillips his hand.

'Thanks for agreeing to come in,' Phillips said. 'I'll take up as little of your day as possible.'

'That's okay.'

'And just to be clear, you're here under your own volition and are free to leave at any time.'

'Understood.'

'So . . .' Phillips flipped open his notebook. 'Anthony Winter . . . I understand there was an argument between the two of you at a gallery opening? The Hecklington and Wearing gallery in Shoreditch. An altercation.'

The hint of a smile crossed Elder's face. 'Altercation would be about right.'

'Can you describe the circumstances?'

'Easy enough. I lost my temper. Punched him. Twice, hard. Hard as I could. Security grabbed hold of me and stopped me doing any more damage than I already had. Deposited me on the pavement outside.'

Phillips nodded, leaning back in his chair, taking his time. 'You lost your temper, that's what you said.'

'That's right.'

'He'd provoked you in some way?'

'Not directly.'

'What then?'

'It was the paintings. His. Winter's. There on display.'

'What about them?' Phillips already knew the answer, or thought he did; Alice had forwarded the images to his laptop on the way down.

'My daughter, Katherine, he'd used her as a model.'

'A life model.'

'I suppose . . .'

'She posed naked, then?'

'Yes.'

'And you didn't approve?'

'It wasn't as simple as that.'

'Perhaps you could explain?'

Elder saw the paintings again in his mind's eye. 'You have daughters, Detective Sergeant?'

Phillips shook his head.

'Any children at all?'

'Unfortunately not.'

'If you did, you might not have to ask.'

Phillips nodded. 'I apologise. I don't mean to be intrusive. I just want to understand.'

'Is that important?'

'I think so.'

Elder looked across at Cordon, who looked away.

'Your daughter . . .' Phillips began.

'Katherine.'

'Yes, Katherine. It was the manner in which she was portrayed that you objected to?'

'Yes.'

'You thought – and this is only my assumption here – but you thought she'd been – how can I put it? – sexualised? Unnecessarily sexualised?'

'Yes.'

'And that made you feel awkward? As a parent especially?'

'Yes.'

'Embarrassed?'

'Yes.'

'Angry?'

'God, yes, how many more times . . . ?'

'I'm just trying to establish . . .'

'Establish!' Elder slammed the flat of both hands down hard. 'I should've thought you've got it nailed to the bloody cross!'

'Frank,' Cordon said quietly, 'there's no need . . .'

But Elder was already on his feet. 'I'd have thought there was a fucking need.'

'Frank, come on. Sit back down.'

Elder waited a few moments until his breathing was under control.

Phillips let the silence settle, keeping his voice even, neutral. 'Forty-eight hours or so after he was the victim of an angry attack propelled by your own admitted loss of temper, Anthony Winter was the victim of a more sustained and brutal attack which resulted in his death.'

'And what? Two and two makes fucking four?'

'Frank . . .' Cordon raised a hand in warning.

'Last Thursday evening,' Phillips continued, 'after, as you said, security ejected you from the premises, what did you do?'

'Do? Made my way to Paddington, caught the sleeper train home.'

'Since which time . . . ?'

'Since which time I've been down here within a twelve-, fifteen-mile radius of Penzance.'

'And there are people, if necessary, who could attest to that?'

'If necessary, yes.'

'So, to be clear, at no time between then and Sunday evening did you return to London?'

'Jesus fucking Christ! Don't you ever listen?'

'I'm listening, Mr Elder, believe me. And what I'm hearing is a man whose temper is on a very short string, a very short string indeed.'

'Well, good for you, sunshine. And now you can hear this into the bargain. Before I answer another one of your questions you're going to have to place me under arrest and caution me, because without that you're not going to get one more goddam thing.'

'Frank . . .'

Cordon moved to intercept him, but Elder swept past and out through the door, slamming it closed behind him.

Sunshine, Phillips was thinking. I'll keep that in store.

20

Hadley sat alongside the detective superintendent at a hastily arranged press conference, saying very little herself, content to let McKeon voice the usual platitudes, dole out assurances, the residue of a Belfast accent lending his words the taint of gritty sensibility.

Both the BBC and Channel 4 News had their crime corres-pondents doing OBs from outside the entrance to the police station on Holmes Road, oiks from one or other of the local primary schools delighting in dashing across in the back-ground, fingers raised.

The swell of journalists of all stripes meant the queues out-side Franco Manca were longer than usual.

Obituaries in the broadsheet press testified to Winter's place amongst those artists who had made a sometimes unfashionable stand against abstraction on the one hand and conceptual art on the other. Richard Cork appeared on *Newsnight*, cementing Winter's place amongst a pantheon of British representational painters which ran from Stanley Spencer and Frank Auerbach to Francis Bacon and Lucian Freud.

Feminist critics railed on social media and in the pages of the *Guardian* about the misogyny at the heart of Winter's work and the tyranny of the male gaze. Rachel printed out the choicest of these and presented them to Hadley along with her granola at breakfast.

'You think one of these could be responsible?' Hadley asked. 'The feminist mafia?'

'I wouldn't discount it. I was at this conference once, I remember. "Psychotherapy and the Visual Arts", something along those lines. This woman came along as guest lecturer, professor in art history from Leeds or somewhere, red hair and red boots up to here. Scared the shit out of me, I don't mind telling you.'

The image stuck with Hadley right up to the start of the team meeting, red boots and red hair, wondering if being seen through a female gaze made it any more acceptable.

The interactive whiteboard was busy but as yet uncluttered. A head-and-shoulders shot of Winter; photographs of the body, in situ, close-ups of the injuries sustained. A detailed map showed the position of the studio, the surrounding streets and buildings. Off to one side a photograph of Frank Elder, blurry and somewhat out of date, and below that, a photo of his daughter, Katherine, both snatched from the Internet.

The report from the Coroner's Office was inconclusive; the post-mortem had been set for that day and then put into abeyance due to personnel issues; still no definite pronouncement as to time of death, somewhere between midnight and 2 a.m. on the Sunday morning seeming the most likely.

A search of Winter's flat had found an iMac computer and

two phones, one landline, one mobile. After the necessary authorisations had been obtained, the Telephone Intelligence Unit had begun logging Winter's calls, starting with the forty-eight hours before his death, examining his emails.

SOCO, perhaps not surprisingly, had garnered a host of prints from Winter's studio, half a dozen of those recurring a number of times – Winter's own, of course, the others in the process of being identified. More specifically, Terry Mitchell said, there were three sets of prints on the manacles and chain, two of those only partial, the one most clearly identifiable belonging to Winter himself.

'Howie,' Hadley said, moving things along, 'where are we with regards to CCTV?'

Howard Dean moved forward to the map.

'Four cameras, boss, for our purposes none of them ideal. Two traffic cameras on the main road, here and here, pointing in different directions. Then there's one camera at the front of this new building – flats and offices – which covers the main entrance and a section of pavement leading to this path, alley, call it what you will, that leads down to the studio. What it doesn't show is the pavement on the other side, so anyone approaching from that direction – east instead of west – wouldn't get picked up at all.'

'And this path leading to the studio, that's the only way in?'

'Unless you climb over three metres of chain fence with a barbed-wire topping, separating the studio from this builder's yard, yes.'

'You said four cameras,' Hadley said. 'That's only three.'

'The fourth,' said Dean, indicating on the map, 'is here, on this stanchion between these two sections of fence. The intention being, I imagine, to discourage anyone from cutting their way through the fence and making off with the equipment kept in the yard overnight.

'It looks to be pointing along the path to the studio, and when it's in neutral position, shall we say, that's what it does. But it's motion-sensitive so all it needs is for a fox to start foraging through these bins at the back of the flats, or for there to be some kind of movement in the yard itself, and it changes direction. Which means it's not focused on the path at all times. Anyone knowing it's there and not wanting to be seen approaching could watch and wait and choose their moment. Added to which, the quality of the image is such that any barrister worth his or her salt would have a good chance, where identification's concerned, of rubbishing it out of court. Like I say, boss, less than ideal.'

Nightmare, Hadley thought, that's what it was.

'How far have you got,' she asked, 'viewing all this?'

Dean shook his head. 'There's hours and hours of the stuff, boss. Without another pair of eyes, one at least, preferably more, be this time next week before we've seen everything.'

'I'll do what I can. Talk to McKeon, see if we can't muster up some help.' She looked across the room. 'Mark, Winter's background. Any skeletons in that particular cupboard?'

'None so far, boss, not that I can see. He was married to a Susannah Fielding from nineteen eighty-nine till they divorced ten years later. She's an artist, too. A painter. Lives in Letchworth, Letchworth Garden City. Two children, Matthew and Melissa, born in nineteen ninety-two and ninety-four respectively. There seems to have been only one significant relationship since the divorce, one that I've been able to track down: another artist, Adriana Borrell. Sculptor, apparently. And that seems to have been a good ten years back if not more.'

'Do we have an address for her?'

'Not yet, I'm afraid.'

'Okay, keep working on it. You never know, it might be useful, maybe not. But good work. Good work, everyone.

Chris is down in Cornwall talking to this man, Frank Elder, about the incident at the gallery, and Alice and I are off to Dalston to talk to the daughter. We'll reconvene tomorrow. Meantime, anything especially significant, groundbreaking, I want to know almost as soon as you know yourselves.'

21

Rachel had teased her more than once about her habit of having her subordinates drive. Status, that's what it's all about, you do realise? That and control. At least, as far as I know, you don't sit in the back, like someone lording it with a chauffeur behind the wheel. In fact, when there were papers to read through, files to check on the laptop, emails to reply to, that was exactly what she did. Not wishing to wind Rachel up further, Hadley kept that to herself.

Today she was sitting up alongside Alice as they made their way around the roundabout on St Paul's Road, Alice's driving totally in character: neat, precise, careful. Not one to take unnecessary risks.

Glancing at her again, Hadley was struck by an image, a flicker of memory, one of those films from the sixties she and Rachel luxuriated in once in a while – or had, before Hadley's promotion to detective chief inspector cut their leisure time by half. Glistening black-and-white, 35-millimetre prints at the BFI Southbank or the recently refurbished Regent Street cinema, a cocktail in the bar beforehand, supper afterwards. Rachel, a film buff since her university days. Bergman, Bresson, Godard. Kieslowski and Kaurismaki. And Alice, Hadley thought, was almost a dead ringer for Jean Seberg in *À Bout de Souffle*: the wide eyes, the dark eyebrows and off-blonde elfin-cut hair. Alice wearing black as usual, black jumper, black trousers, black shoes. Glancing now at the GPS, two more turns before drawing up outside the Wilton estate.

The young woman who came to the door was a little over five foot tall and, Hadley thought, of African parentage. Nigerian possibly? Introductions made, warrant cards shown, they were ushered inside.

Katherine Elder was standing by the partly open door out on to the balcony. Even wearing a shapeless top and ill-fitting jeans, no discernible make-up, hair tied back from her face, there was no escaping the fact, Hadley thought, that she was beautiful.

'Thank you for agreeing to see us,' Hadley said.

Katherine nodded and gestured for them to sit. 'Would you like some tea or anything? Coffee?'

'Thank you,' Hadley said. 'Tea would be nice.'

'There's jasmine, I think, otherwise it's just builder's.'

'Builder's would be fine.'

'I'll stick the kettle on,' Abike said, 'then leave you to it.'

Katherine smiled her thanks.

Hadley offered up a few positive comments about the flat, asked about the area, Dalston not really being a part of London with which she was familiar. Katherine answered in a desultory way, fiddling with the ribbon tying back her hair until it came undone and fell to her shoulders.

'Anthony Winter,' Hadley said, once the tea had been poured and Abike had made her goodbyes, 'it must have been a shock when you heard what had happened?'

'Yes. Yes, it was.'

'And you worked for him, as his model, for how long?'

'Not all that long really. Six months or so, a little more.'

'Even so, working closely as I suppose you have to, you must have got to know one another well?'

'Yes. Yes, I suppose so.' Tugging at the hair now, the ends, grasping and releasing.

'Katherine?'

'I don't . . . Yes, we did.' Tears started to run, soundlessly, down her face.

Alice offered her a tissue.

'I'm sorry,' Hadley said, 'I didn't mean to upset you.'

'It's all right, I . . . It was just a surprise, you know? You never think . . .' She wiped her eyes, blew her nose, crumpled the tissue in her hand. 'Anthony, he was always . . . he was just there, you know?' She gestured with her hands, indicating something solid, a statue, a person.

'A presence,' Hadley suggested.

Katherine nodded. Sniffed. Fiddled some more with her hair.

'So you and Anthony . . . I just want to be clear,' Hadley said. 'You were working for him until very recently, is that correct?'

'Well, no. No, not really. Not very recently, no. The last time, the last time I posed for him, that would have been over a month ago now.'

'And you'd stopped because . . . ?'

'The paintings Anthony was doing, the ones I was modelling for, they were more or less finished. As far as I was concerned, anyway. He'd carry on working on them, of course, till he was satisfied. I think that's what he always did, the way he worked. There wasn't anything else for me to do.'

'And did you see much of him after that? After you stopped working together?'

Katherine shook her head. 'He was busy getting everything ready for this new show.'

'And – I simply want to be clear here – you didn't see him at all during that time, is that what you're saying?'

'Not really. Just the once . . .'

'So you did see him?'

'Yes, once. He asked me if I'd like to see the paintings before they were packed up ready to go to the gallery.'

'And when was this?'

'Last week. The beginning of last week. Monday.' She tugged at a stray hair. 'Yes, that's when it was, Monday.'

'You're sure?'

'Yes. Because at first, when he asked, I didn't think I'd go. I didn't want to.'

'Why was that?'

Katherine fidgeted in her seat. 'There'd been a . . . I don't know what you'd call it . . . a misunderstanding.'

'Between Anthony and yourself?'

'Yes. And I didn't think . . . I didn't think I was going to be seeing him again, so when he phoned and said did I want to come to the studio, I just didn't know . . .'

'This misunderstanding, it was professional? To do with the work?'

Katherine looked away. 'No. No, not really.'

'Personal, then?'

'Yes, but . . . but I don't want to talk about it. Okay? I just don't.'

'All right, let's put that to one side for now.'

'It doesn't have anything to do . . . anything to do with what happened.'

Hadley raised an appeasing hand. 'Fine. As I say, it's nothing we need to pursue. For now, at least.'

The sounds of two dogs barking, one high, one low, rose up

from below; a woman's voice then, clear and commanding, and the barking stopped.

Alice shifted position a little, claiming Katherine's attention. 'When you saw the paintings, on the Monday I think you said it was, what did you think?'

'I don't know.'

'You must have thought something, surely? Now they were finished.'

'I suppose I was . . . I was surprised.'

'What by?'

Katherine thought before answering. 'They looked so . . . I don't know, I don't know if it makes sense, but they looked so, well, real.'

'Lifelike, you mean?'

'No, more than that. They looked raw, somehow. Real but sort of magnified. I can't really explain.' She gave another pull at her hair. 'And they were different. That was the thing. Different.'

'Different how?'

'Things had been added, changed. Made more dramatic, I suppose.'

'How did you feel about that?'

Katherine looked at the floor.

Alice waited, giving her time. 'Katherine?'

'I didn't like it. What he'd done. I mean, I know they're his paintings, it's his work, only . . .' She looked, again, to be on the brink of tears.

'Only what?' Alice persisted quietly. 'What didn't you like?'

'He'd made them more . . . more ugly. Nasty. Like there's one where my arms are up above my head, right? When I was posing, most of the time we used some soft cloth, scarves, to keep my arms steady. It was only right at the end, the last couple of days, Anthony said to use the chains and things and then never as tight as in the painting. Look at it now and it's as if I'm being held prisoner. As if it's hurting.'

'And you weren't?'

'What?'

'Hurting?'

'No. No, of course not.'

'So he changed it later?'

'Yes.'

'Without telling you?'

'Yes, of course. I mean, they're his paintings, I understand that. His work. He can do what he wants. But like I said, it's hard to explain.'

'It made you uncomfortable? What he'd done?'

'Yes. Like that one where it looks as if I'm bleeding . . . you know, from here . . . as if maybe I'm on my period . . .'

She covered her face with her hands. Hadley and Alice exchanged glances and Alice went into the kitchen, returning with a glass of water which she offered to Katherine along with another tissue.

'I'm really sorry,' Hadley said once Katherine had recovered. 'I realise this is distressing. We won't keep you much longer. There are just a couple more things.'

Katherine sniffed, wiped her eyes.

'The incident at the gallery involving your father, you know about that?'

Katherine nodded. 'It was all over Twitter, everywhere.'

'You weren't there yourself, though?'

'The private view? No.'

'And your father, did you know he was going to be there?'

'God, no. And if I had, I'd have begged him to stay away. I don't know what he was doing. What he was thinking of.'

'And were you surprised? At how he'd behaved?'

Katherine hesitated. 'Not really, no.'

116

'He has a temper then?'

'Sometimes, yes.'

'Where you're concerned especially?'

'Maybe.' A shrug. 'Probably.'

'My father would have been the same,' Alice said. 'Just seeing me naked, that would have been enough. But anything more . . . more graphic . . . I don't know what he might have done.'

The sounds of an ambulance, going at full tilt, penetrated the room. Faded away.

'I just wonder,' Hadley said, 'before we go, if you have any idea, any idea at all, who might have wanted to harm Anthony in this way?'

'No, no, I don't.'

'Enemies of any kind? Anyone he might have mentioned.'

'No. But I thought . . .'

'Go on.'

'I thought whoever did this, it was someone who just, I don't know, broke in, I suppose. A burglar, perhaps. Not something deliberate, someone he knew.'

'At the moment, the inquiry's still quite open. We have to consider any possibility. Which is why I asked my question.'

Katherine pushed her hair away from her face, thought some more before answering. 'I don't know of any what you might call enemies, no. I mean, Anthony never went out of his way to make himself liked. Quite the opposite, sometimes, as far as I could tell. But enemies . . .' She shook her head. 'There was a lot of anger over him changing galleries, I know that. From whoever had represented him before. But that isn't the kind of thing people get killed over, is it?'

'Possibly not.' With a quick smile, Hadley got to her feet, Alice following suit. 'Thank you for agreeing to talk to us, thank you for your time. Because of your presence in the

117

studio, we will need to take your fingerprints. Just for the process of elimination.'

'Yes, I understand.'

'If you could pop into the station at Shacklewell Lane later today? Or we could give you a lift down there now if you'd like?'

'I've got to go that way anyway, it's fine.'

'Good. I'll make sure they're expecting you.'

'And if there's a mobile number on which we can contact you? Should we need to again?'

'Of course.'

Alice noted it down and at the door first Hadley and then Alice shook Katherine's hand. 'I'm sorry it's all been so upsetting,' Hadley said.

Katherine smiled weakly in return.

Neither Hadley nor Alice spoke till they were out on the street.

'Did you notice?' Alice said. 'When we were shaking hands?'

'The scars on her wrists, you mean?'

'Yes. Self-harm, you think?'

'Most likely. Unless it was something more serious.'

'Hospitals, we could check, couldn't we?'

Hadley nodded. They were back at the car. A woman in full burqa went slowly past on the opposite side of the street, an orange Sainsbury's bag in each hand.

'You think it could be relevant?' Alice asked. 'To do with Winter somehow?'

'A stretch, perhaps, but yes, possibly. A misunderstanding between them, is that what she called it?'

'Yes. And personal, she said that too. Didn't want to go there.'

'Maybe she'll have to, we'll see.'

They got into the car, Alice switching on the engine, checking the rear-view mirror, indicating.

'You did well in there,' Hadley said. 'Handled it very well indeed.'

'Thank you.'

Looking over her shoulder before pulling out into the traffic, Alice held the position for longer than was strictly necessary in order to hide her smile.

22

By the time Elder had driven back across the peninsula, Penzance to Zennor, he'd calmed down sufficiently to be regretting the hastiness of his actions and much of what he'd said besides. Challenging a detective sergeant from the Met to arrest him for his possible involvement in murder, not the most judicious move. But what's done was done. If they wanted to take it any further, he'd wait for them to come to him.

He wondered how Katherine was faring, assumed someone from the same team would be questioning her too. If he hadn't behaved like such an arse, he could have asked the DS — Phillips, was that his name? — about the inquiry, found out who was in charge. Not impossible, even after all this time, that it was someone he knew from his days in the Met, someone he'd worked with, a junior officer who'd moved up the ladder.

Or someone like Karen Shields.

Just the thought of her name made him smile.

The last he'd heard of Karen, five or six years ago it would be now, she had been a detective chief inspector in Homicide and Serious Crime Command. An investigation she'd brought to a satisfactory conclusion had garnered quite a bit of publicity at the time: the murder of a Moldovan youth whose body had been found trapped beneath the ice covering one of the ponds on Hampstead Heath.

The last time he'd seen her, more or less the last time they'd spoken, had been several years earlier, an occasion he didn't think he'd ever forget. They'd spent the night together, Karen and himself, the first time and the last, both high on the adrenalin that came from a difficult job well done, the case cracked, investigation over, or so it seemed — dinner at Moro in Clerkenwell, wine, brandy — as they were saying goodnight outside his flat, the taxi idling, meter ticking over, she'd kissed him on the mouth. In the early hours of the morning he'd woken suddenly, the space beside him empty, a gun pointing at his head.

Then Karen, stark naked, had come hurtling through from the kitchen, stainless-steel kettle in her hand, swinging it high and wide until it smashed into the centre of the intruder's face as he turned towards her, splintering bone, the flesh either side of the now broken nose splitting open like an overripe plum.

Elder himself a matter of seconds from almost certain death.

It was too much to hope that Karen's team was involved in Winter's murder, that she was SIO. She was still on his mind when he heard Cordon's car draw up outside.

'A right bollocks you made of that,' Cordon said at the door.

'You don't have to tell me.'

'Somebody should.'

'I know.'

'Anger-management course, that'd be my advice.'

Elder nodded. 'Phillips, where's he now?'

'Last I saw him, on the phone to his guv'nor.'

'Deciding whether to arrest me, take me at my word.'

'Serve you right if he did.'

'Apology in order then, is that it? Humble pie?'

'Double helpings, I'd say.'

Elder shook his head.

'What got you so riled up anyway? Wasn't as if anything he said was out of order. Poor guy just doing his job.'

'I know, I know. It's just this whole business with Katherine . . .'

'That time she was taken, you mean, held prisoner, that's what you were thinking of?' Cordon knew the outline of what had happened when Katherine had been abducted; not the details, little more than the basic facts. He didn't want to know any more.

'That's what it comes down to, yes,' Elder said. 'And this now with Winter, it brings it all back.'

'It was you who found her, wasn't it? Where she was being held?'

'I got there first, yes. Just ahead of the rest.'

'Stuff like that,' Cordon said, 'never mind how much help you get, it doesn't go away.'

'She's been in therapy, had treatment, a short spell in hospital. I'm not sure how much good it's done.'

'I wasn't thinking about her.'

'What d'you mean?'

'Maybe you're the one who needs to get some help. Talk to someone, at least.'

'I don't think so.'

'That episode earlier? Flying off the handle the way you did.'

'Phillips. He was goading me.'

'How about up in London? That hoo-ha at the gallery?'

Elder fixed him with a look. 'I lost my temper, okay. But I've got no regrets about that. Far as I'm concerned, he got what was coming to him. Same circumstances, I'd likely do it again.'

'I shouldn't go shouting that from the rooftops. Not with a murder inquiry ongoing.'

'Don't worry, I don't want the Met breathing down my neck any more than I dare say you do. Get me back to the station so I can give a DNA sample, get my prints taken, send Phillips back to London happy. Hope he accepts my apology for anything I said.'

That night he had the dream again. Woke sticky with sweat. Stumbling to the window, he threw it open and breathed in the cold night air. The sky was black, clouds shuttering out the moon. Downstairs he poured whisky into a glass, switched on the stereo, rooted through the small pile of CDs.

The music started quietly, just strings and woodwinds, and then the choir . . .

Elder closed his eyes.

Saw Katherine. Katherine's face. Pale, drawn: afraid.

Before leaving Penzance he'd rung her mobile, but it had been switched off; called the flat and asked if he could talk to Kate.

'She's not here right now,' Stelina had said. 'She's just popped out. I'm not sure exactly when she'll be back.'

'Okay,' Elder said. 'Ask her to give me a quick call when she gets in.'

'Of course.'

He heard nothing. Katherine didn't call. For all he knew she'd been there the entire time, gesturing no with her hand and shaking her head. Mouthing, tell him I'm not here.

When the *Requiem* finished, the best part of an hour later, the first vestiges of light were just beginning to show faintly above the horizon, grazing the edges of the sea.

23

'This guy's paintings,' Rachel said.

'What about them?'

Hadley was at the stove, the coffee just starting to bubble, Rachel halfway through some kind of evil-looking smoothie, kale, spinach and nettles, her iPad propped up alongside the toast.

'This one here, for instance. If one of my clients brought that along after a session of art therapy, I'd be more than a little concerned.'

'Better out than in, surely? I thought that's what those sessions were all about?'

'It depends whether they're getting it out of their system or fashioning some kind of blueprint for something they're going to put into practice later.'

'You think that's what he could have been doing? Winter?'

'It's got to be possible. And if you don't take that coffee off the stove it's going to taste like stewed cat piss.'

'If you can make a better job of it, in future do it yourself.'

'Perhaps I will.'

'Whoa!' Hadley raised a hand in alarm. 'Lesbian bickering warning!'

Rachel laughed. 'Okay, fair enough. But seriously, the minute it starts bubbling . . .'

'Rachel!'

' . . . that's when you should take it off the heat.'

Hadley grabbed the first thing to hand that wasn't a sharp implement, an oven glove as it happened, and threw it at her partner's head.

'You really think,' she said a few minutes later, indicating the screen, 'there's something seriously nasty going on?'

'Don't you?'

'It's art, what do I know?'

'Don't be naive.'

Hadley tried her coffee. It did taste more than a little overcooked. 'When we spoke to the young woman who modelled for those paintings, she said most if not all of that paraphernalia, the stuff you're reacting to, was added later.'

'Lucky for her.' Rachel buttered a piece of toast. 'Even so, it could have been what was in his mind at the time. What he wanted to do but, for whatever reason, didn't feel quite able to. Not with her, at least.'

'But possibly in other situations, is that what you're thinking?'

'Who knows?'

Hadley grinned. 'Well, if you don't . . .'

Chris Phillips was lurking in the entrance, a take-out cup from Bean About Town in one hand, a half-eaten muffin in the other.

'Ought to get up earlier,' Hadley said. 'Have a proper breakfast.'

'What? You're my mother all of a sudden?'

'Heaven forbid.'

'She'll be pleased you said that.'

Hadley had met Chris Phillips' mother on at least two occasions; a nursing sister, now retired, she had come over from Jamaica as a young woman, met his father, a dance-band musician, and set up home in west London, Westbourne Grove. Formidable would be the word.

'How was the West Country?'

'Long way from anywhere else aside?'

'Aside from that.'

'Officially, more than helpful.'

'And unofficially?'

'Elder and this Trevor Cordon, the DI, they're drinking buddies. Conflict of interest, no question. Not that I think it's going to make a deal of difference. Half a dozen people happy to testify to seeing Elder at various times the weekend of the eighth, ninth. Without breaking some kind of land-speed record or chartering a private plane, it's hard to see any way he could have made it up to London, attacked Winter in his studio and made it back again.'

'But not impossible.'

'I guess not. I don't see how, but you're right, we can't altogether rule it out. Not yet, at least. Especially when he's got the temper for it.'

'The incident at the gallery, you mean?'

'Not just that. Lost it under questioning, stormed out. Took Cordon to calm him down, get him to come back in.'

'Anything in particular that got him fired up?'

'The paintings of his daughter, that was the trigger. Not hard to understand why, mind you, seeing a kid of yours like that . . .'

'Not a kid exactly.'

'Near enough, as far as he's concerned. After what happened especially.'

'What happened?'

'Sorry, boss. Somehow I thought you knew.'

'Knew what?'

'His daughter, Katherine, she was abducted. Six, seven years ago now. Held prisoner. Raped. Tortured.'

'Why the hell wasn't I told that before?'

'I'm sorry. Like I say . . .'

'It doesn't matter. Not now.' The expression on her face changed. 'She'd have been just a girl, little more than a child.'

'Sixteen.'

'The person responsible . . .'

'HMP Wakefield. Life sentence.'

Hadley was thinking about the young woman she and Alice had spoken to, nervous, unsettled, pulling abstractedly at her hair, scars that looked fairly recent on her wrists. A history of self-harm?

'Changes the picture, doesn't it?' Phillips said. 'In terms of any possible motivation he might have had.'

'Elder?'

Phillips nodded.

Hadley took a step back, marshalling her thoughts, remembering what Rachel had been saying earlier that morning.

'I wonder,' she said, 'if Winter might have known about what had happened to her, to Katherine, when he made those paintings?'

'As some kind of inspiration, you mean?'

'It could be. Consciously recreating the scene.'

'What kind of sick bastard would want to do that?'

'I don't know. And maybe that's way out of line. But Chris, dig out all the details of the abduction, just in case. And see what's happening with forensics, will you? Howie was supposed to be chasing them up, but who knows?'

'How about phone records, anything there?'

Hadley shook her head. 'CIU, dragging their heels. Richard should be on their case.'

'I'll give him a nudge.'

'Okay, good . . .' She glanced at her watch. 'I've got a meeting, shouldn't be above a half-hour, tops. Till then the ship's yours.'

Phillips grinned. 'I'll try not to run her aground.'

Rebecca Johnson was sitting at a corner table, wearing a pale blue-and-grey dress from Ghost. Hadley had been looking at it online only a week or so before. Exactly why she wasn't sure. She could barely remember the last time she'd worn a dress.

'Rebecca, hello. Thanks for making the time.'

'Not a problem.' Half-standing, she smiled. 'You know, I don't know what to call you. Detective Chief Inspector's such a mouthful.'

'Alex. Alex is fine.'

'All right. Good, Alex it is.'

'Can I get you anything?'

'No, thanks, I'm good.'

At the counter, Hadley ordered a double macchiato and helped herself to water from the jug standing off to the side, careful to avoid both the ice cubes and the wedges of lime falling into her glass.

When she had first been stationed at Holmes Road as a young detective constable, about the best you could have hoped for would have been instant coffee from a greasy spoon. Now there were three chain outlets and four independent coffee shops within easy walking distance. The high street was otherwise dominated by charity shops and estate agents. Maybe that was how the world was now divided: those who'd happily fork out close to three pounds for a flat white and those who could not. The yin and yang of capitalism, as Rachel liked to put it.

'How goes the investigation?' Rebecca asked when Hadley sat back down.

'Oh, you know. Early days.'

'I still haven't quite got over what happened.'

'Finding the body especially, it's no wonder.'

'You must get used to it, I suppose. Dead bodies. Blood and gore.'

'Not really.' Hadley smiled. 'We just have to make it seem as if we do.'

When her macchiato arrived it looked close to perfect, just the right amount of rich crema on the surface.

'What I wanted to ask you,' she said, 'as I understand it, when Winter changed galleries there was a certain amount of ill feeling?'

Rebecca smiled. 'A certain amount? That would be an understatement at best.'

'Somebody's nose was put out of joint?'

'More their wallet. Bank account.'

'There was a significant amount of money involved, then?'

'Thousands. Millions, potentially.'

'I had no idea. I mean, you hear sometimes of paintings going for what seem like ridiculous sums at auction, but that's, I don't know, Warhol or Picasso or some old canvas by Van Gogh that's been lingering in someone's attic for generations. But Winter, I had no idea.'

Rebecca finished her cappuccino, just the foam remaining. A young woman backing her buggy out on to the street managed to get it wedged between a table and the door and a student jumped down from where he was working on his laptop in the window to help.

'What you have to understand,' Rebecca said, 'for years, financially speaking, Anthony was just bubbling under. Not attracting the serious money, the serious collectors, but demanding more than decent sums all the same. Five figures at best and rarely that. Abernathy, they'd been representing him since he left the Royal College. Nothing too pushy, too flamboyant, that's not their style. But respectable, old-school, steady. Then, when Anthony and I became involved . . .'

'Involved?'

Rebecca laughed. 'Oh, not that way. Wrong side of the fence entirely. No, this was strictly professional. I had contacts poor old Rupert – Rupert Morland-Davis, he owns Abernathy more or less – just didn't have. New collectors, new money. Russian, of course, Chinese. I went to work on Anthony's behalf and his prices began to rise. But there's just so much I can do without help. Meanwhile, Rupert's sales through Abernathy were growing through no effort of his own.'

'And the gallery takes how much?'

'From a picture sale? Fifty per cent.'

Hadley emitted a low whistle. 'That much? I'm amazed.'

'Well, it's okay if it's commission they're doing something to actually earn. But if they're not . . . Which is why I arranged for Anthony to move to Hecklington and Wearing. Young, trendy, the right place at the right time.'

'Poor old Rupert, as you called him, he wasn't happy.'

'Practically burst a blood vessel. Threatened to sue, though of course he didn't have a leg to stand on. Anthony never as much as signed a piece of paper. Gentlemen's agreement, that's all it was.'

'And you're no gentleman.'

'Exactly.'

There was something about Rebecca Johnson's eyes, Hadley thought. Did they change colour when she smiled? She reached for her water and almost drained the glass.

'So all of this manoeuvring,' she said, 'has left Morland-Davis more than a little aggrieved, not to say seriously out of pocket.'

'It has indeed.'

'At the time, I assume he'd have done his best to persuade Winter to change his mind?'

'There were a number of heated conversations, I believe. In the end, Anthony refused to speak to him directly, said everything had to be done through me.'

'Which could have made him angrier still?'

'I'm sure it did, but not . . .' She smiled. 'Not enough to kill him, if that's what you're thinking. More of a hissy-fit kind of temper, Rupert. Vicious words at fifty paces.' A smile creased her face. 'He'll be even more put out now, of course. Callous as it might sound, a good dead artist can be worth more than a good live one. The existing canvases take on a special value once it's clear there won't be any more.'

'And Winter's share of the profits? What happens to those now?'

'It depends upon the contents of his will. Assuming there was one. His solicitor would know. Other than that, once I've taken my commission, the rest, presumably, stays in the bank.'

'This solicitor, I don't suppose you have a name.'

'Name and number.' Rebecca reached for her phone. 'Let me have an email address and I'll send them to you now.'

That done, Hadley looked at her watch. 'I really should be going. It's been helpful, filling in the background. I'm grateful for your time.'

She was halfway out of her chair when Rebecca reached out a hand. 'You don't suppose we could meet again some time? Just for a drink perhaps?'

It took Hadley a moment to answer. 'No, no, I don't think so. Nice idea, but no.'

Rebecca smiled, withdrew her hand. 'I understand.'

24

Katherine sat slumped on one of the benches by the path leading to the tennis courts, leather jacket pulled tight around her
shoulders, bottle within close reach. How long she'd been
there she didn't know. A pair of women went by talking loudly
in Polish, pushing buggies, someone else's kids. A gaggle of
schoolgirls, swearing freely, skirts rolled high. Joggers. A
white-haired man pulling a small dog along on a lead, its belly
scraping the ground.

Chrissy had phoned on her behalf again, a little reluctantly,
the third time she'd cancelled a class in as many days. The
thought of anyone looking at her, even fully clothed, never
mind naked, was more than she could stand.

'You've got to pull yourself together,' Chrissy had said
sharply. 'You realise that, don't you? You look a mess.'

Tough love, Katherine supposed.

She glanced up at the woman walking across the grass
towards her; thought for a moment she recognised her, decided
she was mistaken.

'Katherine? Kate?'

She looked up again on hearing the voice, surprised. Padded jacket, black trousers tucked down into silver boots, blue beret covering most of her dark hair.

'V? What are you doing here?'

'Looking for you.'

Katherine shook herself, rubbed her hands across her face.

'Okay if I sit?'

Katherine nodded.

For some moments neither of them spoke, Katherine conscious of the bottle of vodka at her feet.

'London Fields,' Vida said. 'I used to come here all the time. Long time ago now. I was little more than a kid. That novel had just been out. Amis? Martin Amis?' She laughed. 'All changed a lot since then. Trendy now, I suppose. Hackney, the hipster's delight.'

'How did you know I'd be here?'

'Chrissy. Chrissy told me. She's worried about you.'

'There's no need.'

'No?' Vida looked pointedly at the bottle between Katherine's shoes. 'What is it? Close to a bottle a day now?'

'V, don't . . .'

'Pills, too, I dare say.'

'V . . .'

Reaching down, Vida seized the bottle and, fending off Katherine as she tried to grab it back, upturned it, spilling the remaining vodka down on to the grass.

'What the fuck you do that for?' Katherine said angrily.

'I thought you'd had enough.'

'None of your business, is it?'

'No?'

'No.'

'All right then, my mistake.'

She was into her stride before Katherine called her back.

'V, I'm sorry.'

'Okay.' Vida sat and proceeded to roll a cigarette. 'He was a bastard, you know that?' she said. 'Just a wonder someone didn't kill him sooner.'

'Don't.'

'What?'

'Don't say that.'

'Why not? It's true. Never gave a moment's thought for anyone but himself. Mind you, bloody artists, most of them, they're all the same. Selfish through and bloody through. Anthony, if he didn't think there was something in it for him, some way he could use you, he wouldn't give you the time of day.'

'I thought you were his friend.'

'As long as it suited him, yes. Oh, he'd deign to come into my classes once in a while, sprinkle a little praise and bonhomie. But only for what he could get in return.'

'Like what?'

'Like you.'

Katherine stared at her, disbelieving, struggling with the implication of what she'd heard; Vida reached out a hand towards hers and she pushed it away.

'Girls, that's what he wanted. Girls he could use for a while and then discard when he was finished with them. With you, though, it was different. At least, for a time that's what I thought. He saw something different in you. And it shows. It's there in the paintings, the work.'

'What do you mean?'

Vida drew hard on her cigarette. 'I asked him once, what he saw, what it was that made you special, and he said pain.'

Katherine arched her back as if she'd been struck.

Vida reached out her hand again. 'I feel responsible, guilty. For what happened.'

'But surely . . .'

'Not for what happened to him, what happened to you. I was careless, thoughtless. I should have seen you'd suffered enough already. It was there, there in the eyes. And Anthony knew. It excited him. I could tell.'

Katherine hunched her body, turned her face away and cried. After a while, Vida slid an arm round her shoulders and rested her head against the nape of her neck.

'It's all right,' she said softly. 'It's all right.'

'I loved him,' Katherine said. 'At least, I thought I did.'

'I know.'

'And I thought . . .'

'I know, I know.'

25

The sun hung low over the harbour, a disc of pale yellow thinly veiled in mist. Anchored, small boats tilted this way and that on the incoming tide. Gulls swooped and screamed overhead. Elder had walked into St Ives along the Coffin Path, passing small farm after small farm, low stone wall after low stone wall, climbing stile after stile. Burs clung to his trouser legs, mud to his boots.

At Wicca a black-and-white sheepdog ran warning circles around him, barking noisily, harrying his heels along the lane towards Boscubben before dropping back content, job done. It was close to here, where an arm of the path forked down towards the sea, that Elder had first made his home, years back now, in the wake of the breakdown of his marriage and his retirement from the Nottinghamshire force.

Originally a farm labourer's cottage, walls of bare stone save for one unevenly plastered room, in its barrenness and austerity it had suited his mood perfectly. The farm to which it had formerly belonged had stood dilapidated and abandoned, sacking covering the windows, rough hasps and padlocks on the doors — the sad result, Elder had heard, of a family feud that had turned brother against brother, cousin against cousin, father against son.

Only gradually had he felt the need for more company than that of the beasts other farmers paid to pasture in the surrounding fields and the hail-and-well-met of occasional ramblers passing by. Now, both the farm buildings and the cottage had been restored, the farm itself with new owners who had found turning over their fields to the cultivation of maize as fodder for livestock more profitable than keeping the animals themselves, and the cottage was in its second season as a successful holiday let.

Times changed. Some people went under, others survived.

Both he and Joanne had made new lives for themselves, neither perfect, but then whose life was? As his own father had been so used to saying, look around you, lad, there are plenty others one hell of a lot worse off than you.

Which was doubtless true, and amongst those he knew it was Katherine, always Katherine that he worried about most. Now especially, when she had seemed to be getting herself together again after a myriad setbacks: a flat share in London with friends, genuine friends; enough work, almost, to keep the proverbial wolf from the door. Cheerful, almost, on the rare occasions they spoke, the even rarer occasions they met.

Till now.

Those bandaged wrists. Winter's sudden death.

She was still avoiding his calls, not responding to his texts.

Elder had phoned Joanne to see if she'd heard from her and apparently they'd spoken briefly the day before. Aside from feeling a bit under the weather, Katherine had assured her she was okay, possibly coming down with a cold but nothing more. Nothing to worry about though, basically she was fine.

'Are you going to go down and see her?' Elder had asked.

'Are you?' Joanne snapped back.

Elder thought perhaps not: it was a long way to go to have the door slammed in your face as had happened in the past.

It's my life, Dad. Why don't you let me fuck it up whichever way I choose and then you can sod off and find a life of your own. Fuck that up. It's what you're good at, after all.

He pushed his coffee cup aside, folded the paper he'd been sporadically reading, and went inside the café to pay. He'd take a walk around to the other side of the bay, stroll around the island, and then head for home. Vicki was back from what sounded as if it had been a successful trip to South Wales and he'd promised to meet her in Newlyn later.

They had supper at Mackerel Sky — scallops and monkfish helped down with a bottle of decent wine — Vicki keen to tell him about the highlights of their tour. Audiences had been small, she said, but enthusiastic, and there'd been cash in hand enough at the end of the evening to cover expenses, plus the money made from the sale of the band's new CD. Added to which, it had been a laugh. Even when the van they were travelling in broke down on the way from Cardiff to Swansea at three in the morning.

They went for a stroll along the front, the lights of Penzance hazy in the distance, Vicki's hand in his. It didn't have to be true love, not at their age, that was what she'd said. Nor was it. The truth was he felt comfortable in her company, was happy to listen to her stories, laugh at her jokes, liked to hear her sing. In bed, where she took the lead, he was pleased to follow. Her need, he guessed, roughly equal to his own.

'You'll come back?' she said, leaning her head on his arm.

'If I'm invited.'

She thumped him playfully in the ribs.

At her place in Marazion, no need to rush, she made tea, brightened his with a taste of Scotch, poured a small brandy for herself. When she asked after Katherine he shrugged, non-committal, he didn't really know.

'You can't blame yourself for ever, Frank.'

'Is that what I'm doing?'

'That's how it seems.'

'Then maybe that's how I feel.'

'Because you haven't always been there for her?'

'That's part of it.'

She stroked the back of his hand. 'You've been there when it's mattered, that's what's important. When it's mattered most.'

'Have I?'

'That man who took her, when she was just a girl. Keach, was that his name? You were the one to save her.'

'And if it hadn't been for me, he might never have taken her in the first place.'

'If it hadn't been for you, Frank, she'd likely be dead.'

Elder rocked back, pushed her hand away.

'I'm sorry, I shouldn't have said that. I just don't like to see you punishing yourself unnecessarily.'

'It's okay.'

But it wasn't, they both knew that.

Neither spoke for some little time.

'I think I'd better go,' Elder said, edging back his chair.

He got as far as the main door, the street, a jolt of cold air snapping him to his senses.

Vicki was standing in the centre of the room. 'Forget something?'

Elder shrugged. 'I thought I might apologise.'

'What for?'

'My quick temper.'

'Accepted.'

In bed they made spoons, her arms first around his, then his around hers. Closeness, what they both needed then, nothing more. A short while later she was fast asleep, leaving Elder feeling the quiet, settled pulse of her body against his, the night outside vast, unknowable and dark.

26

The atmosphere in the squad room was tense, nervy, slightly charged; a sense that things were at last beginning to move. Outside, the skies were gradually darkening, the storm the weather forecasters had promised finally on its way.

'At least they haven't given it another stupid name,' quipped Howard Dean. 'Doris. Who's going to be bothered about a storm called bloody Doris?'

'Upping the ante, aren't they?' Terry Mitchell said. 'Ever since that bloke went on TV and said there was a zero chance of serious weather and next thing you know one in every dozen trees've blown over and half the bloody country's six foot under water.'

'Okay,' Phillips said, raising both hands for quiet. 'Let's settle down.'

Black trouser suit, white shirt, boots with a generous heel, Hadley took her place front and centre. 'First off, I know you've all been working hard and so far without much thanks. So, due gratitude from me for all that effort. Let's make sure none of it goes to waste.'

A few quiet murmurs of agreement, appreciation.

'The post-mortem, Chris, a summary of the findings?'

'Straightforward enough. Cause of death, as we suspected, blunt-force trauma to the back of the head. Fractured skull and blood clots resulting in severe haemorrhaging. There were also internal injuries to the upper body, principally a ruptured spleen which had led to considerable internal bleeding. Marks on the skull were conducive to the fatal blows being delivered, again as we suspected, by the manacles that were found in the vicinity of the body.'

He took a moment to check his notes.

'There was also bruising and lacerations to the ribs and back and legs, some as a result of being struck repeatedly by an implement, in all likelihood a chain, that had been wielded with force, others most likely the result of being kicked with a heavy shoe or boot. There were also defensive wounds on the victim's hands. And that's about it. Copies of the report itself are available at a click of the proverbial button.'

'Thanks, Chris. Mitch, you've got something interesting, I think?'

'Yes, boss.' Mitchell clicked on his computer and an image like an abstract painting appeared on the whiteboard to Hadley's right. 'Here you can see the victim's blood trail, the well-defined tails on those splashes indicating that the blood struck the surface at an angle of thirty degress or less. Which means he was, almost certainly, crawling along the floor, attempting to get away, while he was being struck, and if you look carefully, those secondary spatters show the direction of movement, left to right across the studio towards the wall furthest from the door.'

He touched the keyboard and a second image appeared.

'And this is from close by that far wall, and judging by the amount of blood that's pooled there, by this point the victim is almost certainly no longer moving, but, again because of the amount of blood, we can surmise that he was still alive.'

Hadley waited a moment for all of that to sink in.

'So, our attacker,' she said, 'our perpetrator, is someone with a considerable temper and the determination to inflict as much damage, as much pain, upon his victim as humanly possible, up to and including the point of death. Which suggests, to me at any rate, that this was not a random killing, a case of someone, say, breaking into the studio and, for whatever reason, carrying out an otherwise random attack on Anthony Winter. I think the attack was purposeful. Almost certainly, therefore, predetermined. I think the victim was known to his attacker and most probably vice versa – there were no signs of forced entry, remember – and . . . Yes, Mark?'

Mark Foster flushed as all faces turned towards him.

'I was just wondering, ma'am, not to disagree with what you've just said, of course, about it being personal and all, but . . .'

'Come on, lad. Out with it.'

'I mean, what if it was someone who gained access by some means or other, someone who didn't necessarily know Winter but attacked him for some reason – robbery, say – and then just got carried away, once the attack had started.'

'You're right, Mark, thank you. The scenario you suggest is equally possible. Perhaps not quite as equally possible as the one I put forward, but one we should certainly do well to bear in mind.'

Laughter. Faces looking towards Foster once more, the young officer blushing furiously yet again.

'By the way,' Hadley said, 'that woman Winter had a relationship with – sculptor, was it? Adriana something – have you had any luck yet tracking her down?'

'Not yet, ma'am. She lives in Cyprus at least half the year as far as I can tell. I've been trying to get an address, but no luck so far.'

'Keep on it.'

'Yes, ma'am.'

'All right,' Hadley said, looking from face to face, 'what else have we got?'

There was not a great deal more. Katherine Elder's prints were amongst those lifted from various surfaces in the studio, but that was only to have been expected. Some of the others had been identified, but by no means all. Katherine's partial prints were also found on the chain, but given the painting for which she'd been the model, this again was unsurprising.

Trace evidence – hair and fibres – was plentiful but inconclusive. Stains from the covers and mattress of the day bed were still being checked for semen and vaginal secretions. Data recovery from Winter's various devices had uncovered a strong interest – not surprisingly, Hadley thought, given the nature of some of his paintings – in various S&M sites, along with a smattering of more straightforward porn. Gambling, too: online poker, a particular favourite. His call history was currently being re-examined, the unit seeking whatever links and connections they could find. Despite the part-time assistance of two other officers, Howard Dean was still working his way through hours of CCTV footage.

Together with Chris Phillips, Hadley went over the findings of the investigation so far, outlining possible further lines of inquiry; she was due to report to Detective Chief Superintendent McKeon on the hour.

27

Despite the various assurances Hadley had felt able to make, McKeon was not a happy man. But then, as she told herself, the DCS was rarely, if ever, a happy man. Possibly at home with his wife and four rumoured children, comfortably ensconced in a detached house in Totteridge on the northern edge of London, with views out towards the M25 and the steadily disappearing Green Belt, he was, indeed, happy. Content, at least. Hadley had met his wife once, a semi-formal occasion she'd been assured she should attend if she were serious about any further promotion. Mary McKeon had proved to be, against all of Hadley's meaner assumptions, a friendly dimple-cheeked woman from a farming community in County Antrim, her accent, by the third or fourth glass of wine, leaving no doubt as to her antecedents. Hadley had liked her a great deal.

She was back in her office, halfway through the mozzarella, avocado and tomato ciabatta Chris had brought her back from the Wine Cellar, when Howard Dean knocked on her door.

'Okay, Howie,' she said, 'I hope you're not looking like the cat that's got the cream for no good reason?'

'No, boss. I don't think so. We haven't got through all the CCTV stuff yet, not by a long chalk. But there is this.'

She set her sandwich aside, opened her computer and slotted the USB stick Dean offered her into place, then clicked on the appropriate file. Looked closely once, twice, once again for good luck.

'I think,' she said, 'I think you might just be right.'

Howard Dean's grin resembled that of the Cheshire Cat.

'Alice,' Hadley called from the door, 'Katherine Elder, we need to talk to her again. If she's not at home, find out where she is. There are some more questions she needs to answer. And this time here at the station. Take Howie with you.'

'Riding shotgun, boss?'

Hadley smiled. 'It is Dalston, after all.'

Katherine was not answering her mobile phone. The landline number rang and rang. When the two officers called round at the flat, Stelina had only just arrived home. At first she claimed to have no idea where Katherine might be, nor when she might return. It took all of Alice's quiet persuasion to gain her cooperation. 'You could try London Fields maybe. Or Gillett Square. She sometimes goes there.'

Stelina watched from the balcony as the two detectives got back into their car, uncertain if she'd done the right thing. Katherine had been fragile enough lately, drawing further and further back into herself and spending more and more time alone. And drinking: after what had happened before that was not a good sign, a safe thing for her to be doing. It might not take too much to push her back to the edge.

Stelina stepped back inside, uncertain what, if anything, she might do to help.

They found Katherine sitting alone in Gillett Square, cross-legged on the ground, head down, jacket collar pulled close. Nearby, a group of rowdy teenagers were pushing and shoving one another, swearing loudly and drawing the ire of a smaller and quieter group of older black men who were gathered round two of their number, engaged in what was obviously a nail-biting game of chess.

'Hello, Katherine,' Alice said. 'Remember me?'

Katherine blinked up into the light. The storm that had threatened earlier in the day had cleared, leaving a patchwork of blue-and-grey sky and a chilly wind that danced the various bits of paper and food wrapping around the surface of the square.

'Alice. Alice Atkins. And this is my colleague, Detective Constable Dean.'

'Hi, Katherine,' Dean said with a hopeful smile.

Katherine didn't respond. A boy, no older than eleven or twelve, crossed the square at speed on the rear wheel of his bike alone, hauling the front wheel high by the handlebars.

Alice squatted low, one hand to the ground. 'You remember, Katherine, we said we might want to talk to you some more? Well, that's what we'd like to do, only this time down at the station.'

Katherine blinked again, as if trying to bring Alice into focus. 'Station?'

'Police station.'

'Shacklewell Lane?'

'No, Kentish Town, where we're based. You don't have to worry, we'll drive you there and back.'

'I don't know.'

'Come on, Katherine. It's just a few more questions. The sooner we get started, the sooner it's over.'

'I don't know,' she said again, angling her face away to avoid looking at Alice, looking at either of them, staring at the ground instead.

'The thing is,' Dean said, 'I'm afraid, when it comes down to it, you don't really have a whole lot of choice.'

She looked at him then. 'What d'you mean?'

'He means,' Alice said, 'if you don't agree to come voluntarily, we'll have no alternative other than to place you under arrest.'

It was quiet in the interview room, just the faint electronic hum of the recording devices, audio and visual; fainter and yet persistent, the slow build-up of traffic along Kentish Town Road. At one end of the table a screen linked to Alice Atkins' laptop.

For the tape, Alice identified herself and Detective Chief Inspector Alex Hadley by name and rank and gave the precise time and date.

'You're not under arrest, Katherine,' Hadley said, 'but you are being interviewed under caution. You do not have to say anything. But it may harm your defence if you do not mention when questioned something which you later rely on in court. Anything you do say may be given in evidence.'

Katherine looked blank, frightened. Tugged at the ends of her hair.

'As I say, you're not under arrest and you're free to leave at any time. And if you wish to obtain legal advice, you're free to do so. All right, Katherine? If you don't know the name of a solicitor, we can arrange one for you.'

Nothing. Katherine bit down into her bottom lip and looked away.

'Katherine, you do understand?'

'Yes.'

'And do you want a solicitor present?'

'No.' Almost too quiet to hear.

'I'm sorry?'

'No.'

'Very well.'

Hadley eased back a little, glanced down at the papers in front of her. 'When we spoke before, you said that the last time you saw Anthony Winter was on the Monday before he died.'

'Yes. Yes, that's right.'

'When you went to the studio to see the paintings for which you'd posed.'

'Yes.'

'And you didn't see him after that?'

'No. That's what I said.'

'You're sure?'

'Yes, of course I'm sure. Why wouldn't I be?'

Hadley shifted sideways so that she was facing the screen. 'I'd like you to take a look at this piece of video taken from a CCTV camera on Highgate Road. You'll see there along the bottom the date and the time: twenty-three thirty-five on Saturday the eighth.'

The apprehension showed clearly in Katherine's eyes.

'Take your time,' Hadley said, 'and tell me what you see.'

Katherine looked at the image, looked away, looked again. 'I don't know, it's too dark to see anything clearly at all.'

'Look again. Look carefully.'

Alice played the same sequence again.

'It's just someone walking. Some woman walking, I don't know.'

'Someone walking along Highgate Road?'

'That's what you said.'

'Close to the path leading down to Anthony Winter's studio?'

Katherine breathed out deeply. 'It could be, I suppose. How can you tell?'

Alice clicked on a second image.

'How about this?' Hadley said.'That's the same person we just saw on Highgate Road, a little over a minute later. Only now – you can just see the flats on the left – they're walking towards the studio. The same clothes, the same walk. It's the same person, you agree?'

'Yes. Maybe. I don't know.'

'Look again.'

Katherine stared again at the picture and saw a woman walking towards the camera, head down, deep shadows to one side.

'It's still not clear. The face, you can't see the face.'

'Then that isn't you?'

'What?'

'That isn't you?'

'What are you talking about?' Voice louder now, the edge of panic, alarmed. 'Me? How could it be me?'

'Look at the build, Katherine, the shape, the way she's walking. Slim, tall, athletic even. The colour of her hair. And the clothes, look at what she's wearing.'

'What about it?'

'A leather jacket, isn't it?'

'It could be. I don't know.'

'A leather jacket and jeans.'

'So? So what?'

'Just like the jacket you're wearing now.'

Katherine reared back in her seat. 'That's . . . that's ridiculous. It doesn't mean anything. There's hundreds of jackets like this. Thousands.'

'Nevertheless, Katherine, I put it to you, that image shows you approaching Anthony Winter's studio at eleven thirty-seven and a few seconds on Saturday the eighth of April, the night he was killed.'

'No, no! No, it's not!' Katherine clawed at her face, drawing blood. A scratch below the left eye, skin caught on a jagged nail. 'No, it's not, it's not me and I want to go. You said I could go, right? Whenever I wanted to, I could go.'

She was on her feet, hands outstretched, fingers spread as if to ward them off, though neither of the officers had moved.

'I want to go, now. Now. Home.'

'Of course.' Hadley pushed back her chair. 'That's your right. Alice will drive you.'

'No. No. I can get home on my own.'

'Are you sure?' Alice asked. 'It's no trouble.'

Katherine nodded, edged towards the door.

'At least let me find a plaster for that cut on your face.'

'What cut?' Reaching up, Katherine wiped blood across her cheek. 'It's nothing. It doesn't matter.'

'How about those other cuts?' Hadley asked.

'Which . . .'

'The ones on your wrists.'

Instinctively, Katherine drew her arms back against her chest. 'That's nothing.'

'Nothing?'

'Nothing to do with you.'

'Nothing to do with Anthony Winter?'

'No!' Leaning across the table, Katherine screamed the word in Hadley's face.

'This interview,' Hadley said calmly, 'terminated at sixteen-nineteen – nineteen minutes past four.'

28

Vicki was midway through a storming version of 'Tain't Nobody's Business' when Elder felt the phone in his pocket begin to vibrate. Outside it was drizzling rain and he sheltered under the archway above the pub entrance while he took the call. Katherine's voice was faltering, weak, broken by small choking sobs.

'All right,' Elder said. 'Just tell me, where are you now?'

'At home.'

'At the flat?'

'Yes.'

'And is there anyone there with you?'

'Chrissy. And Stelina.'

'And all of this happened when?'

'This afternoon. Late this afternoon.'

He fought back the urge to ask why on earth she hadn't called him before.

'Listen, sweetheart, try not to worry. Get some rest. Sleep if you can. I'll be there first thing tomorrow. And don't worry, okay? Try not to, at least.'

'All right. If you're sure.'

'Of course. Of course I am. And just let me have a quick word with Stelina, okay? I'll see you first thing and we'll get all this sorted.'

After a few confused moments, Stelina came on the line. Elder asked her to make sure any pills, ibuprofen, paracetamol, anything stronger, were shut away where his daughter couldn't get at them. Any alcohol. Anything sharp. Keep watch, you and Chrissy between you, it's important.

Stelina assured him she would. They both would. Abike, too.

Elder broke the connection. For a moment he thought about going back inside to explain to Vicki, then thought better of it; he'd phone her later. Right now he needed to make sure he was in time for the overnight train.

Once he was on his way, he called Joanne and alerted her to what had happened. He didn't think it was anything too serious, but he thought she should know all the same. It sounded to him like a fishing expedition on the part of the police and not a whole lot more. Anything more serious and Katherine would have been charged and placed under arrest. From what she had said it seemed as though they were trying to make connections, hoping things would fall into place. He would go in to the police station tomorrow, speak to whoever was in charge and sort things out. Let her know how he got on, good news or bad. If there was anything she could do. And he'd be sure to give her love to Katherine, of course.

He closed his eyes.

Slept fitfully.

At Paddington, he paid to take a shower, bought a bacon

sandwich and coffee from one of the few places he could find open, then took the Tube to Highbury and Islington via Oxford Circus and from there the overground to Dalston Junction.

When Stelina let him in it was still not yet properly light.

Katherine was sleeping with one finger in the corner of her mouth, her other hand clutching at her hair. Careful not to wake her, he lowered himself to the floor beside the bed and sat there listening to the faint sounds of her breathing and watching the quick, occasional tremor of her eyelids as she slept.

Hadley realised she'd read the document on the screen three times without ever fully taking it in, her mind, part of it at least, elsewhere. Had that been a genuine row she'd had with Rachel that morning or simply more bickering? All over an invitation to supper with friends – actually more friends of Rachel's; they were always, almost always, more friends of Rachel's – that she hadn't felt able to commit to.

'It's three weeks away, for God's sake, Rach, how d'you expect me to know for certain?'

'I'd just like to be able to say we'll be there, that's all.'

'Well, do. Say that. Tell them yes, we'll come. I just can't promise, that's all.'

'Can you ever?'

'Now what's that supposed to mean?'

'Oh, never mind.'

'Look, if it's that important, you go. Go on your own.'

'All right then, I will.'

'Tell them I'm sorry, but I just happen to have this job that doesn't allow me to commit myself so far in advance.'

'Three weeks?'

'Yes, three fucking weeks.'

Bickering? Or something more basic? More serious?

The phone went and she picked it up. The officer at the front desk. 'Someone to see you, ma'am. Elder. Frank Elder. He's pretty insistent.'

'Send him up.'

Take it easy, Elder had told himself. Stay calm. Nothing to be gained from losing your temper, storming in there like a bull in the proverbial china shop. Last thing you want to do, get off on the wrong foot, put this officer's back up even further.

The moment he entered Hadley's office all the clichés fell away, unnoticed.

'Mr Elder . . .'

He glared at her, ignoring the proferred hand.

'You're in charge? In charge of this investigation? The murder of Anthony Winter?'

'I am.'

'In connection with which you had my daughter in here yesterday, being questioned under caution?'

'Yes.'

'Then what the fuck did you think you were doing?'

Hadley caught her breath, held his look, walked around him and pushed the office door closed, went back behind her desk.

'Mr Elder, please take a seat.'

'I'll stand.'

'As you wish.'

'You interviewed my daughter without a solicitor being present?'

'She was offered legal representation and declined.'

'And without the presence of an appropriate adult?'

'There was no need . . .'

'What?'

'In my assessment there was no need.'

'Bollocks!'

'Your daughter is how old?'

'Twenty-three.'

'Exactly. No longer a juvenile.'

'That's not the only reason . . . Here, look. Look it up on your fucking computer. Guidance for Appropriate Adults under the Police and Criminal Evidence Act, Codes of Practices, 1984.'

'I'm fully aware . . .'

'Really?'

'Fully aware of the stated reasons for having an appropriate adult present and after taking those into consideration, made my decision accordingly.'

'Mentally disordered or otherwise mentally vulnerable, isn't that what it says?'

'Yes.'

'And you didn't think that applied?'

'No. Clearly not. Or I wouldn't have made the determination I did.'

Elder shook his head in disbelief. 'Do you know anything about Katherine at all?'

'A little.'

'You'd spoken to her before? Before yesterday?'

'Once. Informally. An informal interview.'

'And what opinion did you come to? About her state of mind?'

'I thought she was nervous, perhaps a little more than usual, but in similar situations, as you might know yourself, that can often be the case.'

'Nervous, that was all?'

'Lacking in confidence, perhaps. But still able to express herself clearly.'

'And not mentally vulnerable?'

'No.'

'Did you happen to notice her wrists? I imagine there are still scars.'

'Yes, I did.'

'And what did you think?'

'I thought it was possible evidence of self-harm.'

'But not a sign of mental vulnerability?'

For a moment Hadley closed her eyes.

'I'm sorry . . .'

'Sorry!'

'On consideration, I should have given what I saw greater significance. But if I or my officers have been in any way responsible for causing your daughter undue distress I apolo-gise and I assure you . . . No, let me finish . . . I assure you everything was done to put her at ease. Everything. But, let me remind you, this is a murder inquiry.'

'In which she's a suspect?'

'Not currently, no.'

'Then you were interviewing her as what? A potential witness?'

Hadley shook her head. 'A person of interest.'

'How so?'

'You know I can't tell you that.'

'Does that mean you might have cause to interview her again?'

'It's possible.'

'In which case . . .'

'In which case, I shall do my best to ensure that an appro-priate adult is present to support, advise and assist her throughout the process and to ensure that her rights are respected.'

'And if that person is myself?'

Hadley hesitated before giving her answer. 'I'm sure the

considerable experience I believe you have will enable you to assist her in the best ways possible.'

'Thank you.'

'Now, Mr Elder, as you'll understand, there are things I need to attend to. But please make sure we have your contact details so that we can get in touch with you as soon as possible should it become necessary.'

This time Elder agreed to shake her hand.

Elder rang the flat and Abike answered. Katherine was still sleeping. One or other of them could be there with her for most of the day. Just a little way along Kentish Town Road, he spotted a Turkish restaurant with what appeared to be an old shop sign preserved above. He was enjoying his lamb kebab with chilli sauce when his phone buzzed in his pocket. Joanne, he thought, ringing to find out how he'd got on, but although it was a Nottingham number it wasn't one he recognised.

'Frank Elder, this is Colin, Colin Sherbourne. Notts CID. I don't know if you remember me. Your daughter's abduction. I was just a DC.'

'Yes. Yes, at least I think I do.'

Tall, almost gangly. Thin-faced. A moustache.

'I've been trying to get hold of you all morning. Maureen, Maureen Prior, you'll remember her, she suggested trying the cop shop in Penzance. I spoke to someone called Cordon. He gave me your number.'

'What was it you wanted?'

'Adam Keach.'

'What about him?'

'He was being transferred from Wakefield down to Lincoln and there was an accident. Pile-up on the A1 just short of Retford. He's escaped. He's on the loose.'

3

29

The central police station had moved across town and was now at the head of Maid Marian Way, close by the Playhouse and the cathedral. Colin Sherbourne was gangly no longer, the rest of his body thickened out to match the length of his limbs; moustache still in place, but neater, carefully trimmed. Three-piece off-the-peg suit, pale blue shirt, dark tie. Handshake firm when he met Elder at the lift.

'Frank, long time.'

Elder nodded.

'Could've wished for better circumstances.'

Elder followed Sherbourne into his office, everything neat and stowed away, the faint smell of aftershave, a clear view out through the window onto Derby Road.

'So,' Elder said, 'what the fuck happened?'

Sherbourne sat, waited for Elder to do the same. 'Keach was being transferred from Wakefield over to Lincoln. Coming off the A1 on to the A57 this Ford Mondeo comes straight at them, the van they're transporting him in. Wrong side of the road, must've been doing sixty, seventy miles an hour, out of control. Driver does his best to swerve out of the way, only succeeds in getting hit broadside on. Impact sends the van over on to its side, Mondeo goes through a virtual somersault, spins across the road and ends up upside down like a bloody turtle.'

Elder could do little but shake his head.

'Driver of the Mondeo went through the windscreen – was he wearing a seat belt? Was he fuck! – pronounced dead at the scene. His passenger's in Queen's Meds with more cuts, lacerations and broken bones than you'd care to count. Driver of the van got away with severe bruising, as much from the airbag as anything, cuts to both face and hands. Other prison officer, the one inside with Keach, handcuffed to him, struck his head on the side of the van when it turned, lost consciousness. In Queen's himself, concussion.'

'And Keach?'

'Injuries, no way of knowing. What we do know, before anyone else arrived at the scene he was able to use the keys attached to the officer's belt, unlock the cuffs and do the proverbial runner.'

Elder pictured it for a moment, heard the scrape of metal on metal, the sound of breaking glass.

'Sounds like a right fucking shambles,' he said. 'Starting with whatever box-ticker decided Keach was fit to be transferred from a category A prison to catogory B . . .'

'Been a good boy, hadn't he? Played the game. Said he was sorry, truly contrite. Said his prayers.'

'And why just one escort? I thought two was standard.'

'Two if you include the driver.'

'Jesus!'

'Staff shortage, most likely. Either that or Keach was no longer considered highly dangerous, one officer'd do.'

Elder shook his head. 'Whoever made that decision, let's hope it doesn't come back to haunt them.'

'Amen to that.' Sherbourne glanced at his watch. 'Briefing in ten minutes, why don't you sit in?'

The incident room was crowded. Twenty-plus officers, some in uniform, some not. The blown-up photograph of Keach on the board took Elder by surprise. When he'd last seen him he'd been early thirties, lean-faced, wild-haired, staring eyes; just shy of forty he was fleshier, thick-lipped, all the intensity gone from the eyes. Elder wondered what it would take to bring it back.

Sherbourne stepped front and centre, pointed to the photo.

'Adam Keach, seven years into a life sentence with a tariff of thirty years. Absconded around eleven-thirty this morning when the prison van in which he was being transported from HMP Wakefield to Lincoln was involved in a serious accident and is currently on the run. First indications suggest the accident was no more than that, rather than being orchestrated to facilitate Keach's escape, but obviously that needs to be checked. Car involved in the incident, a Ford Mondeo, stolen in Gainsborough earlier that morning. Couple of scrotes joy-riding, out of their heads on smack most likely, but we'll see. Kenny, that's your bailiwick. Don't let me down.'

A bearded officer off to one side of the room raised a hand in acknowledgement.

'Unfortunately,' Sherbourne continued, 'the helicopter had been called to an incident in the south of the county in which firearms were involved, so there was some delay in getting it to where the accident had taken place. By which time Keach had gone to ground. The area around is largely rural, open fields, a scattering of buildings, farms and the like, though south of the A57 it's Clumber Park and south of that you're into Sherwood Forest.'

'Holed up in't Major Oak, likely,' some wit suggested.

Sherbourne ignored him.

'The nearest village is Ranby, north off the A1. Nearest services some little way north of there at Blyth. My best guess, he'll lay low, hope to wait till dark. What he's going to be looking for, transport, a change of clothes. But for now the chopper's still up, there's patrols on the roads. Catch him before nightfall and we can have him snug inside Lincoln with his mug of hot chocolate before the cock crows. After that, it's the long haul.'

The buzz of conversation in the room rose and fell and Sherbourne's voice rose above it.

'Right, I want a check on all known associates, family, you know the drill. Parents still living fairly locally as far as we know, Kirkby-in-Ashfield. Need to be seen. Jason, down to you. Then there are two brothers, Mark and Dean . . .'

He broke off as one of the officers raised her hand.

'Yes, Simone?'

'Mark, he's known to us, boss. A little form, nothing spectacular, petty thieving and the like. Last known address here in the city, St Ann's.'

'Good. Good work. Pay him a visit, you and Billy. And the rest of you, let's knock on some doors, make some calls. But before you do, wait up, someone I want to introduce you to.'

Elder stepped away from the wall.

'Frank Elder was a DI here on the Notts force quite a few years back. Any of you long enough in the tooth might remember. It was Frank who was largely responsible for putting Keach behind bars. Recently he's been working with the Devon and Cornwall Major Incident Team and in the current situation, I intend to lean on him as much as possible.'

Hands were raised in greeting, sounds of approval.

'Frank, anything you want to say at this point?'

'Thanks, Colin. Just two things, I think. The first is this. When Keach carried out his crimes he was doing so, in part at least, to impress a man named Alan McKeirnan, currently serving a life sentence for the murder of Lucy Padmore in 1989. McKeirnan had an acolyte called Shane Donald who was released on licence some little time back and did have connections with the Nottinghamshire area. It's possible Keach might have known Donald in prison. That might be worth checking.'

He paused, took a breath.

'The other thing is this. Colin chose, for my sake I think, not to mention it, but the girl, the young woman Keach abducted and sexually abused was my daughter, Katherine. So I have the strongest possible motivation for seeing him back in custody as soon as possible – and before he can hurt or harm anyone else. Thank you.'

Elder stepped back, Sherbourne shook his hand, and the team set to work.

30

Katherine rolled over and stretched: arms, torso, legs, toes. Remembered mornings when she would be out of bed at or before first light, splash water on her face, pull on her running clothes, her shoes, and out. A few stretches and then a steady jog, building as she went and hitting a steady pace before picking up speed into a final sprint. Then more exercises, warming down, using weights, and into the shower. Feeling exhausted, refreshed: ready for the day.

Three evenings a week at the track, being put through her paces by the coach; Sunday mornings unless there was a race in prospect. Nervous always as it came closer, the adrenalin starting to kick in. Glancing round the changing room, weighing up the opposition. Girls she'd seen before, seen before and beaten; others from out of the county, tall, sleek and self-assured. All the time the coach's words bubbling under: keep calm, keep cool, keep your form.

Christ, she'd hated it sometimes. Nerves chewing at her gut as she got down into her starting position, spikes pushing back against the blocks. Head up. Head down. The gun. Sixty metres before she seemed to open her eyes, know what was happening, where she was. Runners on either side. Going past. Seventy-five, eighty. Fuck!

The coach with his arms around her shoulders. You did well, you did great. Can't beat everyone, can't expect to win every time. Knocked something off your PB, though, I bet. Second or two at least. His hand for a moment on her back, ruffling her hair. Don't worry, you're getting better all the time.

Another person: not her. A life she'd left behind.

'You used to be a runner, right?' Chrissy had said one day. 'Like what's-her-name? Dina something-or-other?'

Katherine shook her head. 'No, not me.'

Feet on the floor, she waited for her breathing to steady and made her way to the bathroom. Abike had left the radio playing, something classical, Radio 3. A note from Chrissy, lipsticked on to a napkin from Itsu: *Off to get my tits out again − back soon.*

Out of the shower, Katherine dressed and dried her hair. Put bread in the toaster, coffee in the pot. Chrissy's coffee but with any luck she wouldn't notice. Warm enough, maybe, to sit out on the balcony. Someone down there in a parked car, radio turned up loud, the bass echoing upwards. The yapping of a small dog. Police sirens fading into the distance. A plane overhead. Balancing coffee and toast on a couple of upturned flower pots, she unlocked her phone, checked for messages, swiped right for *Top Stories* in the news.

Suspected terrorist attack in Amsterdam.

Hot, twenty, and the world's youngest billionaire.

Escaped rapist and murderer on the run.

Katherine doubled forward as if she'd been punched in the stomach. Dropped her phone and covered her face with her hands. After several moments, she arched slowly back and sucked in air.

Retrieved the phone.

Adam Keach, sentenced to life imprisonment for the murder of sixteen-year-old Emma Harrison and the rape of . . .

Katherine stood up abruptly, stumbled, tried to right herself and stumbled again, losing her balance and falling towards the balcony edge. Pitching forward, she grabbed hold of the rail.

'What d'you think you're doing?' Chrissy called through the open balcony door. ''Cause if you're thinking of jumping it's a long way before you hit the ground.'

Chrissy held her while she cried. Listened as Katherine told her of her ordeal, words spilling from her mouth like stones. The imprisonment, the pain. Waking from some impossible nightmare to the sound of her father's voice – Katherine. Kate, it's me. Then another voice, laughing, cruel. Beautiful, isn't she? At least she was. After that she could recall nothing: nothing until she was in the ambulance, woozy from gas and air, clinging to her father's hand. Alive when she feared she would be dead.

Katherine's phone rang where she had left it, out on the balcony, and Chrissy picked it up.

'Kate,' she said, going back into the bedroom, 'it's your dad.'

Katherine shook her head.

'She's just lying down now,' Chrissy said. 'Why doesn't she call you back in a little while?'

'I was wondering if she'd heard . . .' Elder began.

'About the guy escaping? Yes, she's heard.'

'And she's okay?'

'She will be.'

Chrissy broke the connection and crossed into the kitchen, filled the kettle at the tap. She was still trying to process what Katherine had told her. Wondering how you ever got over something like that happening to you. Realising you never did.

31

The house where Joanne was living was high on the northern edge of the Park, a semi-private estate near the city centre, architect-designed in concrete and glass. From the upper level there were views clear across the Trent Valley to Belvoir Castle and the Leicestershire hills.

She had moved in with Martyn Miles when their affair was at its height, Elder having retreated, tail between his legs, to Cornwall, and then, when the heat had gone out of the relationship and Miles had moved on to pastures new, he'd left Joanne the use of the house, rent free, for as long as she wished. For which kindness, Elder hated him all the more.

He had booked into the Premier Inn and phoned Joanne from his room, explaining why he was there. She'd already heard of the escape on the news. Come round about six, she'd said, six-thirty. I should be home by then.

She greeted him at the door. The hallway deep, faced with pale wood, sunken spotlights pale overhead. 'Frank, come on in. Hang up your coat. I was just getting myself a drink.'

She stood at the centre of the double-height living room, wine glass in hand. Tall, one of the first things he'd noticed about her, tall and slim. Katherine's inheritance. A dinner dance it had been, one of those vaguely formal charity affairs, his commanding officer wielding a three-line whip; Joanne had been there with someone else, arm candy for a local bigwig, a dress that seemed to be painted on and heels that made her taller still. He couldn't believe she'd give him a second look. But she did.

'Time for a little fresh air,' she'd said, taking his arm.

Even then she'd had to make the first move. Smoky brightness in her eyes, taste of cherries on her tongue. 'Wine, Frank?' she said now. 'There's red if you'd prefer.'

'Later, maybe.'

'As you wish.'

There were new paintings on the walls, abstracts of a kind, yellows and greens. Blurry and vague.

Joanne set aside her glass to light a cigarette. 'There isn't any news?'

Elder shook his head. 'Of Keach? Not so far. A couple of sightings, but nothing definite. Nothing that's checked out.'

'You think he'll be found?'

'Sooner or later, yes.'

'And that's why you're here? To help with the search?'

He shrugged. 'Not a great deal I can do. Man in charge, Sherbourne, seems to have it all pretty much in hand.'

'And it was what? Just through some accident that he escaped? That's what it said.'

'Seems that way, yes.'

They sat at either end of a low settee, facing out towards a window that ran practically the whole width of the room; silvered lanterns on the stone patio outside, the garden beyond.

'So,' Elder said, 'you're living here all on your own?'

'Usually. Not always.'

'And now?'

A slow shake of the head. No make-up, no matter how expertly applied, could conceal the darkness hollowed beneath her eyes.

'Kate knows?' she asked. 'About Keach?'

'Yes. I spoke to one of her flatmates earlier. She's taken it pretty badly. You can imagine. Coming on top of everything else. Couldn't be at a worse time.'

'But she's not in any kind of danger?'

'From Keach? No, I don't think so. I don't see how. What he'll be doing, concentrating on keeping out of sight, making sure he doesn't get caught.'

Joanne drained her glass, got to her feet. 'Sure you won't join me?'

'Okay, then. Maybe just one.'

She came back with a bottle of Côtes-du-Rhône and an empty glass. Lit another cigarette.

'I told you they had Kate in for questioning,' Elder said. 'About Winter's murder.'

'I still don't really understand what for.'

'Nothing much, as far as I could tell. Clutching at straws.'

'They don't have a . . . what do you call it? That television programme . . . a prime suspect?'

'If they do, they're keeping it to themselves. But I told them, if they want to question Kate again I want to be there.'

'Can you do that? Insist, I mean?'

'Her state of mind, yes. Now especially.'

'Poor girl.' Joanne lowered her head. 'It's the last thing she needs. Now especially. Just when she seems to be getting over what happened. Injuring herself the way she did.'

Elder went to the window. The garden was slowly fading into shadow, lights coming on at windows circling down the hill: other people's lives. How many families did he know who were truly happy and for how long? How many children? What was it the poet had said? They fuck you up, your mum and dad.

He turned back into the room. 'That business with Winter. Kate getting involved with him the way she did. Did you know about that? When it was happening, I mean?'

'Not really, no. Not at first, anyway.'

'Then you did know something?'

'I knew they were in some kind of relationship, yes.'

'And you didn't say anything?'

'Say anything, what d'you mean? She's not a child, Frank. She's twenty-three, almost twenty-four.'

'And he was what? Fifty-something? Jesus! That's almost as old as me.'

'Yes, Frank. Exactly.'

'Exactly? What's that supposed to mean?'

'It means you don't have to be a psychiatrist to see that's part of the problem, right there.'

Elder laughed, bitter and loud, a bark. 'All of a sudden you're Sigmund bloody Freud?'

'It's not funny, Frank.'

'I know it's not funny. Fucking ridiculous, that's what it is.'

'Not so ridiculous, either.'

'You're not serious?'

'Think about it, Frank . . . How old was she when you disappeared?'

'I didn't disappear.'

'As good as.'

'There wasn't a lot of point in my sticking around here, you'd made that plain enough.'

'You could have stayed for her.'

'What? And slept downstairs on the sofa while lover boy was shtupping you upstairs in our bed?'

'If you'd really wanted to, if you'd thought it was important enough, you could have found a way. Instead of which, what? You go slinking off to bloody Cornwall feeling sorry for yourself. Licking your so-called wounds.'

'You didn't leave me a lot of choice.'

'That's bollocks, Frank, and you know it. You'd been looking for a reason to get away ever since we got here. The minute we arrived.'

'The place, maybe. But not away from you. Not away from Kate.'

'Well, weren't you lucky? I gave you the perfect excuse.'

'Fuck this!' Elder said and hurled his glass to the floor. 'Fuck this and fuck you!'

He grabbed his coat and strode away, slammed the door behind him. When he looked back up at the house from the street he could see her outline, silhouetted against the picture window. The next time he looked she was no longer there.

As he turned left on to Castle Boulevard, the phone buzzed in his pocket.

'One confirmed sighting,' Sherbourne said, 'Blyth services late this afternoon. Threatened some young bloke in the Gents with a knife . . .'

'A knife? Where did he get . . . ?'

'Like I say, threatened him with a knife. Forced him to go to the ATM and take out a couple of hundred quid. Made off with his credit card and pin number and the keys to his car. Honda Civic, metallic blue. Alert's gone out, registration, full description. Likely find it dumped, swapped for something else.'

'You don't know which direction he went off in?'

'What I've told you aside, we know fuck all. But I'll keep in touch.'

'Okay, Colin. Thanks.'

Elder hunched his shoulders and, hands in pockets, headed back to his hotel. He'd phone Katherine from his room, hope that she was up to talking.

32

Elder had slept badly: the same obscene, obdurate dreams. He'd spoken to Katherine last thing and done his best to reassure her that, though he understood her being upset, disturbed, she had nothing to worry about where Keach was concerned; he was the subject of a full-scale manhunt and would soon be back in captivity where he belonged.

The truth, he knew after attending that morning's briefing, was a little different.

There had been several other reported sightings – Sheffield, Doncaster, Leeds – one malicious, two well-meaning, all false. The young man, a trainee supermarket manager, whose car and credit card Keach had stolen at Blyth services, had recouped some of his losses by selling his story – *Terror at Knifepoint* – to the *Sun*. The card itself had been used twice more before the account had been closed.

The surviving passenger from the Ford Mondeo that had caused the accident had turned out to be a seventeen-year-old apprentice welder with an appetite for LSD and cans of

Special Brew. The driver had been his cousin. Neither of them had as much as heard of Adam Keach; there was no connection. Accidental meant accidental. One of the prison officers involved had been patched up and released home, the other was still in hospital awaiting the results of an MRI.

When, on Monday morning, two uniformed officers and a detective called at the small terraced house in Kirkby where Keach's parents lived, the father refused to open the door and would only answer questions through the letter box. Upstairs and down, curtains were pulled tightly across.

'No, he's not here. Not been here and not likely to be neither. Not stupid, is he? Knows this is one of the first places you'd look.'

'I'd like to believe you,' the detective said, 'but we're going to have to check for ourselves just the same.'

From somewhere inside, they could hear the yapping of a small dog.

Only when they threatened to take the door off its hinges was it reluctantly opened. Keach's father, close on seventy, seemed to be shrinking early into the shell of his own body, white-haired and bent at the waist, with trembling hands. Old before his time. His wife sat in a wheelchair behind him, head to one side. The interior smelt of stale cigarette smoke, damp clothes and slow decay. There were neat piles of dog faeces, hard and round like rabbit droppings, on the kitchen floor and here and there on the stairs.

When the animal, a brown-and-white terrier with yellow teeth, jumped up at the detective, he batted it away with back of his hand and then, with a well-placed kick, sent it whimpering into the corner.

Pigeons were roosting in the loft space above the head of the stairs.

Of Adam Keach there was no sign.

'If you do hear from him,' the detective said, handing Keach senior his card, 'you'd do well to get in touch.'

The old man didn't wait till the detective was out of sight before tearing the card into pieces with his shaking fingers and letting them fall to the floor.

Adam Keach's brother, Mark, lived with his wife and family in a terraced house in St Ann's, close to Victoria Park. One of their sons had left home some few years back and now lived across the city between Radford and Hyson Green with a young family of his own. The other son, Lee, still lived at home. Their daughter, Sophie, had been born with learning difficulties and lived nearby in supervised accommodation.

Now in his early forties, the longest Mark had held a steady job was the two years he had spent behind the counter at a newsagent's in the city centre; that aside, he had drawn benefit when he could and taken on whatever casual work, most often cash in hand, came his way. Petty theiving when still in his twenties had first brought him to the notice of the police and when, later, some mates from the pub had roped him into joining them in a spate of house burglaries in Mapperley Park, he'd got caught literally holding the ladder. For this he'd served six months of a twelve-month sentence and, when released, done a further six months' community service.

His wife, Amy, who worked five days a week at Argos and had done for the past fifteen years, told him if he was caught as much as taking the tram without a ticket, she'd have his things out on the street by suppertime and the locks changed.

He didn't doubt she meant it.

When DS Simone Clarke and DC Billy Lavery called at the house that morning, it was Amy who answered the door. Her day off.

She was short, stocky, round face, mousy hair, wearing a sweatshirt and trackie bottoms.

'Thought you lot'd be here crack o' dawn wavin' bloody guns an' that. How you do it these days, i'n' it?'

'Been watching too much telly,' Billy Lavery said.

'Fuck off.'

'Look round first, like?'

'Wipe your feet and mind your manners, then. But he's never here, you know that, don't you? Likes of what he did, them poor girls, not give him house room for a minute.'

'How about your husband?' Simone Clarke asked. 'He feel the same?'

'He feels whatever way I fuckin' tell him and don't you doubt it.'

Simone didn't doubt it for a moment.

Amy Keach stood back and nodded them in. Lee was seated at the kitchen table with a mug of tea.

'Not set eyes on your uncle lately?' Billy Lavery said.

'Which one?'

'You tell me.'

'Me Uncle Dean, saw him Sat'day afore last. Skyped us from Australia, didn't he? Brisbane somewhere. Mind you, picture were terrible. Breaking up all bloody time. Bufferin'. Broadband round here, bloody bollocks.'

'How about Uncle Adam?'

'He'll not come round here.' Said with a vigorous shake of the head.

'How come? Him and your dad, they not that close?'

'Never mind me dad. Me mum'd set about him wi' a pan or two. Part his hair for him proper, no mistake.'

Simone had left them to it, started up the stairs. Halfway she hesitated, hearing a noise, a movement in one of the upstairs rooms, but it was only a cat, a large tabby, big eyes, tail bushed out, looking at her disdainfully before darting past.

The rooms were empty and the beds were made. Air freshener in the bathroom, the toilet.

'You keep it nice,' Simone said.

'And if I thought you were patronising me . . .'

'I'm not. Just with men around it's not always easy. My feller stays over more than a night or two and it's bedlam.'

Amy winked. 'Dare say he's got his compensations.'

Simone grinned back. 'Mark not around?'

'Working. Pal of his, got this white van. Man and van, you know. Removals, the like. No job too small. Brendan, that's his name. Time to time, Mark lends him a hand. Makes me laugh, though, Brendan, white-van man. Black as the ace of spades. Make you look like one of them lattes, no offence intended.'

'None taken. You've no idea when he might be back, I suppose?'

'Hour or so, maybe. Difficult to say.'

'Nor where they're working?'

'Wollaton way I think I heard him say. But, look, phone him, why don't you? On his mobile.'

Simone put the number into her phone.

She spoke to him when they were outside, gave the address to Lavery. 'You go see him, why don't you? I'll get back to the station. Anything doesn't sound right, you can invite him in. Call for backup if need be.'

'Why don't you come with me?'

Simone lowered her voice. 'This Brendan, if he's who I think he is, I went out with him once. A few times, actually. Might be a little awkward.'

'That's always supposing he remembers who you are,' Lavery said and laughed.

Simone feinted to hit him below the belt and when he flinched, clipped him round the side of the head instead, not hard but hard enough.

'Less cheek from you, mister. Unless you want me to pull rank on you.'

'Pull what?'

'Rank.'

'I thought . . .'

'Wollaton. Now. Go.'

'Yes, Sarge.'

'And take that smirk off your face.'

'Yes, Sarge.'

For the life of her she couldn't remember much about Brendan aside from his name and the way the bedside light had shone off his skin.

They were carrying boxes, box after box of books out to the van; a professor of history at the university retiring to a cottage on the Dorset coast and resigning his life's work into storage. Just a few first editions travelling with him, not history, but his other passion, the golden age of detective fiction. Margery Allingham. Michael Innes. Freeman Wills Crofts.

Billy Lavery took Mark Keach aside.

Asked the same few questions again and again.

'How many more times have I got to tell you,' Keach told him. 'I've not clapped eyes on Adam since I visited him in Gartree when he was on remand. Now is it okay if I get on with the job?'

Lavery arrived back just as a report was coming in that Shane Donald had been tracked down to a house in Worksop, the north of the county. Close both to where the accident had occured allowing Adam Keach to escape, and to the last location he'd been definitely seen.

33

'How far off's Letchworth Garden City?' Hadley asked that
morning, pulling on her coat, ready to leave.

Rachel glanced up from where she sat reading the paper.
'Forty, fifty years.'

Alice drove.

After threatening the usual rain, the sky lightened the closer
they came. Their route took them off the A1 and past the
Spirella Building, a former state-of-the-art corset factory,
recently restored to its former glory. Friends of Rachel's had
chosen to celebrate their tenth anniversary there, taking
advantage of the ballroom's sprung maple floor to demonstrate
their best Fred-and-Ginger.

They parked and walked past a row of neat Arts and Crafts
cottages with generous, well-tended front gardens.

'It wouldn't be so bad, living out here,' Alice remarked.

'You could be dead for six months before you noticed you'd
stopped breathing.'

'You might think differently, ma'am,' Alice said, 'if you were living in a flat share behind Finsbury Park bus station.'

'Cheeky.'

Alice blushed.

There were roses, literally, around the door of number 17.

Hadley pressed the bell. Knocked. Pressed again.

After several minutes the door was opened by a woman in her late forties wearing a purple tunic over black leggings, a dark headband holding back a spring of reddish hair. A streak of vermilion on her right cheek.

'Susannah Fielding?'

'Guilty.'

The officers showed their identification. 'I'm Detective Chief Inspector Alex Hadley and this is Detective Constable Alice Atkins.'

Susannah Fielding smiled. 'The distaff side of the force, is it? Sensitivity a speciality.'

'Alice here tackles like a front-row forward and swears like a drunken soldier.'

Alice blushed again.

'You'd better come in. And please accept my apologies for keeping you waiting. When I'm working at the back of the house I don't always hear the bell.'

They followed her along a short corridor, one side of the wall busy with small framed paintings, into a compact kitchen-diner and from there into the rear garden.

'I thought we could sit out here. It's just about warm enough, I think. If you take a pew I'll hustle up some tea. Unless you'd prefer coffee, that is?'

They sat on wrought-iron chairs in a kind of arbour midway down the garden. At the far end the doors were open to the double-width shed that served as a studio.

'There are muffins as well,' Susannah said, reappearing

with a laden tray. 'Apple and pecan. Fresh this morning. When the work's not going well I run off to the kitchen and bake by way of compensation. It's a wonder I'm not twice the size I am.'

'What are you working on?' Alice asked.

'Oh, another still life, I'm afraid. Fruit in a bowl, flowers in a nice vase. Same old, same old. I don't know why I bother. Except there's always the thought that next time you're going to really nail it, the perfect painting. But that's not what you're here for, confessions of a moderately successful artist.' She smiled encouragingly. 'You don't have to be polite any longer.'

A blackbird landed softly on a patch of open ground between two shrubs and began to peck hopefully at the soil.

'You've had a visit from the family liaison officer,' Hadley said.

'Yes, indeed. All very sympathetic. If, perhaps, a little distant. Good at explaining the nuts and bolts, whys and wherefores.' She cut a muffin neatly in half. 'I presume there's still no way the body can be released?'

'I'm afraid not. Not at the moment.'

Susannah bit into the muffin, nodded approvingly. 'It's one of those curiosities of life – your former husband, whom you've barely spoken to, never mind seen, in almost twenty years, dies and you're expected to make the arrangements for his funeral.'

'I'm not really sure how these things work,' Hadley said. 'But if you really objected . . .'

'No, no.' Susannah waved a hand in the air. 'It's fine. Or it will be, I'm sure. There are the children to consider – I say children, but you know what I mean – they kept in touch with Anthony to a degree, Melissa when she was younger especially. And I dare say it's what they'd expect. A family funeral.'

'Melissa, she's what? Twenty-two? Twenty-three?'

'Twenty-three. Matthew's two years older.'

'And they're . . .'

'Melissa's taking a break from university. She started a bit late; couldn't, you know, make up her mind. Thought she fancied art school and by the end of her foundation year found out she hated it. Too much like following in the family footsteps, I suppose, too many expectations. She tried English after that, North Wales, Aberystwyth – that didn't work out either.' She smiled. 'Too many long books, too much reading. I'm not sure what she expected. *Wuthering Heights* on Twitter, possibly. Thomas Hardy on Snapchat. Anyway, now she's at Leicester studying history. Or she would be. If, as I say, she weren't taking a sabbatical.'

'And so, what, she's living at home?'

'Some of the time, yes. She's still got her room, a student house up in Leicester. And a room here, of course. Flits between the two, sort of. Starts her course again properly in September. Or she should do.'

'And Matthew?'

'Contrary to all my wishes, he's in the military – Twenty-six Regiment Royal Artillery.' Another smile, self-deprecating, crossed Susannah's face. 'So much for never letting him play with guns when he was growing up. Now he's a lieutenant in charge of a fire-support team in Afghanistan. What do they call them? The punch behind the iron fist?'

'He's there now?'

Susannah nodded. 'Kandahar. Part of the International Security Assistance Force. Though I don't know for how long.'

'You'll be pleased to have him come home,' Alice said.

The smile this time was wistful. 'Only to have him posted somewhere else. But still' – she sat up straighter, hands together – 'life is what it is, you play the cards you're dealt. And if you'll just excuse me for a moment, I'll get some more hot water for the pot.'

Hadley ran a finger slowly down her cheek to mime tears and Alice nodded.

The female blackbird had been joined by her partner; the scent of flowers was faint in the air. Somewhere in the middle distance a lawnmower started up, stopped, started again. How many young men had been killed with knives in London the previous week, Hadley asked herself? Six? Seven? Enfield, Bromley, Peckham, Brent Cross, Battersea, Bow. How many killed in Kandahar? Maybe living somewhere like this really was little more than an illusion, she thought, life as some Quaker idealist had seen it at the turn of the previous century. Though there were probably food banks here as well. Weren't there everywhere nowadays? Knives, too.

Susannah came back out, red-eyed, carrying a kettle. 'Who's for more tea?'

Hadley held her cup towards the pot, said no to another muffin, asked if, to Susannah's knowledge, Anthony Winter had left a will.

'I'm afraid I've no idea. I haven't heard from his solicitor or anything. But if there is a will, there's no way in which I'd be any kind of beneficiary. The children, possibly, but not me.' She shook her head, resettled in her chair. 'I remember a conversation we had, Anthony and myself, around the time of the divorce. I wouldn't give you, he said, the shit from the sole of my shoe.'

'Nice,' Alice said quietly.

Susannah shrugged. 'Alliterative, at least.'

'His estate,' Hadley said, 'won't be inconsiderable, I suppose. Once the sale of recent work's been taken into account.'

'I do have a few of Anthony's paintings,' Susannah said. 'Early, of course. Before all that latent nastiness had squirmed its way on to canvas. Third-rate pornography, if you ask me. But then who am I? A woman artist painting flowers, what do I know? Just a lady fucking painter!'

More tears. She brought her cup down hard on the saucer, splintering it across. 'I'm sorry, I . . .'

'It's fine,' Hadley said. 'It's okay.'

'No, it's not fine. It's not fucking fine. It's . . .' With a sweep of her arm she sent cup and shattered saucer catapulting across the garden.

Alice arched back out of the way; Hadley was swiftly to her feet. Susannah pushed herself up from the table; stood for several moments, head down, breathing uneasily. 'Life,' she said. 'It's so . . . so fucking unfair.'

'Do you want to go back inside?' Hadley asked solicitously.

'No, no. It's okay. I'm better off out here.' She leaned for a few moments longer against the back of her chair, then sat back down. 'You know, I never used to swear. Oh, sometimes under my breath if a brushstroke went wrong, but otherwise . . . it betrays an insufficient vocabulary, I used to say. But then when Matthew came back on leave – well, I'd heard all the words before, but not necessarily in that order. Even Melissa, since she went to university. F this and F that, the new universal qualifier. It used to be in the papers in asterisks, but now it's spelt out in full. The C word as well.'

She fished a tissue from the sleeve of her tunic, dabbed her eyes and blew her nose. 'You've just heard me swear more in a few minutes than I have in the last six months. But then I suppose you're used to it.'

'We hear the odd word,' Hadley said with a smile. 'Now and again.'

Susannah smiled back.

'You said you'd barely spoken to your ex-husband in twenty years. That would be since the divorce proceedings?'

'Yes.'

'And the occasion on which he made the remark about the sole of his shoe?'

186

'That was the same. July the twenty-sixth, nineteen ninety-seven. Not a date I'm likely to forget.'

'Melissa would have been what? Three?'

'Three and a half, yes. Matthew was just five.'

'It must have affected them badly.'

'Matthew more, possibly. At the time, anyway. He was old enough to know what was going on. Not all the whys and wherefores, but yes, he understood and he was angry. Really angry.'

'At what was happening? The situation?'

'At me. It was all my fault, that's what he thought. What his father had told him.'

'And Melissa?'

'She was too young to really know what was happening. Except that her daddy was going away.'

'And she blamed you for that as well?'

'No, not really. At least, I don't think so. I mean, she may have done later, but then, no, it was Anthony. Anthony she had it in for. From her point of view, why wouldn't she? One minute he was there and the next he was gone. Walked out on her for reasons she didn't understand.'

'But later,' Alice said, 'when she was older . . . ?'

Susannah sighed. 'We come to terms, don't we? On the surface, anyway. It's what we do.'

'And Melissa managed to do that? Come to terms?'

'For a while, yes.' She turned her head away as if something down the garden had caught her attention.

Hadley waited. 'You wouldn't have any idea, would you, who might have wanted Anthony dead?'

'Apart from me, you mean?' Susannah said and laughed. 'But, no. No, I'm afraid I don't. Aside, that is, from probably half the people he ever met.'

*

187

Hadley paused alongside one of the paintings as they were leaving. A portrait, head and shoulders, of a girl of perhaps thirteen or fourteen, soft features, dark shoulder-length hair.

'Is that Melissa?'

'Yes,' Susannah said. 'Shortly after her fourteenth birthday. I had to practically bribe her to sit for it. Six months of riding lessons it cost me.'

'It's lovely.'

'Thank you.'

'She's lovely.'

'She doesn't think so. I wish she did.'

At the door, Hadley offered her hand. 'Thanks for your time.'

'Thank you. Thank you for coming all this way. Whatever I might feel about Anthony, whoever did this, I hope you find them.'

'We will.'

As they reached the gate, Hadley glanced back and saw a movement, faint and quick, at one of the upstairs windows. A hand, pulling the curtain closed.

They were almost at the car when her mobile rang. Chris Phillips eager to update her with developments. Data recovery had unearthed something juicy hidden away on Winter's computer.

'Okay, Chris. We'll be there in an hour, hour and a half tops. Keep a lid on it meanwhile.'

'Boss.'

Hadley closed her phone, snapped open the car door. 'Right, Alice. Time to leave Munchkinland behind.'

34

The house was close to the railway station, a stunted two-storey towards the terrace end and, by the look of it, sorely in need of repair. Sacking had been draped carelessly across one of the downstairs windows, a blanket across the other; save for an accumulation of dirt and dust the upstairs windows were bare. Rubbish overflowed from two plastic bins by the door. A small, square yard at the rear, empty aside from a broken bicycle, led out into a narrow ginnel running off in either direction. Local police from the Potter Street station had confirmed Shane Donald to be in residence.

Two uniformed officers, one armed with a cyclindrical battering ram, waited either side of the front door; two more in the alley behind. Colin Sherbourne had phoned Elder before he and the other detectives had set out from Nottingham, asking him if, given his history with Donald, he wanted to join them.

They waited now for Sherbourne to give the word.

Three . . . two . . . one . . . A single blow with the metal ram and the door was breached, officers quickly into the house with cries of 'Police!' Jason Lake and Kenny Cresswell were in fast and up the stairs, shouting at the tops of their voices, loving every second. After all those hours behind desks, staring at computer screens, this was it, the real thing, the real McCoy. Billy Lavery and Simone Clarke were busy checking the downstairs rooms, Colin Sherbourne hanging back, Elder by his side.

The door to the back bedroom was closed and Cresswell kicked it open, finding Shane Donald stranded between the unkempt bed and the window. The room smelt of cannabis and unwashed sheets.

Donald edged closer to the window and, craning his neck to look down through the tarnished glass, saw a pair of beefy officers smiling back up at him, waving a two-fingered greeting.

'Don't bother, Shane,' Jason Lake said. 'Not without a parachute.'

'Go fuck yourself!'

'All in good time. Right now, why don't you be a sensible bloke and get some clothes on. Catch your death like that.'

Donald was naked save for a pair of yellowing Y-fronts, a few wispy hairs sprouting here and there from his concave chest, ribs fast up against sallow skin. His right eye beginning to twitch.

'I've not done nothing. Not one fucking thing.'

'No one's saying you have,' Kenny Cresswell said.

'Then what the flyin' fuck's all this about? You got no fuckin' right.'

'Few questions we want to ask, that's all, Shane. Friendly chat.'

'What about?'

'Old friend of yours.'

'Who's that then?'

'Adam. Adam Keach.'

'No fuckin' friend of mine.'

Colin Sherbourne appeared in the doorway. 'Place is clear. Let's get him out of here and stop wasting time.'

'You heard what the man said, Shane. Clothes on sharpish. The local nick awaits.'

'And you're gonna stand there, I s'posc, watching me get dressed.'

'My treat.'

Sherbourne and Elder were waiting on the pavement when they came out of the house.

'You!' Donald exclaimed, seeing Elder, recognising him straight off. 'What the fuck you doin' here?'

'Nice to see you again, Shane,' Elder said. 'It's been a while.'

Donald hawked up phlegm and, from less than an arm's length away, spat it into Elder's face.

Sherbourne elected to have Jason Lake do the interview with him, Elder and the senior officer from the local station watching on screen in an adjacent room, listening to the audio.

'Adam Keach, no friend of yours, that's what you said?'

''S'right.'

'You know him, though? Know who he is?'

'Maybe.'

'Shane . . .'

'All right, then, yes. I know who he is, what he done. Read the papers, don't I? Watch the news.'

'Of course. But not just that.'

'How d'you mean?'

'I mean you know him, know him personally.'

'Who says?'

'Met him. Spent time with him.'

'Bollocks, I did!'

'You didn't meet him, talk to him? Not what we've heard.'

'Heard? Who the fuck from? You're makin' this fuckin' up.'

'It would have been a while back, maybe it slipped your mind.'

'Never slipped my fuckin' mind . . .'

'Gartree, that's where it would have been. You were serving time. Robbery, I think. Assault with intent to cause bodily harm. You remember, don't you? HMP Gartree?'

'I was there, yes, but . . .'

'Keach would have been there on remand. While back now, like I say, maybe that's why you're having trouble remembering?'

Come on, Elder said to himself, impatient, watching. Just admit you know him. Why deny it? Unless, of course, you've got something to hide?

'Maybe, yeah,' Donald said, not looking at either of the officers directly. 'Yeah. I remember now.'

'You and Keach, you found things to talk about, I dare say. Things in common.'

Donald didn't answer.

'People, too. Alan McKeirnan, for instance.'

Donald's right eye jumped.

'Bit of a mentor, wouldn't you say, Shane? McKeirnan? Taught you every nasty little thing you know.'

Donald fidgeted in his seat. 'What happened, what he did . . . that was him, not me . . . that girl . . . I never . . . the jury, the jury agreed.'

Like Premiership referees, Elder thought, juries can get conned, judges show the wrong card.

'Have you been in touch with him lately, Shane? McKeirnan?'

'No. No fuckin' way.'

'You're sure of that?'

' 'Course I'm fuckin' sure.'

'And Adam?'

'What?'

'Adam Keach?'

'What about him?'

'You've been in touch with him.'

'Who says?'

'Wakefield. In touch with him there.'

Donald swallowed, glanced up at the camera, then away.

'We can check, you know. Mobile phones, texts, messages slipped under the door.'

'Okay, once maybe. Once or twice. Long time back now. And it was him got in touch with me.'

'Friends, though. Still pals. Friends making plans?'

'What?' That eye again. 'What plans?'

'What you were going to do when he got out. Things you could do together.'

Donald was shaking his head, vigorously, from side to side. You've got something there, Elder thought, watching. Touched a nerve.

'Exciting, was it?' Sherbourne said. 'Gave you a hard-on? Thinking about it. What you were going to get up to, the pair of you. Together. Like old times.'

'No, no!' Donald reared back, rocking the chair on to its hind legs. Jason Lake half out of his seat, ready to intervene. 'Why are you saying that? That's not right.'

'Just trying to get the picture. The full picture.'

'Picture? What you on about? There is no fuckin' picture.'

'You and Adam.'

Donald lowered his head.

Almost imperceptibly, Sherbourne eased forward. Let the moment settle. 'Where are you going to meet him?'

'What?'

'He must've been in touch. Since he went free.'

'No. No, he's not.'

'Come on, Shane. Why not do yourself a favour? Help us and we can help you. Keep you out of it. No blame attached.'

For several moments, Donald looked confused, rubbing his hands together, then pressing them hard against the table edge.

'You've been out of prison a good while now, Shane. Kept out of trouble. Admirable, that. Something to feel proud of. You don't want to take a wrong step now. Put all that good work into jeopardy. Risk going back inside.'

'No.'

'Sorry?'

'No. No, I don't.'

'Tell us where he is, then, Shane.'

'I don't know, do I?'

'Where you're going to meet.'

'We're not. I've not heard from him, have I? I keep telling you. Okay? No matter how many times you ask, I can't say no different. I don't know where he is and I don't fuckin' care.'

His eye had stopped twitching, his hands were still. Watching, Elder knew the moment had passed. They'd had him, almost had him, and then lost him. It happened. Involuntarily, he brought his hand to his face to wipe away the spittle that earlier had run down his cheek.

35

Elder had first set eyes on Shane Donald in an amusement park in Skegness, Donald apprenticing himself to a man named Alan McKeirnan who was working as a mechanic with a travelling fair; apprenticing himself, it turned out, in more ways than one. Not so many weeks before, the fair having pitched up in Mablethorpe, the pair of them had taken a girl named Lucy Padmore, just sixteen, to the caravan where they were staying: quiet, secluded, just inland from the coast. Kept her there against her will for five days before burying her body in the dunes.

After Skegness, it was Rotherham, McKeirnan working in a garage on the Rawmarsh Road; living with Donald in a single basement room in the centre of the town. Earlier suspicion had turned into solid evidence. They kept the house under sur-veillance, hoping to take McKeirnan when he left for work, leaving Donald on his own. Less fuss, less confusion. It was Elder who followed Donald to the corner shop, out to get that day's supply of milk, of cigarettes; a newspaper with the head-line, *Schoolgirl's Killers Still on the Loose*.

Shane Donald had still been a few weeks shy of seventeen.

Maybe the judge had taken the account of his life up to that point into consideration: a miserable, broken childhood; a hapless lad led astray. Mercy, if that's what it was, shown in the length of the sentence, the brunt of the blame falling on McKeirnan.

Released into the care of the probation service, Donald had got into trouble again almost immediately; gone on the run with a girl named Angel Ryan, who had eventually given him up to the police, afraid for her own life, afraid for Donald's if he remained at liberty.

Since then Elder had not set eyes on him until earlier that day.

If Keach were to contact him – a big if – he had no idea how Donald might respond. Besides which there was nothing to suggest that Keach was still in the vicinity. Sightings continued to come in, if sparingly, and all some distance away. Doncaster was the closest – a second time this, and being checked – then Manchester, down by the Albert Dock in Liverpool, a shopping centre in Burnley.

Elder had gone for a quick pint with a few of Sherbourne's team – Billy Lavery, Simone Clarke, Jason Lake – and ended up staying for two. Fending off invitations to join them for a curry, he'd found his way to an Italian place in the Lace Market and taken a table in the far corner, away from the windows and grateful for his own company.

He had spoken to Katherine earlier that evening: 'Dad, I'm okay. I'm fine.' Her voice shrill, nervous, words tripping over each other, giving the lie. Elder had done his best to reassure her, while not wanting her to do anything that might be construed as careless, put herself at risk. But at risk from what? There was no suggestion that Keach was anything less than a hundred and fifty, two hundred miles away.

He was on his way back to the hotel when his mobile rang.

'Tried calling you earlier,' Alex Hadley said. 'Couldn't get through.'

'What can I do for you?'

'Your daughter. Some new evidence has emerged. It looks as if we're going to have to speak to her again.' She paused a moment, waiting for this to sink in. 'After what you said the other day, I thought you'd like to be present.'

'When's this happening?'

'Tomorrow morning. Around eleven.'

'Holmes Road?'

'Yes.'

'I'll be there.'

The temperature in Nottingham dropped that night by at least five degrees and come morning there was a cold wind out of the east. The walk from the hotel to the station took Elder past two shopping centres, one of which seemed to be partly closed, and the boarded-up branches of two well-known department stores. He counted five men and one woman sleeping rough, three *Big Issue* sellers, one busker playing a penny whistle, two out-and-out beggars. At the railway station he bought a coffee and a paper, went down on to the platform and boarded the waiting train.

He'd left a message for Colin Sherbourne, explaining where he was going, asking him to keep in touch; failed to speak to Katherine directly and texted her instead. The news in the paper seemed mostly to be about Europe, Syria, the shenanigans of pop stars he'd never heard of, actors in television series he'd never see. Down near the foot of page 7 there was a single paragraph: *Escaped murderer continuing to evade arrest.* Followed by the briefest summary of Adam Keach's crimes. Of the investigation into Anthony Winter's murder there was nothing. No news was no news.

The train pulled into St Pancras five minutes ahead of schedule. Armed police were patrolling the concourse, either side of the Eurostar terminal, the security level still high after recent terrorist attacks in Paris and Marseilles, a couple of isolated incidents in the centre of London.

On his way down to the Underground he heard people speaking in French and Spanish, Urdu and Italian, Polish and Russian. The two young women sitting opposite him in the carriage wore skinny jeans, bright lipstick and black headscarves tightly covering their hair. At Euston a man got in wearing a kilt, rucksack on his back. At Camden, a nun. The only one showing the slightest sign of surprise at all this was Elder himself. He'd been down in Cornwall too long.

Katherine was waiting by the coffee barrow near the station entrance, take-out cup in her hands. She was wearing black trousers, a denim jacket over a black jumper, dirty white trainers on her feet. Her hair hung shapelessly around her face; her skin was pale, accentuating the darkness round her eyes. Elder wondered how many nights she'd gone without sleep.

She held the cup aside, allowing her father to give her a quick hug and a kiss on the cheek.

'You're early,' she said, stepping back.

'Just a few minutes.'

'You want a coffee or anything?'

'No, I'm fine.'

'I can finish this on the way if you like.'

'It's okay.' Elder looked at his watch. 'We've time.'

'D'you want to sit a minute, then?'

There were several seats, wooden with metal frames, most of them occupied. Drinkers, smokers, down-and-outs. The pair closest to the flower stall were free. Traffic moved slowly past, buses heading for North Finchley or Liverpool Street, Victoria or Parliament Hill Fields.

'Have you any idea what this is about?' Elder asked.

Katherine shook her head. 'Just more questions, that's all they said.'

A man with several days' growth of beard and rheumy eyes stumbled towards them, holding out a hand. Katherine looked away. Elder gave him a hard stare and the man backed away, shaking his head.

'Maybe we should go,' Elder said.

'Yes,' said Katherine, 'maybe we should.'

36

The officer at reception was expecting them. Alex Hadley met them on the landing, shook Elder's hand, enquired about his journey without really listening to the response. A certain amount of deference due but no more.

As they were approaching the interview room, Hadley held back. 'You might find some of this hard going.'

Elder nodded, stone-faced. 'We'll see.'

The room itself was airless, anonymous, little different from the many he had been in before. The other side of the table now, he waited for Katherine to be seated then pulled his chair in alongside her, the two police officers opposite. After they had all identified themselves, Katherine was, again, cautioned. Told, again, she could leave at any time.

'I'd just like you to remind us, Katherine,' Hadley began, 'about your relationship with Anthony Winter.'

'What d'you mean?'

'The nature of that relationship, how would you describe it?'

'I worked for him.'

'As a model?'

'Yes.'

'A life model?'

'Yes.'

'And besides that?'

Katherine blinked, glanced at Elder, reached a hand up to her hair.

'When we spoke before,' Hadley said, 'you suggested your relationship with Winter was also personal.'

A moment before answering. 'Yes.'

'Could you amplify that a little?'

Katherine pulled at a strand of hair. 'We were friends.'

'Friends?'

'Yes.'

'Close friends?'

'Yes.'

'And this friendship, this close friendship, would you say it was physical?'

Another glance towards her father. 'Yes, I suppose so.'

'You suppose . . . ?'

'Yes. Yes, then. Yes.'

'You were lovers?'

'Yes.'

'Up until the time of Winter's unfortunate death?'

'No.'

'No?'

'It finished before that.'

'How long before?'

Katherine shifted sideways on her seat, shifted back. 'A month. Six weeks. I'm not sure.'

Hadley let that slide. 'And who ended the relationship, you or him? Or did it just come to a natural end?'

A breath, long and uneven. 'Anthony did.'

'Did he give a reason?'

'No, not really.'

'He must have said something.'

Katherine looked at her father.

Elder leaned forward. 'Is there really something to be gained from this line of questioning?'

'Yes, I think so. If you'll bear with me a little longer.'

With a brief nod of the head, Elder leaned back.

Hadley refocused on Katherine, waiting.

'He said . . . he said there was nothing more we could do for each other. It was . . . it was time to move on.'

'And you were upset by that?'

Katherine nodded.

'Katherine?'

'Yes. Yes, of course I was.'

'So upset that you cut your wrists?'

Katherine flinched. Elder rose partway from his chair. 'I don't see that has any relevance. Not to your investigation.'

Hadley held his gaze. 'I'm trying to establish the strength of the relationship that existed between Anthony Winter and your daughter, in order to explain any later behaviour.'

'What later behaviour?'

'We'll come to that in due course.'

'Katherine,' Alice Atkins said, speaking for the first time. 'Would you like anything? Some water, maybe?'

Katherine shook her head.

'You're sure?'

'Yes.'

'And you're okay to carry on?'

'Yes.'

Hadley cleared her throat, glanced in Elder's direction before speaking. 'Would it be correct, Katherine, to say that your physical relationship with Anthony Winter was characterised by the giving and receiving of pain?'

Katherine screwed up her eyes, clenched her hands into tight little fists.

Elder began to protest but swallowed his words.

'Katherine?' Hadley said quietly.

'No,' the answer quieter still, eyes still closed. 'No, that's not right. I don't know why you're saying that.'

Hadley's face opened into a faint smile. There, then gone. 'Did you know that Winter was in the habit of filming the various sexual activities that took place both in his flat in Chalk Farm and in his studio?'

'No.' Eyes open wide, voice loud. 'No, he couldn't have.'

'I'm afraid he did.'

'He couldn't have. I'd have known.'

'There were hidden cameras in both locations. We found the results, some of them, on one of his computers. Others stored on a hard drive.'

'But not me. Not with me. He wouldn't have done that.' She turned towards her father, alarmed.

Elder's skin had gone cold. He smiled back at Katherine as reassuringly as he could; rested a hand for a moment on her arm.

Alice Atkins raised the lid of the laptop and, after a glance towards her boss, switched it on.

Katherine glanced helplessly back at her father, head shaking from side to side. 'No, you can't. Please, please. Don't. Not in front of . . .'

As the first image appeared on the screen, she jammed her open hand into her mouth and bit down hard.

Elder slammed his fist on the table.

Alice pressed a key and the image disappeared.

Katherine was rocking backwards and forwards, tears

running down her face and on to her neck, blood speckled across her mouth and cheek, divots of blood on the fleshy part of her hand between finger and thumb.

'We'll take a break,' Hadley said, 'and get that seen to. Continue later.'

'What the holy fuck d'you think you're doing?'

Elder had demanded to speak to Hadley alone and, reluctantly, she had agreed. They were standing in the car park at the rear of the station, Hadley, who never smoked, not since she was in her teens, with a cigarette she'd begged from Chris Phillips.

She drew the smoke down into her lungs and slowly exhaled. 'Pursuing a line of inquiry.'

'Treating my daughter as if she were a suspect. A hostile witness at best.'

'Just trying to get at the truth.'

'The truth is, Katherine had nothing to do with Winter's death and you know that.'

'Do I?'

'You really think she could have been in any way responsible?'

'I think there are questions about her involvement that remain unanswered.'

'Christ!' Elder swung his head away, looked up at the sky.

'What?'

'You ever listen to what you're saying? You sound like some bloody automaton.'

'It's about maintaining a level of detachment. Not getting emotionally involved. I thought you'd have known.'

'Yes? Well, you've got that off to a fucking T and no mistake.'

'I'll take that as a compliment, even though that's not how

it was intended. And I do realise how difficult it must be for you to do the same. These circumstances especially.' Another pull at the cigarette. 'If you'd like to arrange for someone else, someone less close, more detached, to take your place as an appropriate adult, then I'm sure it can be managed.'

Elder shook his head.

'You're sure?'

'Sure.'

'There may be other things which come up that you're going to find difficult to hear.'

Elder looked at her before speaking. 'You can push so far and no further. Anything more aggressive and I'm going to suggest in the strongest possible terms she takes the option to leave.'

'You really think that would be good advice?'

'If you don't like it, charge her.'

'You think I won't?'

'I think if you were going to, you'd have done so already. I think you're still trying to force the pieces together and finding they just don't fit.'

Hadley took a last drag on her cigarette. 'Time we were getting back inside.'

Katherine's face was unnaturally pale; her hand bandaged and resting in her lap.

'Katherine,' Hadley said, 'are you feeling okay to continue?'

'Yes.'

Elder nodded agreement. He'd done his best to suggest to Katherine she should make what she justifiably could out of the injury to her hand and put off the remainder of the interview until later, possibly the following day, but she had wanted to get it over.

'And I must remind you,' Hadley said, 'that you are still under caution.'

'I know.'

'Good. Well, then I'd like to ask you about the last time you say you saw Anthony Winter – which would be the Monday, I think you said? The Monday before the exhibition . . .'

'Yes.'

'The Monday before he died.'

Katherine made no reply.

'You went to the studio at his invitation to see the paintings for which you'd earlier been posing?'

'That's right.'

'And while you were there, did anything else happen? Looking at the paintings aside.'

'I'm sorry, I don't know what you mean.'

'Did anything happen between the two of you, yourself and Anthony Winter?'

'We . . .' Pulling at her hair, avoiding her father's eye. 'We made love.'

'You had sex?'

'Yes.'

'You had sex on the day bed in the studio?'

'Yes.'

'And on the floor.'

'I don't know. I don't remember.'

'You don't remember?'

'No.'

'Perhaps you can remember what else took place? When you were both making love on the floor?'

'No!'

'Not something involving the chain?'

'What?'

'The chain, Katherine. The same chain as in the painting. You don't remember Winter taking hold of it and fastening it across your body?'

Katherine let out an anguished cry.

Elder was on his feet. 'All right, this is going to stop, right now. I assume you know this as it's all there on tape, along with the time and the date. So asking my daughter those details can only be for the purpose of breaking her down even further in the hope that she'll admit to something she didn't do.'

'Or it could be,' Hadley said, 'in order to establish, once and for all, how it came about that, in addition to her prints, there are multiple traces of your daughter's DNA on the implement that was used to murder Anthony Winter.'

Elder slowly sat back down.

'Katherine,' Hadley said, calmer now, 'there's just one more thing. When you were here before we asked you to look at two sequences taken from CCTV cameras close to Winter's studio. Do you remember?'

'Yes, of course.'

Alice positioned the laptop so that both Katherine and Elder could see the screen.

'When you were shown these images before, you maintained that the person in them was not you, is that correct?'

'Yes.'

'You're sure about that? Positive? Having seen them again you don't want to change your mind?'

'No, it's not me, you can see. Dad, you can see, surely? And besides, it couldn't have been me because I was at home.'

'In Dalston?'

'Yes.'

'The flat in Dalston? The Wilton Estate?'

'Yes, where else?'

'The flat you share?'

'Yes, yes. You know all of this.'

'So there will be someone, one at least of your flatmates, who can vouch for you being there, at the flat, between the hours of, say, ten o'clock and twelve on the night in question?'

Katherine looked away, looked for a moment at her father, looked at the floor.

'Katherine?'

'No.'

'So none of your flatmates can vouch for you, is that what you're saying?'

'Yes.'

'Why is that?'

'Because they were out, out clubbing, and I . . . I stayed home.'

'Alone?'

'Yes, alone.'

'How come, when they were . . .'

'I had a headache, a stomach ache, I thought I was getting my period. I took some painkillers, made a hot-water bottle and went to bed.'

'And that's the exent of your alibi?'

Katherine hung her head.

'You've asked your questions,' Elder said, 'and you've had your answer. Either move on or we walk.'

'All right,' Hadley said, 'but first, Katherine, I'd like you to look carefully again at the screen and, in the light of some of the other things we've talked about, things you've admitted, tell me if perhaps you were mistaken and that is, in fact, you?'

'No. No, it's not. It's just not. Dad, it's not – you can see, can't you? You can see.'

Elder was looking carefully at the screen. The build, the shape, what little you could see of the length and colour of the hair, even the way she moved, it could just be Katherine. It just could.

'No,' he said. 'It's not you.'

37

It was five days since Adam Keach had escaped; five days during which he'd been unlawfully at large. Tina Morrison had
finished her shift at Greggs at around three that afternoon,
arms tired after hefting tray after tray of rebaked pasties from
the oven out onto the shop floor; her voice starting to croak
after dealing with a more or less steady stream of customers,
many of whom never seemed clear, even by the time they
reached the counter, what exactly they wanted. Was it two
yum-yums or was it four? The sausage roll, warm or not? That
bag of four jam doughnuts, how long had it been sitting there?
And what if they only wanted two?

She'd be glad to get home and put her feet up, have a bath,
relax, wash her hair. Sandra had said something about meeting
up later at the Black Boy, Tina wondering how much longer
they'd be allowed to call it that, getting so you could scarce
open your mouth these days without someone calling you rac-
ist or sexist or something else she didn't even understand.

She was just turning off Carolgate, crossing Town Hall Yard

into Exchange Street, when she saw him, this bloke, standing there, staring. Making no bones about it, either. No one she knew. Never seen him before, clapped eyes on him. She turned her head away, embarrassed, pretending to look into a shop window, and when she looked again he was gone.

Maybe she'd imagined it. He hadn't been looking at her at all.

A nice enough afternoon, bit of sun for a change, she thought she'd cut across King's Park on her way to Asda.

'Boss . . .' Thursday morning, Billy Lavery knocked on Colin Sherbourne's door and went in without waiting. 'Young woman gone missing, Retford. Not been seen since leaving work yesterday afternoon.'

Sherbourne looked up sharply, a pulse already beginning to tick. 'Any reason to think there's a connection?'

'Two blokes acting suspiciously earlier that day, car park on Churchgate, not so far from where the woman – Tina, Tina Morrison, that's her name – not far from where she was last seen.'

'Acting suspiciously, as in . . . ?'

'Traffic warden, off duty, saw them hanging round, looking in parked cars, reckoned they were out to nick something. Asked what they thought they were doing and got a thumping for his pains. Six hours in A & E. Local police took a description. One of them could be Keach. Nothing definite enough to be certain.'

'And the other? Two, you said.'

'Skinny, trackie bottoms, fairish hair . . .'

'Shane Donald, you're thinking?'

'Could be him. Could be half a hundred others.'

'All right, get yourself up there, talk to this warden, whatever, see if you can't get him to pin down those descriptions, one way or another. And stolen vehicles, that area, last twenty-four hours, we'll need that checked. Car park CCTV. Town centre. If it is them, Keach and Donald, and they've taken this young woman, Tina, you say, it's been — what? — the best part of fifteen, sixteen hours already.' He shook his head, images scuttling across his mind. 'Let's hope for her sake we're wrong.'

When Lavery spoke to him, the traffic warden was still more than a little shaken; strapping around three broken ribs, butterfly stitches to his cheek, plasters to one side of his head where the hair had been shaved away. Faced with photographs of Adam Keach, front and profile, he still wouldn't commit himself one hundred per cent, but when it came to Shane Donald he was more certain. Him, it's got to be. The little shit.

When officers from Worksop went to Donald's house, there was no sign.

'Saw him yes'day mornin',' one of his neighbours said. 'Over 't station. Round ten it'd be, little after. Waitin' for Lincoln train, looked like.'

The 10.15 departure, on its way from Sheffield to Lincoln; next stop Retford just ten minutes later, 10.25.

Early that afternoon, Marek Gomolka, a Polish painter and decorator, reported his van stolen from outside a house on Moorgate Park where he'd been working. Upstairs at the rear, most of the morning, it wasn't until he came down at around 12.30 he realised the van was missing.

It had been Tina Morrison's mother who'd contacted the police when she'd taken her daughter in a cup of tea just shy of 7.30 the following morning — Tina on a late and with the chance of a lie-in — and realised her bed hadn't been slept in. They'd had a row the previous day, the Wednesday, a lot of fuss and rattle about nothing, and Tina had gone off to work in a huff. When she hadn't come back home afterwards, her mother reckoned she'd gone straight round to her mate Sandra's, then from there off on a night out. Nothing unusual in that. She thought she'd heard her coming in later, close to midnight it would have been, but now she realised she must have been mistaken. Wind, most likely, rattling the bedroom window.

Sandra, when Billy Lavery spoke to her, swore blind she'd not set eyes on Tina since the weekend. Meant to be going out last night, but I never heard from her, did I? Texted her but never got an answer. Let her phone go out of charge, that's what I reckoned. Wouldn't be the first time. In the end I went down the Black Boy without her. Thought she might turn up later but she never did. You don't think anything's happened to her, do you? Owt bad?

CCTV from a petrol station on the Welham Road, east out of Retford, showed a white van with three people in the front, a female seated between two males, none of them, however much the image was adjusted, clearly identifiable. Unlike the van itself.

An alert went out to forces in the area – Bassetlaw, Lincoln and West Lindsey – and further afield.

'Could be anywhere by now,' Lavery said. 'Anywhere between here and the Scottish fucking border.'

Sherbourne didn't think so. If this was Keach, and he'd primed Donald to join him, groomed him as it were, he wouldn't be just driving blindly; he'd have a plan. Long time in prison, some of that in solitary, he'd have had time enough to let his imagination fester and blossom. Too much time.

He called Elder, who was still down in London as far as he knew, babysitting his daughter. Filled him in on developments.

'Lincolnshire,' Sherbourne said, 'isn't that where that girl's body was found?'

'Lucy Padmore? Yes, Mablethorpe.'

'And that was Donald, right? Donald and McKeirnan?'

'Yes.'

'You think Donald might have suggested going back there again?'

'He might. Though my guess, it's more likely to be Keach making the running, rather than Donald. Having said that, I'd not rule it out as a location. The east coast, somewhere.'

'Yorkshire, Whitby way, that was where your lass . . . ?'

'Yes,' Elder said abruptly, cutting him off.

Port Mulgrave, he was thinking. The road through Hinder-well from Runswick Bay. A ramshackle collection of huts at the foot of the cliff, close against the sea. Small stones spinning beneath his feet as he made his way down, racing against time.

'You'll keep me in the picture?' Elder said.

'You're staying down in London?'

'A day or two more maybe. I'm not too sure.'

'Okay. Let me know.' Sherbourne finished the call.

Later that day, the van was found abandoned on the Corringham Road Industrial Estate off the A631, east of Gainsborough. Until they got another sighting, they had no idea in which vehicle Keach, Donald and their captive were travelling.

38

A little after 4.30, Friday morning, and Hadley was suddenly wide awake. Two weeks, almost, since the discovery of Anthony Winter's body and how much closer were they to finding the identity of his killer?

Not wishing to wake Rachel, she turned carefully on to her side and slid out from the bed as quietly as she could. Slipping on her dressing gown, she went to the bathroom, careful to step over the floorboard that always squeaked, and from there on down to the kitchen.

First vestiges of light above the rooftops opposite.

Birdsong.

Foxes scavenging amongst the bins.

She could still see Elder's face when he'd been asked if that was his daughter about to enter Winter's studio on the night of the murder. A twitching of the face muscles, almost imperceptible. The slightest of hesitations before his denial.

That song, Hadley thought, the one from the movie where the woman's body's found in her flat in Wood Green. Or was it

Finsbury Park? Not so very far from where Alice lived now. Reggae, wasn't it? Lovers rock? Louisa Marks: 'Caught You in a Lie'.

Elder as uncertain as she was herself, the image obstinate, unfocused. But what did that prove? Other than the presence of doubt. It could be Katherine or it could be, she thought, one of the women it was becoming clear from Winter's phone records and computer data, he was prone, every once in a while, to pay for sex. Mark Foster, she knew, was working on it, doing his best to make connections between those websites Winter had accessed offering specialised services, photographs of known sex workers, and a jumble of mobile numbers that were largely untraceable.

A young sex worker with dark hair wearing a grey hoodie and jeans.

How difficult was that going to be?

Standing by the stove another song came to mind, older, one her mother used to sing when she was clattering pans in the kitchen. 'Needle in a Haystack'.

Just as the kettle was coming to the boil, she heard a footstep on the stair.

'Mint or jasmine?' Rachel asked.

'Fresh mint's all gone.'

'Jasmine, then. Enough for two?'

'Always.'

Rachel brushed the collar of Hadley's dressing gown aside and gently kissed her neck. Not once but twice.

'Careful. I've got boiling water here.'

Rachel laughed, nuzzled Hadley's neck a moment longer, then went over and sat at the kitchen table. 'I imagine this was more than just needing to pee? Up at this hour and not coming back to bed?'

Hadley grunted agreement.

'Bad dreams?'

'Not exactly.'

'Work, then?'

Hadley brought the mugs over to the table and sat down. 'It's this girl, young woman, Katherine . . .'

'The one Winter was knobbing.'

'Knobbing? Charming. Technical term, is it? Something you psychotherapists bandy about at conferences?'

Rachel shook her head, smiling. 'What's the problem?' she asked.

'It's Katherine. I just don't understand her.'

'Ah, well, understanding. That'd be more my province, I imagine. With you it's more a matter of guilty or not guilty.'

'That's bollocks, Rach, and you know it.'

'Okay, okay. But what is it you don't understand?'

'The sex thing, I suppose. That mainly.'

A fresh smile appeared on Rachel's face. 'Isn't it always?'

'I mean, he dumps her so abruptly, so devastatingly, she slashes her wrists, and not much more than a month or so later she's jumping into bed with him again.'

'Oh, come on, Alex. That's not so difficult to understand, surely?'

'Maybe, maybe not. But it's not just any old sex, is it?'

'Isn't it?'

'Handcuffs. Chains. All that S and M stuff. I'm sorry, I just don't get it.'

Rachel grinned. 'Nobody's perfect.'

Hadley punched the table with her fist. 'Don't. Don't do that.'

'What?'

'Make everything into a joke.'

'I know. I know. And I shouldn't trivialise, I'm sorry.'

Hadley rested her face for a long moment in her hands; sat up and sipped some tea. 'When she was sixteen, Katherine, she was abducted by a pair of brutal deviants. Tied up, tortured, raped. You can never get over something like that. Never. It's impossible.'

Rachel nodded agreement.

'And yet, not so many years later, she becomes involved with an older man who gets his kicks from tying her up, hand-cuffing her to the bed, inflicting God knows what punishment and pain. Can you understand that? Because I certainly can't.'

'Specifically, no. Not without knowing a great deal more, and certainly not without having talked to the woman myself. Anything else would just be generalisations and so not particu-larly useful.'

Hadley smiled. 'Believe me, anything at this stage would be useful.'

Rachel eased her chair away from the table. 'The best I can do, based on what you've told me, is make one or two observa tions. When these dreadful things happened to her, her sexual experience may not have been very great. It might not have been much more than the occasional fumble in the bus shelter. She could still have been a virgin, we don't know. But from what we do know, what you've told me, it might be reasonable to assume that what happened to her would have linked sex strongly in her mind with abuse and pain. With being made powerless, per-haps; held prisoner. It could even be that it's only through reliving some kind of rape fantasy that she can reach orgasm.'

Listening, Hadley was shaking her head slowly from side to side.

'Remember,' Rachel said, 'I don't know how far what I've said matches the truth, the truth of her situation. But, if you're looking for an explanation, well . . .' She smiled. 'What it doesn't do, of course, is do anything to help you with your other problem.'

'Which is?'

'Is she capable of murder?'

39

Tina Morrison was found, dazed and bleeding, but still alive, wandering dangerously along the hard shoulder of the M18 motorway south of Doncaster, just short of seven on Saturday morning. Paul Swindells, on his way to the IKEA distribution centre at Armthorpe, pulled his lorry over and climbed down from the cab, hazard lights flashing. Tina screamed when he approached her and struck out with flailing arms. When he tried to take hold of her to prevent her stumbling into the road she turned and tried to run but tripped and fell headlong. Picking her up, he carried her, still struggling, back to his vehicle, lifted her up into the front seat as carefully as he could, and called emergency services.

Two hours later, Simone Clarke was sitting outside one of the cubicles in the A & E department of Doncaster Royal Infirmary, waiting to speak to her. Tina's mum had been allowed in earlier, but asked to leave when she had threatened to become hysterical. Now she sat a short way along the crowded corridor, biting her fingernails and murmuring small, silent prayers.

Police patrols had been stepped up in the area in which Tina had been discovered: Warning Tongue Lane and the Yorkshire Wildlife Park to the east; the A6182, White Rose Way, to the west; Potteric Carr Nature Reserve to the north. After a report of two men behaving in a belligerant manner late the previous day, staff and volunteers from the visitor centre at the nature reserve were questioned, but it turned out to have been nothing more than a couple of ardent birders quarrelling over the sighting of a little ringed plover circling over Decoy Lake.

Finally given the okay by one of the doctors, Simone pulled a chair close to the bed where Tina was stretched out and summoned up an encouraging smile. One quite deep cut running down the side of her neck and along the top of her shoulder aside, the majority of Tina Morrison's physical injuries seemed to be superficial. The others, Simone thought, would take longer to heal.

The version that Simone retold to Colin Sherbourne, back in Nottingham, was basically this: after the van, the decorator's van into which she'd been bundled, there'd been a car — Tina didn't know which make — and then another, larger van. After driving round for what felt like ages, going in circles she'd thought, at least that was what it had seemed like, they'd parked near the edge of a field. One of the men had produced a bottle of vodka while the other rolled a joint.

At first she'd gone along with what they wanted, thinking if she did, they'd let her go, but when it became obvious that wasn't going to happen, she'd tried to get away. Which was when it had all changed. Turned nasty. Really nasty. They'd tied her up and done things to her. Not the one called Shane so much — in fact, he'd tried to talk the other one out of it, some of it — but then, in the end, he'd joined in much the same.

Here Tina had broken down, crying, broken by the all too recent memory, and sobbed her heart out; Simone needing to be at her most patient, most consoling, before steering Tina back to her story.

She must have passed out, Tina said — fainted maybe, she didn't really know — but when she came to, Shane was shaking her by the shoulder and whispering in her ear, telling her he was going to untie her and let her go, and that she had to get as far away as she could and promise never to tell anyone what had happened.

'And that was what she did,' Sherbourne said, 'made a run for it?'

'Apparently. But it was dark and she had no real idea where she was. Must've spent ages just stumbling around, frightened of her own shadow. Till, somehow, she arrived at the motorway.'

'All in all,' Sherbourne said, 'not a bad outcome. When you consider the other possibilities. She's still alive, at least.'

Simone nodded.

'And she identified both Keach and Donald?'

'From photographs, yes.'

'Good. Now we just need to catch the bastards before they can do any more harm.'

But by early evening, when Sherbourne phoned Elder to keep him in the loop, as promised, there had been no further sign. The two men seemed to have disappeared into the earth.

'The young woman,' Elder said. 'How's she doing?'

'Physically, not as bad as might have been expected. But beyond that . . .'

There was no need to say any more. Elder, he knew, was more than capable of filling in the dots for himself. He had seen Katherine that afternoon, the story of Tina Morrison's capture and subsequent release the second item on the news, squeezed between a one per cent rise in the rate of inflation and a fatal stabbing in south London, the second in the past three days.

Katherine had reached out and squeezed her father's hand. 'It never stops, does it?'

'It can seem that way.'

For the news broadcast, Colin Sherborne had been filmed making a short statement in front of the Central Police Station in Nottingham; Tina Morrison's mother had been interviewed earlier, incoherent and weeping, outside Doncaster Royal Infirmary. There were photographs of Tina herself, happy, smiling; a snatch of video taken the year before, on holiday with friends on Ibiza. This was followed by photographs of Adam Keach and Shane Donald, head and shoulders both . . . police are anxious to speak to . . . the public are advised not to approach . . . two numbers to call.

Katherine shivered and looked away.

Elder reached for the remote and the picture disappeared.

'At least . . .' he began.

'At least what?'

'At least he's nearly two hundred miles away.'

'You don't know that. Not for certain. And it's obvious the police haven't got much of a clue.'

'They'll find him, don't worry. And meantime, the last place he's going to come is here. London. Somewhere he doesn't know.'

'How can you be so certain?'

'He'll stick with where he's comfortable. Confident. Notts, South Yorks, Lincs. Somewhere out towards the east coast. That's where he'll be. Not down here in the south. Too chancy. Too much of a risk.'

They went for a walk in London Fields, wandering around the Saturday market and snacking on falafels packed into pitta bread; Katherine hesitated over a velour top at one of the vintage clothing stalls; Elder asked her advice over a sea-glass necklace on a silver chain he thought he might buy for Vicki and, after much umming and aahing, chose a poppy brooch in red enamel instead.

'Missing her, are you?' Katherine asked, teasing.

Elder just grinned.

'You can't stay here for ever, you know. And anyway, there's no need. Not now. Not any more.' She pulled at his sleeve. 'I'm fine, really.'

'Are you?'

'Yes, I think so.'

'You don't think it might be worth getting back into contact with the therapist?'

'No, Dad. No, I don't. I really don't.'

'And if the police want to speak to you again . . .'

'Do you think they will? After last time? I think they believed me, don't you? Even without more of an alibi or anything.'

'Probably. I hope so, but it's difficult to say.'

'Well, either way, I'll be fine. Honest. I was just wobbly for a few days, that's all. You don't need to babysit me any more. And I don't need a bodyguard, either. You said yourself, Adam Keach is over two hundred miles away.' She reached up and kissed him on the cheek. 'But I'm glad you came. Truly. I am.'

As they walked away, she slipped her hand into his.

When Vicki called Elder was half-asleep, the book he'd been reading face down on the bed. Not long back from a gig, she sounded loud, elated.

'It went well, I assume?' Elder said, laughing at her exuberance.

'Great. Fantastic. You should have been there.'

'I wish I had been.'

'When are you coming back?'

'Soon. Soon, I think.'

'Kate, she's . . .'

'She's doing okay. Better than I expected. Either that or she's putting on a pretty good show.'

'Having you there will have helped steady her.'

'I hope so.'

Silence, just the sound of Vicki's breathing.

'I am missing you, you know,' she said.

'That's nice.'

'How about you?'

'Am I missing you, d'you mean?'

'Uh-hum.'

'Not one whit. Not for a minute.'

'Bastard.'

Elder laughed.

'Come home.'

'Home?'

'You know what I mean.'

He hesitated, uncertain. 'Tomorrow. Maybe the day after.'

'Promise?'

'I promise.'

Without being able to see, she knew he had his fingers tightly crossed. Knew that was always the way it was going to be.

'Want me to sing you to sleep?'

Elder smiled. 'The way you sing, I doubt if sleeping'd be what I had in mind.'

After the first verse of 'I'll See You in My Dreams' he blew a kiss into the phone and said goodnight.

40

The Sunday papers were having a field day. Some enterprising crime reporter on the *Telegraph* had made the connection and most of the others had followed suit. Elder picked up a discarded copy of the *Mail* from someone's table when he went into the hotel dining room for breakfast; Hadley and Rachel read the *Observer* over avocado and toast and flat whites, Rachel's treat, in their local coffee shop in Crouch End.

Victim of escaped killer questioned in murder case.

For no doubt a sizeable backhander, someone had leaked the information about Katherine being formally questioned by the police in relation to Anthony Winter's murder and the reporter had taken it from there. Along with a profile of Adam Keach, there was a résumé of the crimes for which he had been convicted, a rerun, more salacious in some cases than others, of the treatment Katherine had suffered at his hands. Just when she seemed to have been gaining in confidence, the last thing she needed.

The account of Anthony Winter's murder was accompanied

by unauthorised reproductions of the paintings for which Katherine had been his model.

There was an up-to-date photograph of Katherine, taken from her Facebook page, several others of her at sixteen which came from various newspaper files. The same pictures of Tina Morrison that had been used before were rolled out again, in addition, somewhat incongruously, to one of her wearing her Greggs' uniform and smiling.

The image of Elder that appeared in most papers was at least ten years out of date and made him look stern and unforgiving. In the *Sunday Times*, it was suggested that he was actively involved in both investigations, the Midlands-based one into Adam Keach's escape and the subsequent attack on Tina Morrison, as well as the London-based hunt for Anthony Winter's murderer.

Cornwall cop comes out of retirement to help solve two major crimes.

Aside from being grossly inaccurate on most levels, what angered Elder particularly was that it successfully identified the area of the Penwith Peninsula where he lived.

When he rang the flat, Chrissy answered. No, she told him, they never have a Sunday paper, not any kind of paper really. But the story he was worried about was all over social media. Katherine hadn't seen it yet, she was still sleeping, but she promised to keep an eye on her when she did.

'Ask her to call me,' Elder said. 'Okay?'

'Okay.'

In the café, meanwhile, Hadley was following up her flat white with a macchiato, anger etched across her face.

'If I find out it was someone at Holmes Road who took the *Telegraph*'s shilling, I'll have him up on charges and out the door before he draws another miserable breath, so help me.'

'You don't think,' Rachel said, 'unpleasant as some of it is, all this coverage might help in some way?'

'You are kidding, right?'

'Mightn't it make it more difficult for this Keach person to stay under the radar? And I suppose it's not inconceivable someone might come forward with new information about Anthony Winter.'

'And Katherine Elder? How about her? Having all that dragged through the papers again.'

'I know,' Rachel said. 'It won't be easy for her. Not easy at all. With everything else that's going on especially. I just hope she gets the support she needs.'

When Katherine made her way to the bathroom a good couple of hours later, Stelina was at the table wearing noise-cancelling headphones and working on an overdue essay, and Chrissy was sitting out on the balcony answering emails on her laptop. As usual on Sunday mornings, Abike had headed off to a concert at Wigmore Hall.

It wasn't until she was out of the shower that Katherine switched on her phone and, having checked her messages, flicked across to the news.

'Fuck,' she said quietly and closed the screen.

When her phone went some fifteen minutes later, she thought it would be her father, but it was Vida.

'Kate, are you okay?'

'Yes, why?'

'I've just been reading all this stuff in the papers. I had no idea.'

Katherine didn't know what to say.

'I just thought,' Vida said, 'right now you probably didn't want to be on your own.'

'It's fine. Chrissy's here. And Stelina.'

'Okay, that's good. Only I was going to say, if you wanted to come over and spend some time with Justine and me . . .'

'Really, it's nice of you, but I'm fine.'

'If you change your mind, it would be good to see you. You could come round some time with Chrissy, maybe?'

'Yes, thanks, I'd like that.'

When she broke the connection, Katherine was surprised to find there were tears in her eyes. Why was it some people were so nice when they didn't have to be?

She texted her dad and assured him she was all right, made herself tea and toast and joined Chrissy out on the balcony. Perhaps, once all the fuss had died down, it was going to be okay . . .

41

Monday morning. The sky a marbled blue. Hadley had set off for work deliberately early, bought coffee from the new establishment close by the Assembly House and carried it the short distance to the station. Spurred on by the weekend's unwanted flush of publicity, Detective Chief Superintendent McKeon had insisted on a meeting first thing.

Alone in the incident room, she stared at the accumulation of items on display – photographs, diagrams, names and times, images snatched from CCTV – searching for a clear connection that refused to come.

As she was certain McKeon would be at pains to remind her, it was three weeks since she had taken the call from the Homicide Assessment Team and made the short journey from Holmes Road to Anthony Winter's studio; since when most of what they'd learned, herself and her team, had served to do little but tease; lead them so far and no further. If you removed Katherine Elder from the equation, which she was increasingly prone to do, they still had no credible suspect. No one in the frame.

No clear motive, either. Sex or money? Someone with a grudge? Jealous of Winter's relatively new-found wealth, his new-found fame? Chris Phillips had interviewed the aggrieved Rupert Morland-Davis at Abernathy Fine Art, who was still intent upon pursuing some kind of legal challenge against Winter's estate, but, Phillips judged, about as likely to have attacked Winter with that degree of force as he was to vote Labour in the next election. Besides which, he had an alibi, doubly confirmed, for the weekend in question.

Hadley prised the lid from her coffee: good crema, still warm.

The photographs on the board made clear the extent of Winter's injuries. The result of a deliberate attempt to do as much damage, cause as much pain as possible, or, as Mark Foster had suggested, had his attacker simply become caught up in the moment, lost control? Could it be the result of a sex game that had gone savagely, wildly wrong?

Winter's recently discovered home movies were still being pored over – sometimes, Hadley suspected, with more relish than was strictly appropriate – in an attempt to identify the participants.

She stepped away from the board.

Sex or money? Which was the most likely? Knowing what she did of Winter's life, his art, she'd go for sex every time. She finished her coffee, dropped the cup down into the bin, and went off to meet her boss.

All too soon she was back in the incident room, smarting from McKeon's thinly veiled accusations of incompetence and lack of leadership, lack of direction.

Conversation hushed as she entered.

'Right,' she said, 'you'll have read the weekend papers and for all I know, we're trending, and not in a good way, on social media. So you can imagine how the conversation just went with the Detective Chief Super. Which means that if you've got anything, anything at all, that's going to progress this investigation further, now's the time.'

Howard Dean and Chris Phillips exchanged glances.

'I think Howie's got something,' Phillips said.

'Then for God's sake let's hear it.'

Dean got to his feet. 'I've been going through all those videos we found on Winter's hard drive . . .'

'It's a tough job,' Terry Mitchell remarked to no one in particular, 'but someone's got to do it.'

Phillips silenced him with a look.

'And there's one face that crops up several times . . .' He moved across to one of the computers. 'If you look here . . . before they really get into it . . .'

All eyes were watching the screen.

'And here . . . It's the same woman, I think you'll agree. Tall, dark hair, slim build, not an ounce of extra fat on her . . .'

'All the exercise she's been getting,' Mitchell suggested.

'Shut it, Mitch!' Chris Phillips snapped.

'Two things,' Dean continued, unfazed. 'One, she looks an awful lot like the woman caught on CCTV close to Winter's studio the night he was killed . . .' Readied in advance, that image appeared on the screen alongside the first.

Murmurs of agreement; nodding heads.

'And second, I think I know who she is.'

'Do tell,' Hadley said with a smile.

Dean grinned back and a close-up image, slightly unfocused, filled the screen: an attractive brunette with a slight overbite, looking seductively at the camera.

'Meet Sorina Nicolescu from Bucharest, twenty-four years of age and, according to the description, feminine, sensitive and emotional. And always open for communication with interesting people. This is from a website advertising, as it puts it, hot Romanian women and girls looking for love, romance and marriage. She also appears on several other sites of a similar nature, including this next one which sets out to appeal to people with certain specific tastes.'

The image showed Sorina in form-fitting PVC, a heavily studded dog collar tight about her neck, holding a riding crop at a menacing angle and smiling provocatively.

'And there's no doubt,' Hadley said, 'that this is the same woman as in some of Winter's nasty little home movies?'

Dean shook his head. 'I don't think so. None at all.'

'Then the sooner we get to speak with Ms Nicolescu from Bucharest, the better. One of you had better log on to a website or two, present yourself as an interesting single male urgently looking for love and friendship and open communication. Mark, something for you maybe?'

All too predictably, Mark Foster flushed a deep shade of red.

42

After years of waking shy of six, stumbling blearily to the bathroom then back to get dressed for work; kettle on downstairs for tea, take a cup up to the wife before leaving – Back the usual time, duck, don't do owt I wouldn't – Gary Talbot found it impossible to sleep in of a morning, even now both work and wife had gone.

By half past the hour, he had his pack-up made and wrapped, thermos filled and ready, notebook, binoculars. Pat had never been able to understand his fascination with birds. She'd go with him on occasion, take along a book or a magazine, more than a few times her knitting; do her best to squeeze out a scrap of enthusiasm when he'd pointed out a flock of Arctic terns circling overhead before flying east, or a marsh harrier collecting material for its nest.

Yes, love, very nice, she'd say without really looking, and recover a dropped stitch, turn a page. He missed her like bloody buggery and he didn't care who knew it. There'd been no more mention of those blokes as had kidnapped that poor lass on the morning news.

Old canvas rucksack on his back, he took the bus from French-gate Interchange towards Lakeside, alighting at the B & Q then crossing the main road before walking along Mallard Way to the reserve.

Willow Marsh he might head for first today, always with the option of crossing Black Marsh Field towards Piper Marsh later in the day. The whole point of it really, what you had to remember, you never knew just what you were going to see and where or when. Like the time he'd more or less dropped off, napping on the job as it were, and snapped awake just in time to see a black-tailed godwit over West Scrape. His first of the year.

By the time he broke out his thermos, mid morning, there'd been nothing but sandpipers and the odd oystercatcher. Quiet but pleasant, decent temperature, a breeze out of the west.

He was screwing the top back onto his flask, when a movement caught his eye away to the left. A bittern, was it? Yes. There in the midst of the reed beds, the curved beak and the long neck. He reached for his binoculars and thumbed them into focus.

No sooner did he have the bird in his sights than, with a splash of water and almost lazy flap of wings, it had lifted away, leaving him staring at what looked like a human face, part-submerged amongst the reeds.

The estimated driving time north from Nottingham to Doncaster was a minute over one hour, but an accident on the motorway and the subsequent detour meant that by the time Colin Sherbourne and Simone Clarke arrived at the Potteric Carr Nature Reserve, the whole panoply of police response was there before them. Divers, Scenes of Crime officers in their blue coveralls, a specialist search team from the Tactical Support Group: South Yorks police pulling out all the stops.

A white tent had been erected on the far side of the marsh. Stretched out inside, Shane Donald's naked, lifeless body — scrawny limbs, pale skin, a withering of hairs across his chest, flaccid penis resting against the wrinkled sack beneath — looked like a failed prototype for something finer, somehow more complete.

The abrupt angle of the head told its story clearly enough: his neck had been broken.

'If pressed,' the medical examiner said, 'I'd say he was caught in a headlock from behind — look at the bruising there and there — one quick sideways wrench and a catastrophic cervical fracture ensued. Paralysis, a certain amount of internal bleeding, he would have been dead within seconds. But better not quote me, at least not yet.'

Sherbourne stepped outside into the fresh air.

'Payback, you reckon?' Simone Clarke said. 'For letting the girl go.'

'Looks that way. Donald no longer the soulmate he had in mind.'

'One thing certain, one man alone, easier to pass unnoticed than two.'

Above them, a flock of lapwings swerved this way and that, making black-and-white patterns against the sky.

The first fresh sighting of Adam Keach came later that same day, a garage near Pontefract, the same MO as before, stolen credit cards, stolen vehicle — a Honda Accord that was found later, abandoned in a Little Chef car park on the Great North Road. With no report of another vehicle being taken in its place, it was quite possible he was no longer driving and had simply hitched a lift.

After that there was nothing until a possible sighting was reported at Glasgow Central station, a man closely resembling Keach's description seen outside the Starbucks on the main concourse. But a trawl through CCTV from the booking office and along the platforms yielded nothing further.

False trail, Sherbourne thought. Until a second sighting was reported a day later, this on the ferry from Mallaig on the Scottish mainland to Armadale on the Isle of Skye. Which, had that indeed been Keach in Glasgow, made a kind of sense, even though the trains to that part of Scotland, he knew from family holidays in the past, left from Queen Street rather than Glasgow Central.

The person who'd reported this had emailed a photograph taken on their mobile phone, the resemblance close enough for Sherbourne's hopes to be raised just a little and to give the local force a frisson of excitement, before the man in question turned out to be an insurance claims investigator set on climbing at least two of the Munros before his week's holiday was over, the visual resemblance to Adam Keach an unfortunate embarrassment.

Wherever Keach was, he was still at large.

43

Sorina's first response on seeing Mark Foster was one of approval: after all those sweaty men who lied by some ten or twenty years about their age, here was someone who looked to be as young as he had claimed. Younger. But when Foster, almost apologetically, showed her his identification, she realised the deception this time had been of a different kind.

Now she was sitting in a stuffy room, faced by two plain-clothes police officers, both equally stern, a woman and a man, and the handsome young detective was no longer anywhere to be seen.

In the first minutes she had been cautioned and informed of her rights, certain basic questions asked and answered: name, age, country of origin, current address. So far, Sorina thought, so routine. It was not the first time she had been questioned by the authorities and would almost certainly not be the last.

She still didn't know what they really wanted; wondered how long it would take them to get to the point.

'You know, I believe,' Hadley said, 'a man named Anthony Winter?'

Ah, Sorina thought, not long at all.

'I'm not sure. Winter, no, I don't think . . .'

'According to his phone and email records, he was in touch with you on at least three separate occasions in the past eight weeks.'

'I still don't think . . .'

'Sorina, you're not in trouble here. All we're seeking is information.'

'Information, yes, of course. I am helping if I can.'

'Good,' Chris Phllips said, with the beginnings of a smile. 'So, Anthony Winter.'

'Yes.'

'You do know him?'

'Yes.'

'You have, in fact, met him on a number of occasions.'

'Yes.'

'For sex?'

'Anthony . . . Anthony was a friend.'

'A friend with whom you had sex?'

'Yes. Of course, there is nothing wrong . . .'

'For money?'

Sorina looked from one face to the other.

'You had sex in exchange for money?' Hadley asked.

'Sometimes he would give me present.'

'Present?' Phillips said. 'That's nice. What was it? Chocolates? Flowers, perhaps?'

Sorina shook her head.

'You had sex with Anthony Winter,' Hadley said, 'sex of a particular kind, the kind of sex in which he was interested, involving the giving and receiving of pain, and in exchange for that, your part in that, you were paid. Isn't that so?'

'Yes.'

'In cash?'

'Yes.'

'And when was the last time this happened?'

'I . . . I don't know . . . I can't . . . I don't remember.'

'Maybe this will jog your memory,' Phillips said, and keyed a short sequence of video on to the screen. 'That is you? Approaching Winter's studio?'

'I'm not sure, you cannot properly see . . .'

'No? Well, look. Look again. I'll freeze the image here. Now . . . is that or is that not you?'

'Yes, I think so.'

'It is you?'

'Yes.'

'Then here you are leaving, a little over an hour later.'

Sorina nodded.

'And you see the date? The time?'

'Yes.'

'Saturday, April the eighth. The same evening, the same night that Anthony Winter was murdered.'

Sorina shivered and clasped her arms across her chest.

'You know how he died? Anthony?'

A quick shake of the head.

'He was beaten. Badly beaten. A sex game that went too far, perhaps, carried on too long.'

Sorina shivered again.

'Is that how it happened?' Hadley said, her voice clipped and brisk. 'Fun and games that got out of hand?'

Sorina shook her head. Her throat was suddenly dry. When she tried to speak, the words refused to come.

'Did you strike . . . did you hit Anthony Winter when you were having sex? Was that one of the things he liked you to do?'

'No. It was not that.'

'What then?'

'Sometimes . . . sometimes he would ask me to tie him up. Like this . . . his hands behind his head. Behind his back.'

'And he didn't ask you to hit him then? Slap him, perhaps?'

'No. It was always the other way.'

'He would hit you?'

'Yes. Later. When I untied him. But not always. And not so hard. You know, it was a game. Like you say before, a game.'

'When you went to Winter's studio that evening,' Phillips said, changing tack, 'how did you go?'

'Go?'

'Yes, travel. How did you get there?'

'Taxi. I take taxi. Minicab. Always.'

'And after? Going home?'

'The same.'

'You're sure?'

'Yes, of course.'

'Which company did you use? One close to where you live? Because, of course, we can check. It will show in their records.'

'I cannot remember. I am sorry.'

'Is that because you didn't go by minicab at all?'

Sorina swallowed. 'Sometimes I get lift.'

'Who from?'

She swallowed again. 'My friend, Grigore.'

'Grigore?'

'Yes.'

'And he's what? Your boyfriend?'

'No. Not really, no. Just friend.'

'Friend from Bucharest?'

'No. Here. Here in London.'

'And would you say he was a good friend?'

'Yes.'

'Who takes you sometimes to meet clients, picks you up afterwards?'

'Sometimes, yes.'

'And you give him money?'

'No.'

'You never give him money? The money from clients? Never?'

Sorina looked down. 'Sometimes, yes.'

'So he's your pimp?'

'No. Friend, only friend.'

'And I suppose the money you give him, it's for petrol, perhaps?' Phillips said and laughed.

Sorina did not laugh. There was fear, instead, ticking at the backs of her eyes. Maybe she had said too much, spoken – how did you say? – out of turn.

'This Grigore,' Hadley said, 'does he have another name?'

Sorina's head dropped even lower. 'Balaci,' she said in a whisper.

'I'm sorry, you'll have to speak up.'

'Balaci.'

'Grigore Balaci?'

'Yes.'

Something in Hadley's brain clicked deftly into place.

44

It had been 2013. Hadley had been liaising with officers from the Vice Unit, working out of West Ham Lane. Preparations for the Olympic Games of the previous year, extensive in themselves, had been followed by a swathe of urban regeneration which had brought large numbers of transient workers to the area and, with them, an ensuing rise in prostitution. Massage parlours, brothels, women working the streets. Many of the women were from abroad, Eastern Europe in particular, some from Africa, trafficked here under false expectations and forced into prostitution to pay back the extortionate cost of being transported.

Getting the women to talk, lay complaints about their situation, name names, was next to impossible: they were too afraid. If they tried to run away, they were swiftly found and made an example of. Beaten. Cut. A razor to the breast, the face. Like something out of *Brighton Rock*, Hadley thought, Britain in the 1930s, not this Brave New Post-Olympic Paradise of glass and shining steel.

And it wasn't only the women who suffered, though they suffered most.

Punters, too. A few.

Gerry Carlin's grandfather had run his illegal bookie's business from the upstairs back bedroom of his house in Bromley-by-Bow; when off-course bookmakers were made legal in 1960, he opened his first shop on the high street; a second, run by Gerry's father, in nearby Stratford. Now there were seven all told, across the East End and out into Essex, overseen by Gerry himself, and despite competition from the likes of Coral and William Hill, profits were steady. Life was good.

Carlin had been married and divorced twice — three children of his own, two of them girls, grandchildren now as well — and though the wrong side of sixty he still had his needs.

For some little time these had been met by Nataliya, a young woman from the Ukraine whom he used to visit in a small hotel off the Romford Road, and who would now call discreetly at his house on St Leonard's Street. A new cleaner, the neighbours thought, if they thought anything of it at all.

It was some two months after Nataliya began coming to the house that Gerry Carlin first encountered Grigore Balaci. There on the doorstep alongside Nataliya when he went down to let her in.

'Mr Carlin . . . I thought time was we become acquainted.'

Malicious, flashily dressed, smiling. Speaking slightly old-fashioned English with an Eastern European accent.

When Carlin tried to bar him from entering, Balaci simply pushed him aside. Thrust him up against the wall. Showed him photographs on his phone. Photographs taken in the Romford Road hotel.

'You would not wish for your family to see these. Your daughters. Your lovely grandchildren.'

Carlin had looked anxiously towards Nataliya, who turned quickly away.

'Fifty thousand pounds or these will be on Internet everywhere, on line, social media. And then one thousand pounds each week, each time Nataliya is here. You understand?'

When Carlin didn't answer right away, Balaci punched him in the stomach, butted him in the face, rested a blade against the side of his neck, just below the ear.

'All right,' Carlin said. 'All right. But I don't have that kind of money here.'

'You lie.' A little blood began to trickle down below the collar of Carlin's shirt.

'I can find maybe two thousand now, that's all. But tomorrow. Come back tomorrow. I will have it all. But you will have to promise me, the photographs . . .'

'Tomorrow. All of moncy. Or . . .' And drawing the knife blade across Carlin's neck, barely an inch away from the skin, he laughed.

When he came back the next day, Hadley was waiting, along with three other officers from West Ham Lane. Balaci was taken into custody and charged with possession of an offensive weapon, causing actual bodily harm and demanding money with menaces.

Held on remand and denied bail, he continued to deny all charges.

Nataliya could not be found.

Six weeks before the case was due to come to court, the front of one of Carlin's betting shops was smashed in, another was set on fire. Shortly after that, Carlin let it be known that he was changing his testimony. He had misinterpreted Balaci's actions, misunderstood the situation. There had been no violence, no knife, he would swear.

Grudgingly, the CPS made the decision not to go to trial.

Grigore Balaci was released.

September 2013.

'You think it's possible,' Chris Phillips said, 'he could have been trying on the stunt here? With Winter?'

Hadley took a drag from Phillips' cigarette; handed it back. They were at the back of the station car park, the road that led down past the recycling depot. Stretching their legs. Thinking time.

'Why not? Winter had money, Balaci would have known that. And a public persona he might not have wanted dragged through the mud. Now especially. After collecting Sorina, Balaci could have come back. He'd have known enough to avoid the CCTV cameras, avoid getting seen.'

They walked on. A council bin lorry went slowly past. A van heading for the Royal Mail sorting office further along.

'That business you were telling me about with the bookie,' Phillips said. 'That was what? Four or five years back now?'

'Four. Since when Balaci's been walking the finest of fine lines. Suspicion of extortion, harassment, living on immoral earnings. Questioned, never charged.'

'Wouldn't do any harm,' Phillips said. 'Invite him in for a little chat.'

'It's something. Otherwise . . .'

'Don't worry, boss. We'll get there.'

'You reckon?'

'Yeah,' Phillips said with a broad grin. 'Got right on our side, after all.'

'If that's all, then God help us.'

Phillips looked up into the sky and laughed. 'The Lord, they say, He moves in mysterious ways.'

Hadley's mobile rang in her jacket pocket. 'Maybe that's Him now.'

45

Grigore Balaci had put on weight since Hadley had last seen him; the beginnings of a paunch that his well-cut suit failed to completely hide. His hair had got thinner, the first suspicions of grey. But the same lean face, the same cheekbones, the same thin lips. Rings on three of his fingers. A gold stud in his right ear. Eyes that were rarely still.

His solicitor was bearded, balding, prosperous. 'My client has agreed to help you in any way he can . . .'

Chris Phillips at her side, Hadley let the platitudes wash over her.

'Mr Balaci,' she said when the formalities were through. 'Do you remember me?'

'No. Should I?' The tone insolent, the look.

'Perhaps not. After a while, I imagine one arresting officer must look much like another.'

Balaci's tongue slithered between his lips. 'Not when they're as pretty as you.'

Hadley's distaste was etched on her face.

JOHN HARVEY

'I should remind you,' the solicitor said, 'my client has never been prosecuted for any offence, and we strongly resent any attempted slur on his character.'

'I doubt,' Hadley said, 'if it would be possible to demean Mr Balaci's character any further.'

'If that is your attitude . . .' the solicitor began, rising from his seat.

'You are the owner,' Chris Phillips said swiftly, addressing Balaci, 'of a metallic grey Volvo S90, registration DR66 TDP.'

Balaci shrugged. The solicitor sat back down.

'Said vehicle,' Phillips said, 'was seen twice on Highgate Road between Linton House and the Forum late on the evening of Saturday, April the eighth'

'ANPR,' Balaci said with the edge of a smile. 'Of course. I saw the sign.'

'Then you admit to being the driver of the car?'

'Who else?'

'Perhaps you could tell us what you were doing there?'

Balaci shrugged. 'A favour for a friend.'

'A friend?'

'A young lady.'

'Does this lady have a name?'

'Naturally. Sorina. Sorina Nicolescu.'

'And what is the nature, would you say, of this friendship?'

Balaci leaned his head to one side. 'We are compatriots, that is all. From Bucharest.'

'And that was enough for you to leave whatever you might have been doing and not only take her to her destination, but collect her afterwards?'

Balaci shrugged. 'She asks, I oblige.'

'Why, I wonder, didn't she simply take a taxi? Rather than risk inconveniencing you?'

He shrugged his shoulders again, lazily. 'Women some-times, who knows?'

Hadley stared back at him, stone-faced.

'You knew where she was going?' Phillips said. 'Sorina. Where you were taking her?'

'To visit a friend.'

'A friend of a friend, then?'

Balaci smiled.

'You know this friend's name?'

Balaci shook his head. 'Only that he is artist, I think.'

'You don't know his name?'

'No.'

'You're sure?'

'You are badgering my client,' the solicitor said. 'He has already answered your question. He did not know the man's name.'

'Not then,' Hadley said. 'But later, surely?'

'I'm sorry, I do not understand.'

'Later, when it was all over the news, all across social media that this same artist, Anthony Winter, had been murdered.'

Balaci casually crossed one leg over the other. 'I did not — what is your expression? place two and two together.'

'Do you remember, from what you heard, how exactly he was killed?'

'No, but he was stabbed perhaps. It happens so often now in London, stabbings all the time.'

'He was beaten to death. Beaten to death with manacles and an iron chain. Beaten in a frenzy.'

'Manacles — sorry, I do not . . .'

'Handcuffs. Old-fashioned handcuffs.' Hadley leaned for-ward. 'You understand handcuffs, surely?'

Balaci didn't answer.

'I think, Detective Chief Inspector,' the solicitor said, 'this line of questioning is oppressive.'

'I'm sure Mr Balaci can stand up for himself, can't you, Mr Balaci? A little to and fro, a little banter, that's nothing to you? A little give and take.' She leaned forward, engaged Balaci with her eyes. 'The kind you exchanged with Gerry Carlin, remember? Is that what it was like with Anthony Winter? When you called round again later demanding money? A little push and shove?'

'Money? What money?'

'However much you thought you could get.'

'Get? Get for what?' He glanced at his solicitor and the solicitor raised a hand, palm outwards, fingers outstretched. 'All right, this has got to stop.'

'Photographs, probably,' Hadley said, 'like it was for Carlin? Photos you were threatening to put on social media? Video? Little games he played with your friend, Sorina. The kind of games he might pay to have suppressed. That might be bad for his reputation.'

The solicitor was on his feet. 'This interview is over. You have nothing, no evidence that my client has been involved in wrongdoing of any kind. This has been nothing more than a fishing expedition of the worst kind, fuelled only, it appears, by your personal animosity. We are leaving. And rest assured, I shall be lodging a complaint at the highest level.'

Balaci was on his feet now, too, the smile in Hadley's direction offset by a quick glimpse of lizard tongue. The solicitor stood to one side to let his client exit first, then closed the door firmly behind them.

'Fuck!' Hadley said. 'Fuck, fuck and double fuck! I let that smarmy, smug bastard get to me.'

Turning, she kicked her chair hard against the wall.

'We didn't have him, boss,' Phillips said. 'We never had him. Never even came close.'

He bent down and set the chair to rights.

46

Elder climbed over the granite stile and made his way between patches of brightly flowering yellow gorse, across a paddock of coarse grass and bracken and down towards the sea. To his left, the old engine houses of the Carn Galver mine stood out against the sky. A buzzard hovered overhead, buoyed up by the wind. It was almost a week since he had last seen Katherine, two days since he had spoken to her on the phone. Three days now since Shane Donald's body had been found. Rumours of Adam Keach being seen in Scotland that were difficult to believe.

Katherine had sounded chirpy enough, considering all she had had to contend with; together with her friend, Chrissy, she had been round to the house of an art teacher they knew – Vida, was it? – eaten too much good food, laughed a lot, drunk too much wine. She thought in a week or so she might even feel up to returning to work, doing some modelling again. The rent still needed paying, after all.

Elder had made encouraging noises, wanting to believe;

fearful that this new-found confidence was a carapace waiting to crack. Ahead, the buzzard swerved suddenly and plunged, faster than the eye could follow, down on to its prey.

Colin Sherbourne, it was clear from the brief conversation they'd had, was almost as dubious about the recent sightings of Keach as Elder himself, but in the absence of anything further, what could he do but watch and wait?

Elder hated it, the waiting and, in his case, hundreds of miles distant, the feeling of helplessness that went with it. It was all he could do not to board the next train, or jump in the car and drive.

'He'll not thank you, you know,' Cordon had told him. 'Sherbourne, that his name? Breathing over his shoulder, second-guessing. Think how you'd feel if it were your investigation. That detective chief inspector up in London the same. Cop comes out of retirement to solve crimes might make a good headline, but we both know that doesn't make it true.'

Elder realised that made absolute sense and bridled against it all the same: the powerlessness, the inability to influence what was going on – to crack the case, solve the crime – it was as simple as that.

'I fucked up,' Hadley said that morning, standing by the kitchen worktop, waiting for the toaster to do its job. 'Totally, inexcusably fucked up.'

'What it sounds like to me,' Rachel said, 'all you're guilty of, if anything, is an error of judgement. A relatively small one, at that. And you do know, don't you, if you stand there like that over the toaster, the bread'll never brown in a month of Sundays.'

'I ignored the facts, such as they are. Let my emotions get the better of me. And made myself look foolish and incompetent in front of a junior officer.'

'And that's what's really getting to you as much as anything. You do realise that?'

'Yes, well, I could do without the analysis, thank you very much. Now, marmalade or jam?'

'Marmalade. No, make it peanut butter.'

'I don't think we've got any.'

'I bought some the other day.'

'Where? I don't see . . .'

'There in the cupboard, right in front of you.'

Hadley reached for the jar and it slipped through her fingers, fell to the ground and smashed.

'Fuck! Fuck, fuck and fuck.'

'It doesn't matter. Just make sure you don't cut yourself, step on any of that glass. Here, look, I'll sweep it up. You sit down a minute.'

'I'm okay.'

'Are you?'

'Yes, I'm fine.'

Rachel gave her a quick hug, kissed her on the cheek, and fetched the dustpan and brush. Marmalade would have to do.

There was worse waiting for Hadley when she arrived at Holmes Road. Detective Chief Inspector Andy Price, head of the Met's Modern Slavery and Kidnap unit within Human Exploitation and Organised Crime Command. Hadley knew him from conferences, knew his face, his name, his reputation. Fools, suffer, gladly — rearrange into a well-known phrase or saying.

Worse still, it looked as if Price had been in conference with the DCS; was, in fact, on his way from McKeon's office when Hadley bumped into him.

'Alex,' he said brightly. 'Well met.'

They went to her office, closed the door. Offers of tea, coffee, water politely refused.

'Grigore Balaci,' Price said. 'What was all that about?'

Hadley took a deep breath. 'Error of judgement,' she said, remembering Rachel's words. 'Wading in before properly checking the background, checking the facts. Which, if I had done, might well have meant we'd never have gone after him at all.'

'You thought he might have been involved in your murder? The artist, Winter?'

'I thought it possible, yes. His name came up and . . . well, I acted, shall we say, precipitously. And Balaci went off laughing.'

Price nodded, pushed a hand up through his hair. 'In the long run, maybe no bad thing.'

'What's your interest, anyway?' Hadley asked.

'In Grigore, to be honest, very little. As far as we're concerned, small beer. It's his uncle, Ciprian, we're interested in. Along with Immigration and HM Revenue and Customs, we've been building a case against him for the best part of a year. More. Trafficking, abduction, procuring and trading in prostitution, all on a major scale. I just wanted to make sure your interest in one of the family didn't clash with ours. But it seems as if that's all fine. In fact, if anything it might do us a small favour.'

'How so?'

'If the old man or any of the Balacis were getting wind of us sniffing round, you bringing Grigore in the way you did might throw them off track.'

'How close are you to making your move?' Hadley asked.

Price held up forefinger and thumb and brought them close together until they were almost touching.

'Good luck,' she said, getting to her feet.

They shook hands at the door.

*

By the time Elder arrived back in the village it was late afternoon. Still several hours off sunset, the temperature had already started falling as clouds shunted heavily across the sky. He was on the path between the church and the pub, on his way back to the cottage, when the pub landlord called his name.

'This came for you,' he said, holding an envelope aloft. 'Someone who didn't know your exact address. Maybe forgot.'

Elder thanked him, glanced at the envelope, and, not recognising the writing or being able to read the blurred postmark, pushed it down into his pocket. Time enough, once he'd unlaced his boots and set the kettle on for tea.

Peckish after his walk, he cut off a wedge of cheese and a hunk of bread, took an apple from the bowl and carried them all out into the back garden together with his mug of tea. Moved the bench so as to get the last true warmth of the sun.

Using the same knife with which he'd cut the apple into quarters, he sliced the envelope open.

A postcard, overbright colours, Skegness, donkeys on the beach.

He turned it over.

STILL GOT A DAUGHTER, FRANK?
UNFINISHED BUSINESS THERE, KNOW
WHAT I MEAN?
YOURS, ADAM

47

Forensic records confirmed the presence of Keach's finger-prints on both the card and the envelope; the lettering of the message similar, if not identical, to examples of his penman-ship on record. The card had been posted in Skegness early on the morning of the previous day, CCTV showing someone with a close resemblance to Keach in the vicinity of the post office on Roman Bank, in the centre of the town.

Lincolnshire Police were informed, officers from the Coast and Wolds district covering Skegness and the surrounding area, put on high alert.

Katherine, having turned down the suggestion of moving temporarily into a hostel, was issued by the police with a panic alarm which was patched through to the personal radio net-work and would be acted on immediately; her mobile number was flagged on to the system and linked, on speed dial, to a priority number which only needed one or two digits to be pushed in order to elicit a response. Two officers from the Safer Neighbourhood Team went round to her flat and offered advice as to locks and general security. Foot patrols in the area would be stepped up, checks and drive-bys scheduled. What more was there they could do?

Elder talked to Katherine on several occasions, wanting both to warn and reassure her, striving for a balance between the two. At first she had sounded shocked, frightened; then calmer, on the surface at least, more matter-of-fact; keeping her fears under control, under wraps.

When Elder offered to come up to London she told him there was no need. With what seemed like half the local police force calling round all the time, what possible difference would him being there make? And neither, thank you, did she want to go running off down to Cornwall to stay with him. She had a life to live, after all – she was just starting to get it back on track – and she wasn't going to be frightened out of it by a few words scribbled on a postcard.

Be careful? Of course she'd be careful. What did he think?

He thought she was foolish; he thought she was putting on a brave front. He thought, after discussing it with Cordon, and then with Colin Sherbourne, that the card could well be a red herring, a way of laying down a false scent, setting a false trail.

'If that's really his intention,' Cordon said, 'going after Kate, why give fair warning? Surely that's the last thing he'd do? No, I think, giving wrong information aside, he just wants to get up your nose, make you worried and angry. Taunting you, that's what he's doing. Letting you know he's still free. And besides, how does he even know where she lives? If he's IT savvy enough, he could use her social-media footprint to track her down, but I doubt if he is. He couldn't even find out your exact address, remember, just the name of the village from it being all over the papers.'

'Looks as if you were right,' Sherbourne said, 'about Keach sticking to the east coast, where he knows. Skeggy,

Mablethorpe, up as high as Whitby, maybe. Saltburn. That's where we'll find him. And we will.'

That weekend, the proprietor of a crazy golf course in Ingoldmells, two miles north along the coast from Skegness, thought he recognised Keach from his photo on the television news and notified the police accordingly.

'Right shifty, if you ask me,' he told the officers who attended. 'Saw me looking at him, interested like, and buggered off sharpish. Up towards the dunes.'

Monday morning, Maureen Tracy, a single mum living on Richmond Drive, close to the Tesco superstore in the centre of Skegness, went into her sixteen-year-old daughter Jessica's room and found the bed had not been slept in. She'd gone off to a party with friends and not returned home.

48

Hadley's team redoubled their efforts: checked back again through all the available CCTV, traced the owners of vehicles seen in the vicinity of Winter's studio on the night in question, reinterviewed people living in the flats nearby. Because of the hour, there had not been a large number of pedestrians using that stretch of Highgate Road and they assiduously tracked down as many of them as they could. A man who had been seen on camera ducking into the path leading to the studio, and who they thought might be of interest, was eventually found to be someone who, after several hours in the Bull and Gate, had simply been looking for somewhere to take a much-needed piss.

Mark Foster continued to burrow into Winter's life, personal and professional, hoping to turn up something that might provide a fresh lead, a clue worth following. Through Rebecca Johnson and Vida Dullea, Alice Atkins contacted the models who had posed for Winter in the years preceding Katherine, one of whom admitted having participated in a short-lived sexual relationship, another claiming that she had been propositioned, but declined to be involved. With some striking exceptions – a West African, tall with severely cropped hair, and a petite Chinese woman with tattoos on much of her body – the models Winter favoured, Alice noted after going back a dozen or more years, were very much of a type, a type exemplified by Katherine Elder: the same cut and colour of hair, the same hazel eyes.

Howard Dean, meanwhile, continued the slippery task of tracking down the women Winter had contacted through various sites on the Internet. A task made all the more difficult by the fact that as soon as one site closed down, it reopened under a different name. As did the women whose sincere friendship was advertised: Valeria from the Ukraine looked an awful lot like Valmira from Albania.

Earlier that morning, 5.30 precisely, fifteen minutes ahead of officially designated sunrise, some seventy officers from units within Human Exploitation and Organised Crime Command had raided the Epping home of Ciprian Balaci and other premises belonging to him in Romford and Walthamstow. Thanks to a friendly tip-off which had resulted in a *BBC News* camera crew being conveniently present at Balaci's address, Hadley had been able to watch edited highlights on her mobile phone over breakfast. Ciprian Balaci being bundled into the back of a van before being charged, later that morning, with false accounting and fraudulent evasion of tax, controlling prostitution for gain, and human trafficking for the purpose of sexual exploitation. Somewhere out of picture, Hadley thought, Andy Price must be feeling pretty pleased with himself. She wished she could feel the same.

She was on her way back to her office after another chastening meeting with McKeon, when Mark Foster intercepted her.

'A moment, ma'am.'

'Yes, Mark, what is it?'

'Adriana, ma'am.'

'Who?'

'Adriana Borrell, the sculptor. Winter's girlfriend from way back.'

'What about her?'

'She's just returned from Cyprus, apparently. Finally responded to one of my messages.'

'And you're telling me this why?'

'Just checking we still want to speak to her.'

'Speak to her? Yes, of course, why not?'

Leaving him standing there, Hadley hurried on into her office. If that boy doesn't develop some initiative sharpish, she was thinking, I'm going to have to ship him off back into uniform.

Elder got back from his run that morning to find a message from Trevor Cordon on the answerphone. A body had been found in Penlee Park in the middle of Penzance, would he be interested in taking a look? Anything, Elder thought, for a diversion. Even another dead body.

Cordon met him at the Trewithen Road entrance, Scene of Crime officers already evident, the area roped off, tent erected round the corpse. Elder found a spare set of protective clothing in the boot of Cordon's car. The dead man was young, mid-twenties at best, possibly younger; reddish hair, a fashionable amount of stubble. A dark gash like a second mouth where his throat had been cut.

'Poor bastard,' Elder said softly, as much to himself as anyone else.

'My first thought,' Cordon said, 'before I got a good look, another druggie. They tend to congregate here some of them, this end of the park. But, no, he's too well dressed. Casual, but smart. Certainly not been sleeping rough. And altogether too healthy-looking. At least, he was.'

'Killed here?' Elder asked.

'Close, I'd say. Signs of some kind of struggle down by the gate. Killed there and then dragged into the bushes would be my thinking.'

'Robbery, then?'

Cordon cocked a head to one side. 'No wallet, no phone. Just 15p in his pockets and a train ticket, return to Falmouth.'

'Student, maybe?'

'It's possible. We'll get his ID checked as soon as we can.'

'No one reported missing?'

'Not as yet.'

Elder leaned closer, looking at the face which had settled into some kind of strange repose. The same age as his daughter, more or less. A life snuffed out too soon. He called Katherine the moment they moved away from the scene, no reason other than to hear the sound of her voice, reassure himself she was okay.

The recorded message was short and to the point. 'Sorry I can't talk to you right now, please try again later.'

He was halfway across the park, heading back towards the police station, when his phone rang and he thought it might be Katherine, returning his call.

Colin Sherbourne's voice was flat, matter-of-fact. Jessica Tracy, the girl who'd been reported missing, had been found and returned home, safe but sorry, nursing a sore stomach and an aching head after a night of too much vodka, too much cheap wine, too many pills.

'No further sign?' Elder asked.

'Of Keach? No, since Ingoldmells, not a thing. But we'll keep looking.'

As he was passing the tennis courts, his phone went again.

'Dad, hi. Sorry I missed your call. I was off out for a run.'

Smiling, Elder veered off the path towards an empty bench and sat down.

49

Adriana Borrell was tall, taller still thanks to boots with a serious heel. She was strikingly dressed: a suede jacket, several sizes too large, hanging loose over a pink shirt with a ruffled front; camouflage trousers secured by a scarlet leather belt and a patterned scarf tied loosely around her head. Her face was leathered and deeply lined. Her voice, when she spoke, suggested someone for whom the health warning on cigarettes held no meaning.

Her grip, when she shook Hadley's hand, was firm and strong. 'Your boy said you wanted to see me.'

Hadley suppressed a smile. The word 'catamite' flashed wickedly across her mind.

'I thought we might talk about Anthony Winter.'

'You still looking for the bastard who killed him?'

'Yes.'

'Ten, twelve years back it could cheerfully have been me.'

Hadley smiled. 'I take it this isn't by way of a confession?'

'Call it more wish fulfilment, if you like.'

'You weren't sorry, then, to hear what had happened?'

A smile creased the sculptor's face still further. 'Opened a bottle of Chablis I'd been saving and drank a toast. Or two.' Her laugh was as rough and robust as her voice.

'Your relationship ended in what? Two thousand and eight? Nine?'

'Fifth of November, two thousand and eight. Gatwick to Larnaca. When we took off you could see the first of the fireworks. Seemed kind of suitable. Celebratory.' She looked around. 'I don't suppose there's any way I can smoke in here, is there?'

'I'm afraid not.'

Adriana laughed. 'Infringement of my human rights.'

'Two thousand and eight,' Hadley said, pressing on. 'Ten years ago, give or take. It's a long while to stay angry, harbour that much hate.'

'Oh, don't worry yourself. I haven't exactly been sitting around dwelling on it. Don't suppose I gave him a thought for months at a time. Over there especially. Too much living to do. Too much work.'

'But still you cheered when he died?'

Adriana shrugged her shoulders as if to say, why not?

'What was it, made you so angry?'

'At Winter? You mean, aside from him being a total shit? Which is what most artists, those that are any good and know it, have to be just to get on, get noticed.'

'Yes, aside from that.'

Adriana stretched her arms sideways and flexed the muscles in her back. 'Are you sure I can't sneak a cigarette?'

'Sure.'

Now Adriana stretched her arms in front and spread her fingers wide. 'Sorry. Sit too long in one position, I seize up.'

'Would you rather walk around a little? Talk somewhere else?'

'Can we do that?'

'I don't see why not.'

Adriana's eyes lit up. 'And then I could smoke?'

'No rules to say you can't.'

They crossed the car park and turned right along Regis Road, crossing at the lights towards the open space by the railway bridge and the seats between Natasha's Flowers and Bean About Town.

Hadley nodded in the direction of the coffee wagon and Adriana shook her head and took a slim packet of cigarillos from her pocket.

'Each to her own addiction,' she said, when Hadley came back with a double espresso.

'Okay, so now . . . Anthony Winter . . .'

Adriana took smoke down slowly into her lungs; released it through her mouth and nose. 'I think I knew from the start he wasn't going to be what you'd call faithful. And I took that on board. Or thought I had. But it was the lies that went with it that got to me, undermined whatever it was he had. And then the tying up, the bondage . . . I was happy to go along with a little of that. Nothing, you know, too serious. Nothing that was going to really hurt. But Winter, he got into it more and more. It got so normal sex – whatever that is, but you know what I mean, I think – it got so normal sex simply wasn't on the menu. And I got a little tired of being tied to the bed or whipping Winter across his backside just so he could have an orgasm.' She tapped away a sliver of ash and watched it fall towards the ground. 'And then there was the business with the girl . . .'

'The girl?'

'Melissa.'

'His daughter?'

'His daughter, Melissa.'

Hadley's skin felt electric. 'What about her?'

'She modelled for him. I don't think at first she wanted to. I don't think her mother wanted her to, either. But somehow he persuaded them.' She gave a quick shake of the head. 'He wasn't easy to say no to, Winter.'

'And that was it? She modelled for him, that's what you didn't approve of?' Hadley's mind was racing back through the reproductions of Winter's paintings she'd seen. 'Modelled nude, you mean?'

'Yes, of course. With Winter, what else?'

'And she would have been how old? Fourteen? Fifteen?'

'Somewhere round there, yes. You'd have to ask the girl herself if you want to know for certain. Ask her mother.'

Hadley held the question for a second longer, tasting it on her tongue. 'Aside from the modelling, was there anything else you didn't approve of? Between Winter and his daughter?'

Adriana stubbed out the cigarillo. 'I've said all I'm going to. I'm sorry.'

Hadley was already selecting a number on her phone. 'Alice, drop whatever you're doing. Time to go back to Munchkinland.'

50

This time the weather was less welcoming: a constant mithering rain. The kind, Hadley thought, that soaked through clothes and skin down into your very soul. Overhead, the sky was a leaden, uncompromising grey. There would be no sitting in the arbour, enjoying the scent of flowers, the touch of the sun.

There was a light dully shining in one of the upstairs rooms, the curtains not quite closed. They could hear Susannah Fielding's hurried footsteps on the stairs before she opened the door with a look of half-surprise.

Following her through into the kitchen, they politely declined the offer to take a seat.

'Tea, then, it won't take a minute. I could make tea . . .'

Hadley shook her head. 'We just wanted to ask you a few questions about Melissa. It need not take long.'

'Melissa, yes, I'm afraid she's not been well.'

'About her relationship with her father.'

'With Anthony . . . ?'

'When she was younger, she posed for him, I believe?'

'Yes. Yes, she did.'

'And this was after she'd posed for you? The portrait we were looking at before.'

'Yes.'

'The riding lessons,' Alice said with a helpful smile.

'Yes, that's right.' She smiled back. 'You remembered.'

'When she posed for her father,' Hadley said, 'it was different.'

'I don't . . .'

'She posed in the nude.'

'Well, yes.'

'And at the time she was how old?'

'She . . . she would have been, I think, fourteen. Yes, fourteen.'

'And how did you feel about that? As her mother, I mean?'

'I don't know, I mean, I really can't remember. I . . . And why, anyway? Why does it matter now? I don't understand.'

'I'm wondering how you felt about Melissa posing in that way?'

'I thought . . . I thought . . .' Susannah's left eye was starting to blink, almost uncontrollably. 'I thought since he was her father it was all right.' Leaning sideways, she reached out a hand towards the back of the nearest chair.

'Maybe you should sit down?' Alice said, moving towards her, concerned that she might fall.

'Yes, I think . . .'

Alice took hold of her arm and helped her into the chair while Hadley fetched a glass of water. At the far side of the room a clock was quietly ticking; muffled, the sound of footfall overhead: all the colour had gone from Susannah Fielding's face.

'Did Anthony behave inappropriately towards your daughter, Mrs Fielding? And if so, were you aware . . . ?'

'No, no! Of course not! Of course . . .' Susannah brought her head down hard and fast, face first, against the kitchen table.

Alice let out a small, involuntary cry and, darting forward, reached for Susannah's shoulders, easing her gently back. Blood was beginning to run from her nose and there were the first signs, already, of a swelling above her right eye. Hadley ran water on to a clean tea towel and held it against her face.

In the commotion, the sounds of someone descending the stairs had gone unnoticed.

'It's me you should be talking to,' Matthew Fielding said.

The air in the interview room was heavy and still. Matthew Fielding sat beside his solicitor, upright and steely-eyed, lean face, closely cropped hair.

'My client is prepared to make a statement,' the solicitor said.

The pulse in Hadley's temple quickened and, alongside her, she sensed Chris Phillips tense momentarily, then relax.

'Mel had been ill for years,' Fielding began, his voice even, matter-of-fact. 'Little things, off and on. No particular reason, no particular cause. Doctor would examine her, find nothing, prescribe a few pills. Then, when she went to university, she had this kind of breakdown. I suppose that's what it was. I was off in the army by then and all I knew was little bits Mum'd tell me if I asked. Fobbing me off, really, I suppose. Not wanting me to worry. Enough to worry about out where you are, she'd say. But then this last time, when I came back on leave – just a few weeks back, this – Mel and I, we went for a drink together. Something we'd hardly ever done. Not talked either, I suppose, really talked, not properly, seriously, not since, well, not since we were kids. And not much then. But she started telling me – we'd been talking about something else at the time – suddenly started telling me about what had happened. With . . . with, you know . . . with . . .'

Pausing, he glanced from Hadley to Phillips, from one face to another, then up for a moment at the ceiling.

'I went round there. That evening. She tried to stop me, Mel, said what was the use, it wouldn't do any good. But no, I wanted to have it out with him, see his face when I made him tell me . . . tell me what it was he'd done. At first he wasn't going to talk to me at all. Point-blank refused. Then came over all friendly, offered me a drink – I think he'd been drinking pretty heavily already. Put his arm round me. Tried to. That was when I hit him first. Not hard, but he went down all the same, and I could see the fear in his eyes. And seeing him like that, it made me think of how he'd fucked up our lives, Mel's and Mum's and mine, and I hit him again. And made him tell me about what happened with Mel. And I think he knew then I was going to kill him. He started yelling, yelling and screaming and trying to get away and I grabbed him and got hold of this chain and started swinging it round my head and . . .'

He broke off again, steadying his breathing; his voice, when he resumed, quieter, back under control.

'The thing is, I no longer knew what I was doing. I've seen it happen, in a fire fight, the heat of the battle, you lose control. It's not you. There's something else takes over, driving you on. As if, for those moments, you've literally gone out of your mind.'

He looked across the desk evenly and folded his arms across his chest.

'What d'you think?' Phillips asked. They were in Hadley's office, Matthew Fielding in a cell below, waiting to be charged.

'I think he'll try to plead manslaughter, some kind of diminished responsibility, temporary insanity, whatever. The CPS will go for murder, straight and simple.'

'Is it ever?' Phillips asked ruefully.

'Is it, fuck!'

51

The body in Penlee Park had been identified: Scott Masters, twenty-two, in the final year of a BA honours course in photography at the University of Falmouth. The rucksack he had been carrying was found, discarded, in one of the gardens on Trewithen Road, some sixty metres from the park gates. His notebooks, together with a small book of photographs by Saul Leiter, were still inside; his Nikon D5600 digital SLR camera was missing.

'Expensive?' Elder enquired.

'Quick check on the Internet,' Cordon said, 'a few quid short of a thousand.'

Elder let out a slow whistle.

'I've sent out a description to all the camera shops in the area, pawnshops, anywhere whoever did this might be looking for a quick sale. His mobile the same.'

'And Masters, do we know if he was over from Falmouth on his own?'

'Apparently so. There was an exhibition at the Exchange he

was interested in seeing. I spoke to one of his friends at the university. Until more or less the last minute, he'd been going to come with him. Feeling like shit now, of course, that he didn't.'

'What about family, they've . . .'

'They've all been informed.'

'And the murder weapon? No sign?'

Cordon shook his head. 'Still searching. What we can tell, long blade, seven or eight inches, inch and a half wide. Kitchen knife, that kind of thing. If he's got rid, a good chance we'll find it. Unless he's chucked it out to sea of course. Then we'll have to wait on the tide. Meantime, we're talking to the staff at the Exchange, checking their CCTV, see if anyone remembers Masters being there. If he was seen talking to anyone in particular. Taking his photograph round to other places he might have visited, stopped for a drink, coffee, whatever.'

'You think he might have struck up a conversation with someone? Whoever it was attacked him later?'

'It's possible.'

'What doesn't make sense to me,' Elder said, 'if whoever did this didn't know his victim, which is what, for the moment, we seem to be assuming – if it was a matter of sheer chance, opportunity – all right, threaten him, overpower him, attack him from behind, but why kill him? And why in such an extreme way?'

'Maybe he panicked,' Cordon said. 'Either that or the adrenalin kicked in and he couldn't stop.'

Or maybe, Elder was thinking, he just enjoys it for what it is. Not the first time and possibly not the last.

After leaving the police station, and enjoying what was, for him, the relative luxury of a good phone signal, Elder called first Katherine and then Vicki.

'What is this, Dad?' Katherine said. 'Twice in two days. Anyone'd think you were stalking me.' But she said it with a smile. And after ten minutes or so of small talk and having assured him she was absolutely fine, no one lurking in the shadows, no weird phone calls – his aside – said she had to go.

'Take care,' Elder said.

'You take care yourself.'

Vicki didn't want to talk very much at all. With two gigs coming up later in the week, she was worried about getting a sore throat and was keeping out of draughts and gargling every couple of hours with salt water.

'I might call round later, Frank. We could have a drink at the Tinner's. But I'm not promising, okay? I'll see how I feel.'

Back at the cottage, Elder realised he'd scarcely eaten all day and hastily made himself beans on toast, stirring a good dollop of Worcester sauce into the beans as they were heating, then grating cheese on top once it was on the plate.

It was that time of the day, no longer afternoon and not yet evening, when he always felt most restless, unable to settle. He picked up a book he'd bought at the charity shop in Newlyn and set it down again less than ten minutes later, realising he'd read the last few pages without taking in a single word.

Nothing else for it, he pulled on his boots, lifted a coat down from the peg and, remembering to put the key under the stone by the door in case Vicki decided to risk her throat and arrived before he got back, set off down the path. Instead of going to the headland, he took a left turn through the village and crossed into the lane that would take him alongside the stream and up the rocky path towards Zennor Quoit.

By the time he arrived at the top, calves beginning to ache, the first lights of the village were beginning to show. Beyond the cluster of houses, beyond the fields, the sea was a faint greeny-grey, wrinkled and still.

He breathed in the air and turned for home.

When he arrived, the key was gone.

Smile on his face, he called Vicki's name as he pushed open the door.

The first blow hit him on the top of the right shoulder, jarring his whole body, splintering the bone. The second, delivered as he turned, struck him high to the side of the head, sending him, stumbling, back against the wall.

In the half-light he saw his attacker step back, raise what looked like a pickaxe handle above his head, and, instinctively, he thrust up an arm to ward off the blow. When it smashed against his elbow at the end of its swing, he yelled with pain and fell to the floor.

A boot drove into his ribs as he tried to crawl away.

Hands grabbed at his clothes and hauled him to his knees, dragging him into the centre of the room, then forcing him down on to his back.

'So, Frank, how d'you like it so far?'

Elder blinked upwards, left eye all but closed, to see Keach standing over him, straddling his body, tapping the pickaxe handle against the palm of his hand.

'Not quite, I'd guess, what you had in mind.'

Elder kicked out as best he could and was struck, several times more, in return. Then, tossing the pickaxe handle aside, Keach drew a long-bladed knife from inside his coat.

'Time to talk about Katherine,' Keach said, and resting the point of the knife against Elder's Adam's apple, drew a bead of blood. 'Unfinished business there, like I said. You did get my card? Nice touch that, I thought. But what I didn't say, this time I'm going to be dealing with you first.'

'Bastard,' Elder spat out and, in response, the tip of the knife slipped a little deeper beneath the skin.

'No last-minute rescue this time, Frank. No prince, no

knight in shining armour. No daddy, saving his little darling . . .'

Summoning every last vestige of strength, Elder struggled to lever him away and Keach simply laughed and increased the pressure. 'One last thing, Frank, it was you who got me sent me to prison, remember? All those years locked away, I owe you for those.'

He leaned down on the blade, twisting it across Elder's throat before, with a suck of air, pulling it free.

'Say goodbye, Frank . . .'

Crouching over him, he drove the knife between Elder's ribs.

52

Vicki had hummed and hawed for the best part of an hour before deciding yes, she'd drive across and keep Frank company for an hour or so. But not stay. Back in her bed before the witching hour and enjoying all the benefits of a good night's sleep.

His car wasn't parked in the usual place and she wondered if maybe he'd taken it into his head to go off somewhere without letting her know. The door to the cottage was open though, left ajar, so she assumed he was still home.

Stepping inside, she switched on the light.

The first thing she saw was Elder, stretched out, face down, on the floor. Her immediate thought, he'd fallen, knocked himself unconscious. Or that he'd had a heart attack, a stroke.

And then she saw the blood.

Kneeling, hands trembling, she turned him over as best she could. When she lowered her face to his, she could just feel the slightest breath, faint against her cheek. One of his eyes flickered momentarily and a tight gargling sound came from his mouth as if he were trying to speak.

'Keach,' he managed, the word just audible, her ear pressed close against his mouth, a bubble of blood breaking on her skin.

Standing quickly and stepping past him, she reached for the phone and dialled 999.

The ambulance was there within fifteen minutes, the first of the police not long after. Cordon found Vicki, ashen-faced, in the garden, unable to go back inside.

'It's okay,' he said. 'He'll be okay.'

She let her head fall against his chest and cried.

Paramedics carried Elder out past them on a stretcher.

'Did you touch anything?' Cordon asked. 'Inside. Anything at all?'

Vicki nodded. 'I turned him over. Just to see . . .'

'It's all right,' Cordon said. 'Don't worry . . .' A woman PC appeared at his shoulder and he released Vicki's grip on his arm and stepped away. 'Later, when you're up to it, the officer will take your statement. But now there are things I have to do.'

'Frank's car . . .' Vicki said.

'What about it?'

'It's not here.'

No mobile signal, Cordon was forced to use the landline. He was patched through to the Operations Support Commander at headquarters and within minutes the Firearms Unit of the Force Support Group had been dispatched and the police helicopter was in the air.

The assumption was twofold. Either Keach would seek to avoid capture by sticking to the side roads, travelling under the cover of night, or he would take the most direct route east, the A30, driving as far and fast as he could.

After very little time, the helicopter picked up Elder's car

277

heading towards the Oakhampton bypass on the northern edge of the Dartmoor National Park. A decision was taken to set up a roadblock on the eastern section of the bypass and force Keach to take the B road that would lead him into the park in the direction of Coombe Head Farm. There it would be easier to position armed officers and execute a hard stop. Less danger of civilians being involved.

Even as he sped down there, Keach must have known.

A tractor partly blocked the road ahead of him, three police cars closing fast behind; the leader sweeping past him and then swerving sharply inwards, forcing him to brake.

As he skidded to a halt, armed officers ran fast towards both sides of the car, shouting instructions, headlights illuminating the scene.

'Armed police! Armed police! Get out of the vehicle. Put your hands on your head.'

'Get out of the vehicle. Put your hands on your head.'

When Keach pushed open the door on the driver's side and started to get out there was a knife in his hand.

'Drop the knife! Drop the knife now! Drop the knife!'

The armed officers moved closer on all sides.

'If you don't drop the knife we will shoot.'

Keach smiled.

And, smiling, took a step forward, still brandishing the knife.

Oh, fuck! the officer in charge thought, he wants us to do it. That's what he wants. Suicide by fucking cop!

'Drop the knife! Drop it! Now!'

Keach lunged at the nearest officer and in that instant three others opened fire.

He was dead before he hit the ground.

'Bastard,' the lead officer said quietly and shook his head. Already he was thinking about the debrief with the Chief

Superintendent, the written reports his team would have to make, the photographs, the video, the inevitable investigation by the IPCC. And for what? Looking down at Keach, he cleared his throat and, not wishing to contaminate the scene, swallowed hard.

Vicki had been sitting in the corridor outside Intensive Care for several hours; if she'd been asked how many it's doubtful she'd have known. One of the nursing auxiliaries had brought her a cup of tea and it sat beside her feet untouched. Trevor Cordon, concerned, had been there and gone, work to do, promising to return. Elder's ex-wife and daughter were on their way.

When one of the doctors came out, walking briskly, she intercepted him and asked about Elder's condition. Was he conscious? Was he going to be all right? Was he in a lot of pain?

'All I can tell you right now,' the doctor said, 'we're doing everything we can.' He avoided looking her straight in the eye.

53

Katherine was holding his hand when he died. Felt the last involuntary flinch of the fingers, saw the life fade from his eyes.

There had been a moment, some little time before, when he had blinked his eyes open and, seeing her, had weakly smiled, and she had thought her heart must break.

After a decent interval they raised her gently from her chair beside the bed and led her carefully away. There were procedures to follow, things they had to do.

Outside, she clung helplessly to her mother, sobbed against her breast.

The chapel was half full: music playing, nobody seemed to know exactly what it was. Cordon was there in uniform, the first time he had worn it in years; other officers from the local force. Colin Sherbourne sent his apologies and a wreath. A scattering of neighbours attended, some of whom Elder would barely have known; the landlord from the Tinner's Arms.

Karen Shields arrived just after the service had started, her train from London delayed. Vida Dullea had driven down, bringing Katherine's flatmates with her and they sat together – Abike, Chrissy and Stelina – in the second row, behind Katherine and Joanne.

The Priest in charge leading the service had asked if there was any family member who would like to speak about the deceased and Katherine had said she thought she would, but, in the event, she was too upset and the Priest in charge said of course, that was fine, she understood.

Vicki sang 'Body and Soul', a cappella, faltering only in the final verse.

Two days later, Joanne and Katherine took the urn containing Elder's ashes out to the headland beyond the village, Vicki walking a little way behind. It was a day of patchwork clouds moving fast across the sky. Below them, as they stood, the sea drove in against granite rock and splashed back in a spume of silvered foam.

Urn held tight in her hand, Katherine moved closer to the edge of the land: prised open the lid, and after a moment's hesitation, cast her father to the wind. A few last ashes clung to her hand and, raising her arm skywards, she shook them free and he was gone.

ACKNOWLEDGEMENTS

You can learn a great deal from the Internet these days, some of it even true. For myself, I've always found there is more to be gained from the advice of friends with different areas of expertise; during the writing of this book I've leaned quite heavily on Jon Morgan for his knowledge of police procedure, while taking advice from Caroline Walker on art, artists and the art world in general. Caroline's own work can be seen at carolinewalker.org. I'm grateful also to Anna Deighton and Jane Morris, who read and commented on sections of the manuscript, and to the Two Stephs for the concept of Lesbian Bickering.

Both my partner, Sarah Boiling, and our daughter, Molly Ernestine Boiling, read early drafts of the manuscript and made cogent suggestions, Molly being especially atuned to the mysteries of young women's lives and scrupulous about correct punctuation.

As has long been the case, my editor, Susan Sandon, has been unstinting in her encouragement and meticulous in her attention to detail; without her enthusiasm it is possible this book would never have been written – or, at the very least, finished once it had been started. My agent, Sarah Lutyens, has been equally encouraging throughout, and Mary Chamberlain has proved herself, once again, to be amongst the very best of copy-editors.